NORTHERN BLOOD 2

The second collection of crime writing with a northern theme, including stories by Peter N. Walker, Ann Cleeves, Reginald Hill and Robert Barnard.

NORTHERN BLOOD 2

edited by
Martin Edwards

Magna Large Print Books
Long Preston, North Yorkshire,
England.

British Library Cataloguing in Publication Data.

Edwards, Martin edited by
  Northern blood 2.

  A catalogue record for this book is
  available from the British Library

  ISBN 0-7505-1027-7

First published in Great Britain by Flambard Press, 1995

Copyright © 1995 by Flambard Press

The contributors have asserted their moral rights in accordance with the Copyright, Designs and Patents Act 1988

Published in Large Print February, 1997 by arrangement with the copyright holders.

Magna Large Print is an imprint of
Library Magna Books Ltd.
Printed and bound in Great Britain by
T.J. International Ltd., Cornwall, PL28 8RW.

CONTENTS

ACKNOWLEDGEMENTS

The Two Talks by Ngaio Marsh are published by kind permission of the Ngaio Marsh Estate and the Alexander Turnbull Library, Wellington, New Zealand. 'Dog Television' by Robert Barnard first appeared in *Malice Domestic 2* (ed. Martin Greenberg, Pocket Books, USA, 1993). An abbreviated version of 'Where the Snow Lay Dinted' by Reginald Hill first appeared in *The Mail on Sunday*. Gerard Benson's poem 'R. I. P.' is taken from his collection *In Wordsworth's Chair* (Flambard Press, 1995).

R.I.P.

Poor Tom lay dying. Faithful at his side
His wife and helpmeet sat, a tireless nurse,
Fixing his dosage, watching, anxious-eyed,
His laboured breathing sink from bad to worse,
Wiping his fevered forehead. He, poor soul,
With aching conscience, tried in vain to pray;
Then hot, remorseful tears began to roll
Across his cheeks. "There's something I must say:
I have deceived you, Peg my dear," he said,
"With cousin Beattie and your sister Joan.
I've lain with both, here in this very bed."
"Don't fret, my love," his wife replied. "I've known
For years." He stared. "You knew?" "Of course I knew.
Why else, dear Tom, would I have poisoned you?"

GERARD BENSON

FOREWORD

This is the second anthology published by crime writers in the North of England, and it illustrates the commitment of its authors to the regional work of the Crime Writers' Association.

The CWA was founded in 1953 by the energetic writer John Creasey who produced 564 books. He knew that authors endured a lonely working existence and his concept was a friendly but professional organisation which would allow them to meet socially and at the same time provide access to professional information through meetings and lectures. His ideals have been successfully achieved; the CWA now boasts more than 400 members in the UK and overseas. It hosts a monthly meeting in London, supports an annual conference and presents the Cartier Diamond Dagger at a House of Lords ceremony every May to a writer whose work has been consistently meritorious. This year, 1995, the recipient of the Diamond Dagger was

Reginald Hill, a member of the Northern Chapter of the CWA and a contributor to this book. The CWA also arranges the prestigious awards dinner every December at which the coveted Gold and Silver Daggers are awarded for the best crime fiction of the year, with another Gold Dagger for the best non-fiction and a number of other awards.

When annual conferences were proposed, it was decided that they should be held out of London to make it easier for country members to attend; hitherto, London meetings could only be visited on very rare occasions by writers living beyond commuting distance. An annual conference would provide a further opportunity for members to socialise and attend professional lectures.

It was at the first CWA conference in the North of England, at Harrogate in May 1973 (coincidentally the year John Creasey died), that I first came into contact with CWA members. I was to give a talk about police work and, as a young policeman, was flattered by the advice so readily given by some big names of the crime writing genre. I realised just what friendly and helpful people they were and vowed to attend other conferences.

But even though the national conference provided succour to a Northern lad struggling to be a writer, a year was a long time to wait for another. Writers do need other writers and at later conferences I chatted to a Yorkshire-based author whom I had met and befriended at Harrogate. We felt there should be a meeting for Northern CWA members, but it took a while for that to become a reality. Eventually, in 1987, I rang that same writer and sought his views on actually forming a Northern Chapter. 'I'll help you,' said Reginald Hill, who now shares the task of arranging the Northern Spring Symposium. And so the Northern Chapter of the CWA was formed, our first meeting being at Boroughbridge in November 1987.

We hold a quarterly lunch and an annual Spring Symposium which alternates between Yorkshire and the Lake District. Our lunches attract around thirty people, while the size of the Symposium depends upon the small hotels we use: at least forty attend each year. In addition, the Northern Chapter has hosted two of the CWA's annual conferences since its inception and will do so for a third time in 1995.

As current Chairman of the CWA and convenor of the Northern Chapter, I am gratified by the dedication of Northern members. They conquer tempests, drifting snow, floods and long distances to attend our lunches and they come from both sides of the Pennines between the Trent and the Scottish border, an area larger than Wales. Such dedication must be placed on record.

At our Northern meetings we take the business of writing very seriously. We have discussed the important question of the moral responsibilities of those who work in the genre: this debate, which is likely to run and run, has also been conducted at national level by Northern Chapter members. We have also discussed the future of the Crime Writers' Association as it heads for the next century and we have worried about declining book sales, funding for libraries, the possibility of VAT on books and a host of other matters of importance to authors and their readers.

It was from these meetings that Martin Edwards produced the idea of an anthology of Northern crime writing. It is thanks to his efforts that the first *Northern Blood* was published, and to him we owe thanks for this second volume. Almost all the work within these pages is by Northern CWA members, and it is this kind of cooperative spirit, now being emulated by other regional Chapters, which will ensure the CWA reaches its centenary in good health.

PETER N WALKER
CWA Chairman, 1995–96

INTRODUCTION

Welcome to a brand-new collection of the best in Northern crime. The region's leading mystery novelists and specialists in true crime have joined in putting together a book which demonstrates, we hope, that Northern crime writing is not only remarkably broad in range but also consistently high in quality. And because we believe in providing value for money, we also offer a special bonus: two previously unpublished pieces by one of the most popular detective-story writers of the twentieth century, Ngaio Marsh.

Members of the Northern Chapter of the CWA have been keen to build on the success of *Northern Blood* (Didsbury Press, 1992), the first anthology of regional crime ever published in the UK. To our delight, the book was greeted by enthusiastic reviews in the national press. *Northern Blood* reflected the growing popularity of regional mysteries and started a trend: the East Anglian Chapter of the CWA has now produced *Anglian Blood,* whose contributors include P D James.

We have again mixed fiction with fact. The four real-life stories are supplied by one serving police officer, Roger Forsdyke, making his first contribution to an anthology, and two former policemen, Alan Sewart and Peter N Walker, together with true-crime expert Douglas Wynn. Peter is currently Chairman of the national CWA and in this capacity has provided a Foreword, for which I am grateful. The three fiction writers who make their regional anthology début in this book are amongst the most talented of our younger crime novelists: Barbara Crossley, Val McDermid and Kay Mitchell.

Variety is the hallmark of the contributions. Ann Cleeves and I have allowed our series detectives, Inspector Ramsay and Harry Devlin, to take a break whilst we tried our hands at a different kind of story. Reginald Hill, however, provides a treat for all fans of Dalziel and Pascoe with a story hitherto seen only in truncated form in a holiday edition of a national newspaper, and Barbara Whitehead continues her York mysteries in the short form. Bob Barnard and Eileen Dewhurst are represented by

18

characteristically entertaining stories, while Stephen Murray—with a monologue in the Stanley Holloway tradition—and Chaz Brenchley show the versatility of the new generation. And from Margaret and Peter Lewis, better known for their non-fiction, come stories in pleasing contrast.

Margaret Lewis is the biographer of Ngaio Marsh, and while researching in New Zealand she came across some unpublished material by Dame Ngaio, including the two items included here: a broadcast heard only once on New Zealand radio in the 1950s, and the text of a talk she gave to the Times Book Club in London a few years earlier. We felt that as this year sees the centenary of Dame Ngaio's birth, on 23rd April 1895, crime buffs everywhere would be glad if we seized the opportunity to bring these hitherto-overlooked pieces into print. In the classic tradition of ingenious, if improbable, detective reasoning, we would like to claim Dame Ngaio as a Northerner by adoption, not only because of Margaret's association with her work but also because in 1978 she accepted a commission from Granada Television to write *Evil Liver*, a script for the *Crown Court* series. Be that as

19

it may, her observations on the craft of writing detective fiction will surely strike a chord with modern practitioners, and 'Shakespeare's Lost Whodunit' is highly enjoyable. We are most grateful to the Ngaio Marsh Estate for permission to publish these two talks.

I would like to thank all the contributors for their support, but in particular Margaret and Peter Lewis for their hard work in preparing this book for publication. We are also indebted to Chaz Brenchley for his contribution to the production process.

When Joan Hickson, later to find fame in the role of Agatha Christie's Miss Marple, showed Dame Ngaio round the Manchester studios of Granada twenty years ago, the great lady remarked, "I do think that this would be a marvellous place for a murder." We hope she would agree that, in fiction terms, the North today offers more marvellous murders than ever.

MARTIN EDWARDS
Editor, *Northern Blood 2*

Robert Barnard

DOG TELEVISION

The cat-flap was a success from the start. For the first week or two the perspex door was secured up, and Gummidge was convinced that this hole in the door was God-sent, and a secret known only to her: she used to look round to see if anyone was watching before jumping through it, preening herself on the other side that her secret was still safe. When the flap was let down she was suspicious and resentful at first, but she soon learned to pat it with her paw, like a boxer being playful, and march through. Now her attitude to it changed: this is for ME, she seemed to say. It is MINE, and MINE ALONE. She looked with pity at Jaggers. If he had had a flap of his own it would take out a quarter of the door. So much better to have the petiteness and delicacy of a cat.

But in fact the cat-flap was a godsend to Jaggers too. He began to sit on the doormat, his head on his paws, gazing through the perspex at the human, animal and ornithological cavalcade which changed minute by minute, making the back garden a fascinating, endless soap opera: garbagemen came, and postmen, both to be barked at; birds swooped down on the breadcrumbs left out for them, fought each other endlessly over the nut-holder, dive-bombed the rough vegetable patch and bore off worms; male cats came in search of Gummidge, who was on the pill but still retained vestiges of her old attractions. There was always something going on. It was like one of those endless wildlife programmes on television.

And in this case the screen image could literally leap into your living-room. One day when Jaggers was not on sentry duty a tom leapt through the flap in search of Gummidge. Then there was mayhem. Peter was not at home, so the pursuit went on, with barks and feline shrieks for all of half an hour, before the tom found his way out of the flap again. When Peter got home from school he found the living-room so impregnated with tomcat smells that no amount of open windows or deodorant sprays could make it liveable-in for days.

The flap was wonderful for inspecting callers too. This was the North, and the front door was for 'special' callers, the back door for everyday. Jaggers could crouch and size up the dark blue trousers of gas or electricity meter readers, the bare legs of children wanting to be sponsored for this or that, or singing carols at Christmas, the varying garb of political canvassers. All were barked at, but the barks were subtly graded, from the downright threatening for garbagemen to the joyful welcoming of children.

Was it a child, that evening in March? The legs were bare and thin, and rather dirty too, and the skirt was above the knees. Still, the heels of her shoes were higher than children wore, except in play. Jaggers barked on, a middle-of-the-road, could-go-either-way kind of bark. Anyway the ring on the door got Peter up from the pile of exercise books that he was marking in the front room to open the door.

'Oh, hello,' he said. Friendly—yet somehow guarded. Jaggers wagged his tail tentatively.

'Hello again. Long time no see.'

The tone of the visitor was cheeky, with an undertone of aggression. Jaggers

23

recognised it. There was a Jack Russell that came to the Park who took exactly that tone. It tended to run around, barking and snapping. This girl—woman—just stood there with her hands on her hips. Jaggers couldn't see her face, but he always judged more on body than on face.

'Come on in,' said Peter.

They went through to the living-room. Jaggers had realised by now that he had smelt the girl before. Not recently, but many seasons ago, when she had really been a child. Now she was dirtier, smelt stronger and better, but it was still the same human person. He wagged his tail and got a pat, but no more acknowledgement. The woman sat on the sofa, waiflike but not weak, not begging. The aggressive stance was still there, hardly hidden by any social veneer.

'I'll make you a pot of tea,' said Peter.

'Haven't you got anything stronger?'

Jaggers' master paused for thought.

'I've got a bottle of beer... Oh yes, and there's still some gin left over from Christmas.'

'Gin, then. With whatever you've got.'

Social gestures, then, were being made, however reluctantly. Jaggers wagged his tail—*thump,* and then *thump* again. He was rewarded by a caress of his ears, which was an acknowledgement of his presence that always delighted him. She wasn't a bad girl. He remembered that she had caressed him often, those times she had come before. Peter had liked her too. They had gone upstairs together.

Peter came back with the gin, and a little bottle of ginger ale. He put it down on the table beside her chair. She raised her eyebrows at the single glass, but Peter shook his head. He wasn't having anything, didn't want to make that social gesture. He sat tensely in his chair and waited. The girl-woman filled her glass from the bottle and drank half of it down. Then she slapped the glass down loudly on the table.

'You put me where I am now,' she said.

'Where are you now?'

'On the streets.'

'I did nothing of the sort.'

Jaggers, his nose on the carpet under the table, was exploring her feet, delicately. They certainly were like no feet he had ever known before. He had known and appreciated Peter's feet after he had come

25

back from a walk across the Pennines, or after a strenuous game of rugby, but these were different—or rather, *more so*. Much, much dirtier. Layer upon layer of dirt—a dirt that extended, less concentrated, up her legs. It was on the feet that weeks, months, of living outside, living rough, showed most tellingly. Jaggers thought they were wonderful.

'It started upstairs here. It was my first time.'

'You were as eager as any girl I've known.'

'What kind of schoolteacher is it that takes his pupils to bed?'

'What kind of schoolkid is it who drags her teacher upstairs to bed? A slut, that's the answer. You were determined to be a slut.'

'I'm on the streets. I'm not on the game.'

The voices were getting raised. Jaggers no longer thumped his tail. He removed his head from under the table, to be ready if anything happened. The girl was shouting, accusing. She could attack Peter, throw herself at him. It had happened before, with other women.

There was a lull. The girl began jiggling

her empty glass on the table. Peter sighed, got up and took it for a refill. Jaggers experimentally licked the feet, but got no answering caress. He lay there, unhappy at the situation.

'I want money.'

'You'll have a job—getting money out of a schoolteacher!'

'You inherited this house—you told me. You can raise money on it.'

'I've no intention of doing so.'

'I'll take a hundred pounds.'

'You won't. A hundred would only be a start.'

'It might. But if I don't get it I'm going to your headmaster. If he doesn't listen I'll go to the Press. And if they don't listen I'll go to the Police.'

The row didn't get any louder, but it got more intense. They somehow shouted at each other in voices that were hardly raised above a whisper. Jaggers found it unsettling. Peter was getting red in the face, and the girl was too, and her voice kept breaking as if she was going to sob. Eventually she shouted:

'What's a girl have to do to get a drink in this dump?'

When Peter went for her second refill

Jaggers made a mistake. He looked at the girl to see that all was well, and then went to check up on the cat-flap. It was a good hour since he had barked at those dirty legs. Dark had come, and there were no birds around any longer. Now there was only the odd luminous eye of a tomcat, on the prowl in hopes of an amorous encounter with Gummidge.

When he had done his couple of minutes on sentry-go, he went back into the hall and found the living-room door shut.

Jaggers was unhappy. He had gone to fulfil one duty, and now found himself shut out from fulfilling another. He could not protect Peter now, nor even provide distraction. He lay with his nose against the bottom of the door, his tail quiet. Of the voices he could now hear no more than their rise and fall, the hiss of accusation, the suppressed fury of Peter's angry retorts. Surely soon he'd come out again?

But he didn't, and the curve of the voices became a continual rising one, not in volume but in intensity. Jaggers heard chair springs go—they were no longer sitting, but were confronting each other standing up. The curve continued upwards, the girl's voice like a whiplash with words of scorn and accusation. Jaggers was considering barking when he heard a tremendous thump, a shattering of glass, and then another bump—to the floor, on the other side of the room to the door. Then silence.

Jaggers whined, unhappy. Glass—he knew the sound of breaking glass. But what he'd heard wasn't like a breaking wineglass; it was something heavy, thick... The thick grey glass ashtray, which had sat on the mantelpiece since Peter had given up smoking.

Still silence. Jaggers' nose was firmly inserted into the tiny crack along the bottom of the door, as if by smell alone he could understand what was going on. He was just thinking that he might understand when Peter came out the door and shut it firmly behind him, then leaned his head against the door-jamb, sobbing.

The brief moment that the door was open had told Jaggers. It had given him the whiff of something he came across now and then in his walks in woods and moorlands, a phenomenon that was sometimes exciting, sometimes disconcerting. It was Not-Being. An End to Being. Lying there without Being.

He went to the front door, whining, and lay there on the doormat. He no longer wanted to be near the living-room.

Peter stood by the door, still sobbing, otherwise motionless, for some minutes. Then he went upstairs. Jaggers heard the lavatory flush, then water running in the bathroom. When he came down he was looking more normal, but Jaggers could tell from the way he came down the stairs that he was still tense. He looked in the mirror in the hall, to see that he did look normal. Then he fetched Jaggers' lead from the kitchen.

A walk at this hour! Unheard-of! Jaggers was more than usually beside himself because he was happy to get out of the house. The air outside was fresh and...free from that blight that was now pervading indoors. They walked to the Jug and Bottle, and Peter took him into the Saloon Bar.

'Have you got such a thing as a bottle of whisky I could buy? And I'll have a half of bitter while I'm waiting.'

Jaggers curled up contentedly by the brass rail around the floor of the bar. He saw no need to behave other than ordinarily.

'Having a party?' asked the landlord

when he came back from the cellar.

'Not really. An old rugby friend rang up—may drop in later. Likes a drop of Scotch.'

'Show me a rugger player who doesn't,' said the landlord. 'When they've tanked up on beer.'

On the way back Jaggers showed signs of reluctance. He didn't want to go back into the house. But where else was there to go? Peter let them in the front door, then shut Jaggers and the whisky in the dining-room. Jaggers sat listening. Peter didn't go into the living-room. He went to the kitchen and soon returned with a jug of water and a glass. He poured whisky, then water, then sat at the table drinking. Jaggers sat close, watching him, waiting for some sign, some revelation of intention. Occasionally he wagged his tail, occasionally a hand would come down and caress his head. He was still unsettled. It was a comfort.

It was well after midnight, with the whisky bottle a third empty, when Peter made a move. He got up, only a little unsteady, and left the room. Shutting the door behind him. Jaggers sat by the door, straining his ears. The house was surrounded by a tremendous night silence. Peter opened the back door, leaving it open, and Jaggers heard his steps go to the garden shed. Something taken from it—two heavy implements that clanged when he let them come together.

He was going to the vegetable plot—that large oval that he turned over every year, but somehow never seemed to do very much with. Jaggers jumped up against the bookshelf under the back window, peering into the darkness. Yes—Peter was forking over and then digging. He was in condition—he kept himself in condition. Jaggers lay down on the floor again, waiting.

After what seemed like an eternity Peter came back into the house. He came back into the dining-room, chucking Jaggers' ears. Then he went to the whisky bottle, pouring himself a stiff one. He took his time drinking it: getting his breath or summoning up courage. Then he went out, shutting the door. Jaggers heard the living-room door being opened. That was where the Not-Being thing was. He heard something heavy being dragged. That would be It. Little clinks as bits of glass knocked together on the floor. Peter dragged It into the hall. It seemed heavier than he had expected, or perhaps now he was tired. He had difficulty dragging It round from the living-room through to the kitchen and the back door. He bumped into the dining-room door and it came off the latch. Jaggers watched, giving the tiniest thump of his tail, but did nothing.

The unmistakeable sound of the back door being closed. In a second Jaggers was up and nosing at the dining-room door. That was the first trick in the book. A moment and he was through it, and on his haunches in front of the cat-flap, on duty again.

Peter had something in his arms. It. By the time he got to the vegetable patch they were nothing but shapes, but Jaggers could see that Peter had put It down. There was another, a new shape there. A mound. That must be it. A mound of earth. There were tiny, distant sounds. More digging. Peter had found that he needed more digging. Then Jaggers saw the shape of Peter come round the mound, take up It, then lay It down, right in the hole.

Again he saw Peter come round the mound, spade in hand. He stood by the mound, and, using the spade with strong, practised motions, he began rapidly filling the hole. Shovelful followed shovelful, the man powered by alcohol and desperation. In ten minutes the mound was nearly flattened again.

In the kitchen Jaggers still kept watch. His tail went thump, thump, thump regularly on the linoed floor.

What had been buried cried out to be dug up again.

Chaz Brenchley

DROWNING, DROWNING

She was dead, and I held her in my arms, and it was raining. That was all the space there was, all the world allowed.

Then there was a weight, a blow, a body hurtling into me; and she was snatched from my arms and I was shoved away, and the intrusion was so great that I could do nothing but howl.

Then I would have fought, seeing a stranger take her and lay her out, dead on cold stone, like an affirmation. But I was gripped and held, another unknown with his fat arms looped around me, and he was shouting as I was shouting and he made no more sense than I did.

I felt the slickness of his waterproof against my sodden shirt, I felt the warmth of him against my chill; and I saw the man who had my Beth bend himself across her, mouth to mouth.

And that was it, that was what I needed, *mouth to mouth.* A cue for some seed of rationality, a moment's clear thought: I ceased struggling, stood utterly slack within the circle of the second man's arms and meant to say, *It's all right, I understand, you can let me go now.* Nothing of that came out, though, above a grunt; and that was absolutely right, because my Beth still lay there under the stranger's mouth, still dead, and nothing should be coherent in such a world, nothing should work as it was meant to work.

And he understood me anyway, or the message he had from my body. He unlocked his hands and stepped away, took a pace or two towards where his friend worked on her slack, slack body, left me standing.

Amazing that I could stand, that she being dead allowed it. I should be there beside her, I should be utterly with her, pale and supine and destroyed.

Unable to watch this desecration, a man with his mouth so hungry and his hands so hard on her body, working so hard, I turned away; and saw how gulls hung still in the wind above deserted rods and bags, and knew at last who these men were in

36

their yellow rainslicks and their urgency.

They were the men who had let her go, who had turned their backs and hunched their shoulders and let her come to this.

Too late, too late for redemption, she was dead. No breath, no stirring in her body or her blood. Nothing left, nothing left for me now...

Until she coughed. Until she coughed thinly and I saw her fingers stir as if the tide were moving them, but she wasn't underwater now, the water was inside her. All the water that mattered, she contained.

And she coughed again, more than just his rough hands forcing her; and a dribble of those foul waters came from her mouth, and her hand moved in protest, such indignity.

And she was mine again, back in my world, lying at my feet and breathing, sharing the air with me as she was meant to. I would have pulled the man from her body then, I would have hurled him from the pier if he'd resisted; but she didn't need me, seemingly, she could look after herself. She rolled onto her side with a great flapping of her arms to move her, she rolled away from him and was sick on the stones. He crouched back on his heels to watch her, looking for an excuse, I thought, to maul her again; and bless her, she lifted her head to find me, before even lifting her hand to wipe her mouth.

'David...?'

More than permission, that was a summons and a demand. And I was there for her on the word, as she was there again for me; I fell to my knees beside her and gave never another thought to the fisherman or his friend.

Until that evening, taking flowers to Sunderland General, finding them both already there at the foot of her bed: and me with that evening's *Echo* in my pocket, where they had spoken of her and made her humiliation public.

I gave her the kiss of life, the man said in the paper. Had said in real life to the reporter, and smiling no doubt, smiling I was sure, lips that had touched her lips leering now in memory. *Her bloke got her out of the water,* the man had said, *but he didn't know what to do, we had to get her off him. My mate had to hold him back, he was frantic,* the man had said. *No use to her,* the man had said.

No use to her.

I could have killed him then, when I first read it; or I could have killed him now, finding him here in the hospital with his fat friend when she was mine and I wanted her, I needed her to myself.

'David,' she said, 'look,' she said, 'Tony and Andrew have come to visit me, isn't that kind?'

'Kind,' I repeated dully. Fat Andrew reached out to shake my hand, which I was too distracted to resist; Tony, lean and dark with hands that handled other people's women, merely nodded. I suppose I nodded back.

'And see, they're in the paper, they brought it in to show me. It says how Tony saved my life, I never thought I'd be news, did you...?'

I never thought she'd be anything but mine. Never thought she'd be anything at all after she ran from me on the waterfront, after I took her from the sea and she was dead.

Never thought she'd be smiling at another man, touching his hand, smiling at her own degradation; and all of it so utterly, utterly wrong, never thought she

39

could be so misguided and confused.

I'd have to set her straight, it shouldn't have been necessary but there it was, there to be done; but not to be done until they were gone, those men, and they showed no signs of going.

I couldn't even kiss her under their eyes, I didn't dare. She might not lift her head to receive it. She wasn't looking for it, certainly, when she should have been, herself in hospital and me just come with flowers; they were taking too much of her attention and I was fearful, I thought she'd turn her face away, "Not now, David," and right in front of them.

So I fetched a chair and sat on it, as much possession as I could claim, *I have this right, I have a place here;* and she said, 'Oh yes, bring chairs, sit down, are there enough, can you find some, David?' and I could have screamed, I could have screamed at her.

But I fetched chairs for them, because she asked me to; and I sat quiet while she talked to them and said very little to me; and I said almost nothing, to them or to her.

'You're making too much of this,' she said

later, a day later and home again, in bed only because I insisted.

'Too much, what do you mean, too much?'

'It was an accident, that's all. I had an accident.'

There's no such thing as accidents, I could have told her, *everything is planned.* If not by God, then devil-planned for sure, no room for chance in such an ordered world.

But she knew that already, she didn't need telling. It was only her stubbornness talking, saying, *I don't want to be in bed.* So I smiled, all patience, and said, 'You nearly died, Beth.'

She went still and quiet for a moment, considering that; and then, 'Yes,' she said, 'I nearly died. But I'm all right now. You don't have to treat me like an invalid.'

'I have to know where you are.'

'For God's *sake,* David...!'

And we were on shifting sands again suddenly, without warning, as we had been on the beach. She'd run from me then, run down the pier and slipped on wet stones and gone headlong into the water, and didn't that only prove my point?

I said that, I said all of that and more. I

reminded her that she'd needed fishermen to save her after I'd pulled her from the water, fishermen and strangers; and she said, 'So what are you proposing, are you going to keep me in bed all the rest of my *life*, is that it?'

'I want you to be safe,' I said. *Safe and mine, and no fishermen between us.* 'That's all,' I said, 'I only want you to be safe...'

'Oh, for God's sake.' The words the same, but the voice entirely different, warm and smiling now, as it ought to be. 'You want to know where I am, there's only one way to be certain. Only one sure way to keep me in bed, come to that, if I'm not sleeping...'

All night I held her in my arms; and she did sleep, but I kept myself wakeful, to make assurance doubly sure. I smelled the sweet, heavy smell of her, and traced her features with my eyes; and sensed how fragile her life was, contained within so thin a skin, so little protection. Resented her for being so foolish, for running risks she had no right to, running away from me. She was mine, she knew that, I'd told her often and often. She was my miracle, twice given now: once from nowhere, God's gift to me and all undeserved, and now again she'd been given back from death, because she belonged to me and even God wouldn't take her until I gave her up to Him, until I let her go. Even God wouldn't trespass on so right, so perfect a possession...

Next day her mother came, my relief, a trusted substitute; and so I was free, she was in safe hands and I could go to church.

We'd bought one of the new riverside houses, as soon as they became available. They were expensive, but Beth had a good wage and we lived thriftily, with care we could manage the mortgage; and I'd never liked the other thing, knowing that others had lived and died in my own home before me. I could smell their sweat in the plasterwork, and see the marks of their feet on the floorboards. Like a used car or used clothes, you could never clean a used house properly; and I would never have allowed Beth to buy one. We deserved better than that.

So we lived by the Wear, on the new estate; and the sea was five minutes' walk one way—only we wouldn't be walking that way any longer, I'd nearly lost her once and wouldn't take the risk a second time—and the church the same distance in the other direction, upstream.

It felt like coming home, to come to church. Here it didn't matter that I trod in others' footsteps, that I sat in pews their bodies had worn to a gloss and swept up the dust of their skin from the flagstones. My home, their home: this I could share with everyone, so long as my other home I only shared with Beth.

The path led straight from the gate in the railings to the side door, where my key would let me in; but I didn't follow the path, not ever. Unlucky, to walk even a little way widdershins around a church. Besides, I liked a minute to encompass the building, to walk the bounds and settle my soul within them.

St Peter's was an old, old building. The Victorians had extended and expanded and elaborated, and a more recent vicar had persuaded his bishop and his PCC that it needed a new chapterhouse built onto the back; but the original bones were still there to be seen, and nobody had touched the tower since the Saxons came. Blunt and square and barely higher than the gable roof, it was all history and truth and no adornment, something to cling to, something to be certain of. I loved that tower.

Halfway up was the ghost of a window long since sealed, only its outline still to be seen in the weathered stone. From the inside, it was impossible to tell that it had ever been there. I loved that too, I loved to tell people about that and hear them speculate on what its purpose might have been, or why it had been closed up so long ago and never opened since.

I had an answer of my own but that was private, I kept it to myself. I thought it had been closed up simply because it was a window, and a window was wrong in that tower. It gave access to the world, the other world outside; and towers are built to contain, to deny access. Churches are built to focus people's gaze towards God, not to show them a view down the valley.

No, seal up the windows, close the doors. What God has, God holds; that's what churches say, and their towers speak most loudly.

It stirred me, every time I came to the church it stirred me. That day as most days I reached to touch the old stones of the tower, to feel their strength, looking to gain from them a little of what they had, certainty and endurance and possession, *none shall trespass here.*

Then round to the door again, coming at it deasil, sure that God would never condemn me for a little superstition; and so in, my latchkey one of the most treasured among those things I owned, one of the most jealously guarded of my rights.

The vicar was in the vestry with his paperwork. A smile and a word from him, and I went through into the church. Turned on the lights, unbolted the big door, fixed the *Church Guide* badge to my lapel and sat down to wait.

We had a constant stream of visitors in the summer; fewer in winter but they were better informed, they asked more sensible questions. I enjoyed that, when they wanted to know more than they could read in the brochure. Even the vicar deferred to me, on matters of church history; and so he should have, I'd been there longer. Ten years, I'd been showing people round.

It was autumn, and the storms were coming in: high seas, high winds and the church quiet, visitors falling off. It suited me well, that day. I'd been keen to come, I was on the rota and I never liked to miss; but once there I was restless and impatient, not welcoming, not doing my job.

Luckily I wasn't on shift alone. It was that awkward time of year when there weren't really enough people coming to need two guides, but were often too many for one. In another month we'd be changing the rotas, but for the moment we still had double cover. So I was able to ask my companion to stand in for me, to call if she needed help; and then I was free to go up the tower, through the hatch, out onto the roof.

I did this sometimes, climbed up high at a time of crisis, in search of peace and isolation. Not to look down, the tower-top wasn't simply a higher window to me, or an open window. No, I came here to look up.

The tower points like a finger, direct to heaven; I liked to lie spread out with my eyes and my aspiration upward, my body under God's burning, cleansing eye if the sun were shining, under His blanket of protection if it were not.

That was all I sought, all that I ever

sought up there: only to be that much closer to heaven, that much further from the earth. No matter how high I went, I could never be far from Beth; I carried her with me wherever, a picture in my wallet and more than a picture, the reality of her in my head. I knew her utterly, better far than she knew herself. Better than God could know her, I thought sometimes. I thought God might be like the vicar, he might come to me with questions.

That day, though, it was different, there was more. I lay down and stretched myself wide, the stones cold under my back and the parapet rising all around me, cutting me off from everything except the sky; I watched the scudding clouds, felt how they made patterns of light and shadow across the land, all part of God's greater pattern; and I heard voices.

I heard voices coming to me from below, from the wide slopes of grass that had been the graveyard once, that must still hold the bodies although the stones had all been cleared now.

Not seeking to listen, still I heard; and there must have been Another's hand in that, having them say these things there, and loud enough to lift their voices up to me.

'You really going down there, then, are you?'

'Aye, why not? She's canny.'

'Her man's not.'

'So? I'm not going to see her man, am I?'

'You know what I mean, though. He finds you there, he's not going to be happy. Christ, he never said a word to us, hardly, in the hospital. He's that kind, you know. Possessive, like. That's what I reckon. And I wouldn't like to get across him, he's a big lad.'

'He's no lad, he must be forty, that gadgie.'

'All the more reason to keep out of his road.'

'I'm not in his road.'

'You are if you start playing around with his wife.'

'She's not his wife, they're not married. She's got that much sense, not to marry him. Not enough, mind. If she had enough sense, if she had the sense she was bloody born with, she'd leave. I mean, she never said, even before he turned up she never said it straight; but some of the things she did say, she tried to hide it maybe but you could tell, you could see she wasn't happy.'

'You could, maybe. Maybe that's just what you wanted to see.'

'Oh, come on, Andy mate. I mean, you've met him too. How's any woman going to be happy, with a man like that?'

'Yeah, but he wouldn't be like that, would he? Not normally. It was just because we were there...'

They moved off then. I moved too, I had to; I needed to check, to be sure. I got up onto my knees, to see over the parapet. Yes, there they were, two men carrying rods and bags away from the river, cutting over church grounds up to the main road. Like two cattle, one fat and one lean: Andrew and Tony, and Tony's lips still desecrating her, as truly as if he lay upon her still, mouth to mouth and heedless of my rights.

I felt sick, I felt violated in her violation; I felt murder in my heart. I wanted to tear the stones loose from the parapet and hurl them down, I wanted to crush both those men into the earth and let the worms have them, send them back to God for retribution.

But they were gone, too far away; and it was not mine to do, in any case. They were God's creatures, not mine. He would take them in His own good time, and I had nothing to say to that.

I huddled my head in my hands, there under His eye, and tried to learn patience.

A little later I was called down, because a group had arrived with questions; but I humiliated myself and couldn't answer, I was too distracted. I had to hand them on to the vicar; and that done, all my responsibilities abandoned, there was nothing to keep me at the church.

I could make my excuses, and go home.

So I did that; and there were rods and bags stacked in the hallway, laughing voices in the lounge, death in my fingers as I opened the door.

Beth, her mother, and the two fishermen fishing, angling to find corruption, scattering foulness for bait; and the women so easy with them, so pleased to have them there. I could have wept, except that I found it hard even to speak in their company, even to say hullo was an effort.

Her mother I wasn't so surprised at, she was so innocent, so eager to see good in everyone; but Beth, oh, Beth should have been seeing more clearly than this. She shouldn't have been so easily fooled. She'd lived with me long enough. I'd told her and told her, *You can't trust men,* I'd said.

You're a man, she'd said.

That's different, I'd said. *I'm different,* I'd said.

And, *You certainly are,* she'd said. And smiled just a moment, just a beat late, just to tease.

But today she wasn't teasing, she was sitting there in her night-clothes with nothing but a bathrobe to cover them, her legs showing bare to the knee sometimes when she moved; and that man Tony was watching her legs as much as her face, he was ogling all of her, and I wanted him dead.

Not my place, though. *Not my place.*

And Beth, I didn't understand Beth, she knew his interest and she was acting up to it, she was encouraging him. Flirting, I would have said, if such a word could ever apply to my Beth. It wasn't right, it couldn't be right; but that was how it seemed to me. Always moving, she who usually sat so still; showing knee and ankle and smiling, smiling. Laughing at his clumsy stories, barely acknowledging me except to send me out, 'Make us a pot of tea, would you, darling? This one's done.'

And the *darling* only there for irony, she didn't mean it. He grinned when she said it, and I could read the contempt right there on his face, no attempt to hide it.

Oh Beth, Beth, this from you? I don't need this from you, I don't deserve it...

And what I did deserve, support and strength in the face of the invader, none of that. No trace of that. No. She smiled and smiled, but not for me. He told his filthy fisherman's stories, not fit for her ears, and she smiled and smiled. He talked, she smiled, he watched her legs.

And they stayed far, far too long. Five minutes would have been too long, but they were there for hours, and she seemed so glad. They wouldn't stay for tea, but that wasn't for want of asking. She pressed, she urged them to it, and her mother backed her up, no ally she. They were expected home, they said, the only good thing I heard them say, all there was to be glad of; but another time, they said, they'd love to.

In the end I left them, I couldn't bear to stay.

'I'll be in the garage,' I told Beth. 'If you want me.'

'Going to play with your trains, dear?' She said that often, it was a little joke between us; but that night it wasn't funny, she didn't say it funny. She said it sneering, almost; and as I closed the door I heard the two men laughing, and her mother joining in a beat behind.

And *Beth, Beth,* I was all but crying inside when I left her in their company, where she should have hated to be. *Beth, what's happening to us...?*

And oh, I hated those men, and I wanted to see them dead.

I sat in the garage at the pulsing heart of my system, the full timetable in operation all around me; but I couldn't bear to watch the trains at work, they worked so well. They ran to time and to command, everything happened as it ought, and my life used to be like that but we had lost it. There was too much pattern here, it spoke too clearly of the chaos outside.

So I powered the system down, and meant to enter some few timetable changes into the computer. But I spent a long, long time listening, waiting for their footsteps on the path and the door closing behind them, waiting for them to go; and all that time I was staring with my fingers still on the keys, seeing images that were not on the screen.

I spent a lot of time with my trains, the next few days, and achieved very little. I couldn't bear to be much with Beth, she was so altered suddenly, so wrong; and I could think of nothing else, when we were apart.

'Let's go out,' she said. 'Can we?' she said. 'For a drink?' she said.

'We don't like pubs,' I said.

'*You* don't like pubs,' she said.

Time was when that was the same thing, when it was the same things that we liked and didn't like. Time was when she was mine and I was hers and there was no space between us.

No space broad enough to allow a cigarette paper to interrupt us, let alone a fisherman.

But we went to the pub and the

fisherman was there, and he sat between us. My hands clenched under the table, so hard; if I'd held him in my hands he would have died at that moment, and quite rightly.

I went to the toilet and came back, and sat on the other side of Beth. She barely noticed me. Her shoulder hunched, her head turned, her body slipped an inch along the seat away from me, towards him; and none of it was conscious, couldn't have been. Not my Beth in control of those muscles, no. Not possible.

But she spent all evening twisted like that, twisted away. Her hand lay on his arm, not on mine, and all her attention was his. I sipped a lager-and-lime, just the one and I bought it myself, I would take nothing from him though he was taking everything from me. And I watched him drinking pint after pint and remembered that alcohol was a poison, *too slow, though, it works too slow.*

And Beth was matching him, drinking halves, she who only ever drank sherry or snowballs with me, only ever in our own home. He went back to the bar again and she said yes please, every time. And she couldn't take it, she got drunken and foul, not my Beth at all; and I couldn't take her home till it was closing, she wouldn't have come.

When we did leave, he came with us, 'just for a coffee,' she said, 'round the night off nicely.' And she tucked her arm through his to keep her upright, giggling as she swayed and staggered in the public street, no Beth of mine.

He stayed till three in the morning. They were talking, she said; and yes, I heard their voices. Sometimes I heard their voices, sometimes not. They played cards also, she said.

I had gone to bed, long since. Gone to bed and not slept, not hoped to sleep; only lain there listening, listening and hating, hating.

At the weekend she wanted to fish, to learn how. She who'd flinched from needles all her life, who'd said so often how cruel it was, catching fish on steel hooks and hauling them out of water to drown in air, a terrible death, she'd always said, terrible: and now she stood on the pier with him behind her, his arms around her, sometimes helping her to hold the rod, showing her how.

Sometimes not.

I stood on the bank above, watching until I couldn't bear to watch any longer; and then I walked home with death in my thoughts like a resurrection man, needing a body from which there could be no resurrection.

Christians have it wrong. The symbol of God is a circle, not a cross. Everything circles, it comes around and comes around, world without end amen.

And you can cheat death for sure, you can even cheat God maybe, but you can't cheat the circle.

And so she came to me, when I was with my trains; and she said, 'God, would you look at you? I mean, just take a *look* at yourself, will you, take a look at your *life?*'

'I don't know what you mean,' I said, not looking up from where I was making an adjustment to a locomotive's bogie.

'I *know* you don't, that's the *problem,* that's what I'm *saying.* You ought to know, you ought to find out. See yourself how others see you, just for once...'

'You've changed,' I said.

'I've changed, that's right. I have

changed. I was changing anyway, but I've done it properly now. Which means I can see what you need, you need to change too. Brother, do you need to change...'

'What, then? Why should I change,' *why have you changed,* 'what's so wrong with me, the way I am? It satisfied you before.'

'No, David. I wouldn't say that. Not satisfied. It kept me in quiet desperation, that's what I'd say. But I'm not going to be quiet any longer, I can't afford to. I've got my life to live, I've given you too much already. You're not worth it to me, David, unless you can change...'

Then she enumerated all that was wrong with me, she said, all that made me different from the fisherman: from my speech and dress to my interests to my innermost secrets—secret no longer, I thought suddenly, she would have told him all—and my aspirations for myself and Beth together.

If ever we were together any more, because we weren't now. Only in the same room, not at all together.

She listed me, all the sum of my parts; and she condemned me, each individual part and the whole that they comprised.

Coldly, clinically, surgically she said what should never have been said, what my Beth never would have said; and all I said, all I could say was, 'Come for a walk.'

'What?'

'Come for a walk,' I repeated dully.

'David, it's dark out there, it's *cold* out there, it'll likely start raining any minute; why the hell should I want to go for a walk?' *With you,* unstated but underlying, very much there.

You'd go with him. But I only stood there mutely, looking at her, waiting; and at last she said, 'Oh, for God's sake, come on, then. Let's go, let's do it. We've got to talk anyway, maybe it'll be easier on the move. Maybe you'll find it easier in the dark,' with a brisk contempt in her voice, unrecognisable, not my Beth.

She walked beside me down to the pier, where I'd thought we'd never walk again. Too much risk of losing her, I'd thought, not realising how she was lost already. *Not my Beth,* the constant theme, the chorus of this time: and how true it was, nothing but simple truth. Something else animated her body now, something given or taken from the fisherman's mouth when he breathed his life into her, none of her own; she'd been gone then, dead and gone, and something other had been given back to me. Something vile, that used her body and her life as its own but was never her, was seeking only to corrupt what had been so clean...

But it had come full circle now, the wheel had turned and turned and brought us here where it had started, where I had lost her and thought her found again, where now I chose to accept that dreadful loss in preference to this.

I took hold of her at the pier's edge and jumped down to the lower level ten feet below, where the sea swirled and broke at high tide. High now, it tugged at my knees and taunted me, thief of my woman; but though she struggled I held her body in the water until the sea had cleansed it, until it was mine again, hers again, all things as they had been and the wheel turning on.

And this was all the space there was, all the world allowed: that it was raining, and I held her in my arms, and she was dead.

Ann Cleeves

THE HARMLESS PURSUITS OF ARCHIBALD STAMP

I read the report in the *Journal*. It was very brief. The Magistrates' Court had ordered the destruction of a collection of birds' eggs, which had been found in an attic in a house in North Shields. The collection had been discovered by the police after the death of an elderly man. Hidden in a safe in the same house were notebooks which showed that the eggs had been illegally taken. They had not been inherited from a Victorian grandfather. In the newspaper a name was given, but at first it was unfamiliar. To me he had always been Dr Stamp. The first name seemed strangely theatrical. It reminded me of a music-hall comedian.

The eggs were destroyed at the insistence of the Court and the implication of the newspaper report was that this was unnecessary, rather a shame. They were beautiful objects in their own right. What harm could it do to keep them? Perhaps they could be donated to Newcastle's Hancock Museum, where schoolboys could marvel at them and become interested themselves in the natural world. They were meticulously catalogued in the hidden notebooks. All had been taken from the north of England. Mr Archibald Stamp, for that was how his neighbours had known him, had not liked to travel far in pursuit of his pleasures.

There was an address in the newspaper too, and the next day I went to visit it. The house was a substantial Edwardian semi with a large and overgrown garden. A moth trap had been left outside to rust and two bamboo poles were set at each end of a niche through the bushes. Between them Dr Stamp would have strung a mist net to catch migrant birds and ring them. He had always been an exceptional naturalist.

When I knew him he had lived in Jesmond, Newcastle's superior suburb. He had rather a grand flat, which I fancy he must have inherited from affluent parents. He wouldn't have chosen it himself. He had worked at the University, hiding from students, immersing himself in his botanical research. He was an expert on grasses. I thought he must have moved out to the coast on retirement, attracted by the thought of a garden.

I had opened the gate and walked halfway up the path without thinking, then paused, feeling ridiculous, wondering why I was there. I imagined the neighbours staring at me and could not turn and run away. Instead I walked on to the door and rang the bell. I did not expect a reply but a woman appeared. She was small, attractive, in a well-groomed WI sort of way. I was astounded. It never occurred to me that Dr Stamp might have married.

'Yes?' she said. Her voice was pleasant, not in the least off-putting.

'I was looking for Dr Stamp.' It was all I could think of to say.

'Oh, dear,' she said, and very kindly she explained that he was dead. She invited me in for tea but I said I would not intrude. Even from the doorstep the house smelled like the Jesmond flat, of his tobacco and books. I was not sure I could control myself if I saw the familiar furniture. I knew he would not have changed that. So we talked on the doorstep. She was a neighbour, it seemed, and had taken on the task of going through his things. There was no one else to do it.

She broached the subject of the egg collection herself. She thought it a pity that the authorities had made so much fuss. Perhaps stealing birds' eggs was against the rules but it wasn't a real crime, was it? Not like burglary or assault. It was a gentle, harmless occupation and they should have left well alone.

'Did you know him, then?' she asked, just before I left. 'You were friends?'

'I suppose we were at one time,' I said. 'I owe my interest in natural history to him.'

'Ah,' she said, sadly. 'He was a great example.'

I first met Dr Stamp when I was eleven. It was a time of change—the year of the eleven-plus and the first Beatles hit. We lived in a neat little council house on the edge of the city, my mam, my dad and me. My dad was a nervy man. Mam had married him because he looked like a film star, thin and soulful, but he hadn't lived up to expectations. He worked for the Post Office as a sorter, the long fingers which had attracted Mam and made her think of a violinist were useful for flicking letters into pigeonholes.

By the time I was eleven Mam had given up trying to improve him and turned her attentions to me. She had plans which involved my going up in the world and providing her with the lifestyle she had always wanted, a lifestyle which she had seen in the films. She had taken me to the pictures since I was a toddler—not to the Saturday club which she thought common, but to adult afternoon matinées. She always dressed up for these outings in a hat and high-heeled shoes. When I passed the eleven-plus she chose the Grammar School in the middle of town because the uniform was smarter though it was two bus-rides away. There was no Metro then.

That spring I joined the Ornithological Society. There was a poster in the library advertising for junior members. I took the details back to my mother hesitantly, afraid that she would think joining was common too, and refuse me permission, but she was surprisingly encouraging.

'They meet in the University,' she said. 'You'll get to know all sorts of nice people there.'

The first time she took me herself, came with me to the lecture-theatre door and pushed me through it, half-hoping, half-afraid that she might be invited in too. She sent my father to collect me. After that Dr Stamp always delivered me home.

He must have been there at that indoor meeting though I don't remember it. I noticed him first on the field trip to the Farnes which took place on an unusually hot afternoon in May. There was a coach to Seahouses, then Billy Shiel's boat to Staple Island. My mother had given up her weekly visit to the pictures to pay for it. I still remember it as the happiest day of my life. Better than sex when I finally made it with a woman, or finding out that I'd got a first at university.

Everything glittered that day. There were puffins and guillemots and scaly, reptilian shags. So close I could reach out and touch them. The smell of guano and seaweed. And Dr Stamp explaining, lending his binoculars so the birds hit me in the eye, naming everything for me.

He was a tall man with a slightly misformed spine which gave him the air of always looking on the ground. But when he *did* tilt back his head to look at you he had startling eyes which glittered like the water and a sudden shy smile that included you and made you feel special.

There was only one other recruit from the poster campaign and he was on the Farnes trip, sharing Dr Stamp's attentions. His name was Will Pickering and he was a year older than me. He had red hair and the sort of freckles you usually only see on a girl. He lived in Jesmond too, in a big terraced house full of children. His father was a solicitor, and his mother wrote articles for women's magazines. They never seemed much like parents to me. They listened to rock music and according to Will, they took drugs. I had never met adults like them before.

The three of us—Will, Dr Stamp and me—became unlikely companions. Will and I were friends though I always felt that in some sense we were rivals for Dr Stamp's admiration. He suggested trips into the hills, and to Holy Island, early in the morning before the trippers arrived. But not every weekend. Some days he claimed to be busy.

These excursions may not sound much now, but for Will and me they were adventures. My parents had never owned a car and were frightened anyway to leave familiar territory. We never took a holiday. Will's parents were always busy, wrapped up in work and the yearly babies, desperate not to miss out on the Sixties, and they had little time for him. So our birdwatching expeditions into the Northumberland countryside were an escape and a revelation. Dr Stamp was our hero. We would have done anything for him.

He waited two years before he initiated us into the mysteries of egg collecting. I suppose he wanted to be sure of us. He did not attempt to justify or explain. He told us flatly that it was illegal and if we wanted we could have nothing to do with it. With a shy pride he showed us his collection in the flat in Jesmond. In a room we had never been in before, there was a huge mahogany cabinet of the sort you'd see in a museum, with tray upon tray of eggs. He could tell us where each of them had come from. He said it was a scientific study. His real life's work. And they *were* beautiful. Even I could see that.

Then he explained the delicate operation of preparing the eggs. Only schoolboys poked a hole at each end and blew them, he said, with disdain. He showed us his tools—a dentist's drill to puncture the side of the egg, a pipette and a syringe. Air was introduced through fine tubing to remove the contents, then water to flush out the shell. The trick was to collect the eggs early, before the chicks had started to form, and when the contents were sufficiently liquid for easy removal. That was the skill. Occasionally he'd misjudged the timing, he said regretfully, and he'd had to use embryo solvent to dissolve the chick inside. That could take weeks and it wasn't ideal. Even that did not put us off. Perhaps it even encouraged us. We had to prove to him that we weren't squeamish.

'Well?' he had said, flashing us one of his magic smiles. 'Are you on then?'

Of course we were on. How could we refuse him? The trips to the hills took on a new significance. Winter was spent in planning, in marking the maps. Dr Stamp belonged to a network which shared information. There was the challenge of avoiding detection by wardens and police officers, though I believe that Dr Stamp exaggerated this danger to thrill us. We never saw anyone on our raids to the Tyne Valley, the Simonsides or the Cheviot.

There was a ritual to the preparation on the day of the theft. We always took the same equipment: maps, thermos flasks lined with cotton wool in which to hide the eggs, climbing gear. Sometimes a rubber dinghy to get to islands or lakes where grebes or ducks bred. I see now that this had much in common with a heroin addict preparing a fix. Much of the pleasure came from anticipation.

In the breeding season we thought of little else. Quite often we spent the whole weekend with Dr Stamp. He had a tent and there was a ritual in setting up camp too. Everything had to be done in the correct order. He was firm about that. My mother was delighted that I went out with him so often. She had convinced herself that when the time came he would obtain a job for me. Something clean and secure. It did not appear odd to her, or apparently to anyone else, that a middle-aged man should enjoy the company of young boys.

There was only one comment so far as I can remember. A sixth-former in my school who was going to Oxford to read zoology bumped into me in the library and seemed to recognise me.

'Oh yes,' he said. 'You're one of

Doc Stamp's little boys, aren't you?' And sniggered. I didn't know what he meant. You must realise that although it was supposed to be a permissive age, that was a much more innocent time. And in fact nothing overtly sexual ever occurred on the trips into the hills, though we always shared the same tent. I do recall physical horseplay, slaps on the back, wrestling, but it seemed quite innocent. A part of the experience, like collecting the eggs. What Dr Stamp got out of it I really can't say.

Will grew up quicker than me. I see that now. I suppose it was the family he came from. He had to stand on his own feet. It made him more sexually aware. He began to resist the contact, the arm around the shoulder. It made him question the whole set-up.

We were on Cuthbert's Crag, a rocky outcrop of Cheviot which formed a cliff where peregrines breed. It was one of our regular sites. Dr Stamp liked to get there early in the season before the illegal falconers who collected the eggs for their own use: to incubate and hatch. It was a cold day. There was still a patch of snow on the tops.

It was Will's turn to go down on the

rope. He was poised at the top, leaning back with the rope taking his weight when he said suddenly as if the words had just come into his head:

'This is wrong, you know. Illegal.'

He was always impulsive. It wasn't the best moment for a confrontation.

'You've always known it's illegal,' Dr Stamp said.

'You should stop,' Will said, 'before you get caught.'

'Oh, I'll never get caught.' The words were slow and pedantic, slightly chiding, as if we'd misidentified a plant he'd pointed out only the week before. We should have known better.

'We could tell someone.'

'I don't think so.' Dr Stamp gave each word consideration. 'After all, you are involved too. And who would the authorities believe?'

He let out the rope and Will jerked several yards down the cliff. Dr Stamp held him there. He was a strong man, very fit.

'If I let go,' Dr Stamp said conversationally, 'you would probably lose your balance and fall. I'd say it was an accident. Davey would back me up, wouldn't you, Davey?

Davey wouldn't let me down.'

He smiled across at me as if he knew me so well that he did not need an answer.

'Bring me up,' Will shouted. His voice seemed distant and thin.

'Oh no,' Dr Stamp said. 'Not without the eggs.'

So with the female peregrine screaming around his head, Will had to climb down to the eyrie, not knowing whether Dr Stamp would pull him back or not. There was a ledge where he could stand. He took the eggs and wrapped them in cotton wool and put them into a box and then into his rucksack. Only then did Dr Stamp take the strain of the rope and bring him back. We behaved quite normally for the rest of the day. What else could we do?

I tried to persuade myself that the conversation on Cuthbert's Crag had never happened or that it was some sort of joke, but it affected Will badly. He became nervy and tense, reminding me, in a strange way, of my father. I think it was my fault. I think he felt betrayed. If I'd shouted at Dr Stamp, 'No, I won't back you up, no way,' Will might not have been so shaken. He avoided me, though his parents had me round one evening when he was out. They sat me in their big chaotic kitchen, with kids' paintings on the walls, amid the dried flowers and cookery books and asked me what was wrong. Even they had noticed.

'You're his friend, David,' they said. 'Is something worrying him?'

I just said no, not as far as I knew.

Even now I'm not quite sure why I lied. Partly it was because you never told parents important things, and if Will hadn't chosen to confide in them that was his business. But that wasn't the real reason. The real reason was Dr Stamp. I knew the conversation on Cuthbert's Crag hadn't been a joke.

That summer Will failed his exams and despite their socialist principles, his parents sent him away to boarding school in Scotland. I think he asked to go. I never saw him again. Later I heard that he hadn't settled and there'd been some sort of breakdown.

I saw less of Dr Stamp. I still went to the Ornithological Society meetings and the field trips, but when he invited me for weekends away I pleaded too much homework, or said that my father was ill, which was often true. He made no effort to persuade me. I realise now that young boys came after me as, no doubt, there had been others before. He collected us as he collected successive clutches of eggs. I went away to college and took up my own life.

I came across him again six months ago. He was in a dinghy on a small lake where shelduck breed, so I knew what he was up to. I was surprised that he was still alive. I saw that although I'd always thought of him as old he hadn't been in those days when we'd spent so much time together. He would have been much the same age as I am now. That made a difference to my opinion of him. What is a permissible eccentricity in an elderly man seems squalid, rather disgusting, in someone younger.

I was counting merlins on the moor. My obsession, you see, had taken a different turn. I was now a bona fide ornithologist with a Government licence to approach the nests of specially protected birds, and had trained for a ringing permit. I used the skills taught by Dr Stamp to find the nests. I would stare at the eggs in a rather voyeuristic way, like someone looking at a pornographic magazine, but

I would not touch them. I would make a careful record of the site and walk away. When the eggs hatched I would ring the chicks. My pleasure came in holding the warm and downy birds in my palm.

Dr Stamp was alone in the dinghy. He had no boys to wade ashore for him. I suppose times have changed. Everyone now can get into the countryside and the pursuits he had to offer must have seemed tame to a new generation.

I stood at the boggy edge of the pool and watched him. He was intent on rowing to the bank and did not see me until he was almost upon me. I think he must have recognised me because he half-stood in the boat and gave me that sudden, boyish smile which had charmed me all those years before. Perhaps he thought I was there for the same reason as him, that I had been corrupted after all.

The movement unbalanced the boat. He lost his footing and tipped into the water. It was not deep there but he was encumbered by his rucksack with its eggs, and his binoculars and his waders. Perhaps he hit his head as he fell. It all happened so quickly that I do not remember. The surface was covered with weed and I could not see below it.

Of course I could have saved him. I don't know why I didn't wade in and pull him out. I never hated him as Will did. I wouldn't have pushed him in deliberately, even if I'd had the chance. Perhaps I'd grown into the habit of passivity since being too scared to speak up that day on Cuthbert's Crag. Perhaps I just didn't fancy getting wet on a cold morning. I had a long walk back to the car. In any event I turned away and left him to drown. Even now I don't have any feelings about that either way. Not guilt or jubilation. It wasn't revenge on Will's behalf. Nothing like that.

A month after my visit to the house in North Shields there was an obituary to Dr Stamp in a natural history magazine. It was embarrassed, understated, and I realised that I wasn't alone in my uncertain response to him. I wondered how many others had guessed at his egg stealing and why none of us had considered his activities sufficiently harmful to make a fuss. Perhaps we were all, in one sense, his boys.

Barbara Crossley

RIGHT BETWEEN THE EYES

So this was what it felt like to be shot, right between the eyes. Hanson Gray's vision cleared. His life was over.

How could he still be in his seat, no blood on the office floor? Why was his body still functioning inside its Austin Reed suit, when to all intents and purposes he was dying? Where was the smoking gun?

Simon Miles, oblivious to the explosion he'd just caused, sat opposite Hanson, his face a composite of embarrassment and grim implacability.

'You do understand why we're having to downsize?' he asked of Hanson's breathing corpse.

Hanson barely had it in him to croak, never mind reply.

'Because of difficult trading conditions and increased competition,' parroted Miles patiently. The words echoed emptily in

Hanson's head, for all he was hearing was his inner voice: 'I'm redundant, I'm forty-nine, I'll never get another job worth a damn. We can't exist without my salary, my pension-plan doesn't mature for six years, there's no way I can disguise this as early retirement and I'd never make enough as a consultant. What will I say at parties when people ask what I do? Nothing. I am nothing. I'm no one.'

'Why me?' he managed to whimper, gathering his strength with the force of desperation. 'I've given seventeen years to this company, I'm a senior accountant.' The title sounded hollow even to Hanson's biased ears. 'Don't experience and—and loyalty count for anything with you people?'

Miles—whose career had progressed in two-year leaps from company to company —gave a placatory gesture. 'Outplacement is a fact of commercial life these days. It's to do with the normal ebb and flow of business cycles, nothing personal, Hanson.'

Nothing personal? Then why was he hurting in every molecule of his being, why did his brain feel about to implode? He was the one who'd have to go home and explain to Charlotte that life as they knew it was about to end—no more Caribbean at Christmas, no more antique-buying, no more shooting parties. He was the one who'd have to take their sons out of private school and watch them sulk indoors, too ashamed to tell their friends the reason why. He was the one who'd have to suffer his parents' wordless sniff which meant 'Of course, we expected this—you never did have enough drive.' They'd never let him forget it, none of them would. What was to be their life after this death?—a scuffed semi, shopping at Scrimp'n'Save, loading jumbo economy packs into a second-hand saloon? He could imagine Charlotte's disgust. He might as well go down to the car park, attach a pipe to the company-car exhaust and lay out his body to die in a brand-new Ford Mondeo. Then at least the family'd get his life insurance, he'd be good for something.

But of course, they wouldn't. A suicide would make the policy void. He'd have to drive home as normal. He'd have to present Charlotte with the burden that was himself: he could see her sighing, giving up on him, launching into the development of her dried flower sideline as a full-scale business. Could he bear to live off her dried flowers, his life hollow as an empty vase? He had a sudden vision of throttling Miles with his own silk tie, throwing the body down the garbage chute, pretending this conversation never happened, carrying on as before. But there'd always be another Miles to take his place, clone upon clone, all of them programmed to pronounce the death sentence on Hanson Gray. No, he was the one who'd have to die. He could rig up an accident. A car crash? He shuddered—too frightening—and he'd run the risk of hurting someone else.

As he left Miles' office, grey-tinged, he shrank from facing his colleagues' condolences. He loosened his tie, suddenly claustrophobic in the building that had been his security, his bolthole from the family. Charlotte's voice could grate, and the boys were wearing; now he couldn't seal himself off any more.

He wandered out into Manchester's summer-stifled streets, clutching his briefcase to his chest like a comfort bear, his chin contorted. He wondered why his face was wet, and was astonished to realise he was crying. He hadn't known he was capable of tears. What would people think?

They passed him by, uncaring—what did it matter any more what they thought? He could cry, laugh, dance in the road like a drunken beggar, stripping his clothes off one by one. Hanson Gray didn't exist any more, he was nothing, no one who mattered.

When the tears cleared he found himself sitting on a kerb at the scruffier end of Deansgate, and through the crowd's bustle he was staring at a travel agency. Outside the shop was a board, and on the board was 'Today—Express Coach to Blackpool'. The resort was the antithesis of all the Grays' aspirations—cheap, brash, vulgar—the sort of place Charlotte could only be bribed to visit, and then wearing a surgical mask. But he'd been there on a conference and felt curiously liberated by it: no longer judged, no one's eyes poring critically over his wardrobe, no one estimating his worth by address or occupation, no longer waiting for a glance of dismissal or a welcome to the coterie.

Blackpool suddenly seemed to him a desirable place to be.

'I'm terribly sorry, darling,' he said in the phone booth, 'something's come up at work, I've got to zip across country for a meeting. Bit of a crisis, I'm afraid. I'll be staying there overnight...maybe longer. I'll keep in touch.'

'But Hanson,' replied his wife resentfully, not even concerned where he was going, 'you know I've invited the Morleys for drinks and a bite of supper, and I only did it for you. We need to keep in with Piers Morley, he'll get you a leg-up on the shooting club committee.'

A leg-up on the shooting club committee —the words followed him from his other life, up the coach steps, getting fainter with every mile of the way to Blackpool. Charlotte was cultivating the country set, and had turned out to be a keen shot: game or clay pigeons, depending on the season. Hanson felt more like a beater. There was no way he'd get a leg-up, or even a toe-hold on the club committee now. Old Hanson the accountant was dead, and Piers Morley wouldn't want to retrieve his remains.

The coach disgorged its passengers on the tarmac and a salty sea breeze blew up Hanson's nose, drawing him down the street, across the main seafront road to the promenade. It was mid-afternoon, a July day, warm, humid, plenty of trippers lounging on the beach who'd never had need of an accountant and never would. They hardly noticed him; he mattered nothing to them. He tramped over the sand in his black leather lace-ups, still carrying his briefcase, full of redundant matter—a report he'd never give, a memo he'd never read—but he couldn't let go of it yet. Maybe, he thought miserably as he trudged steadily towards the sea, maybe he'd find the strength to throw it in. And then strip off his Austin Reed suit, his Gieves and Hawkes shirt, his Tissot watch, and follow it: knee-deep, waist-high, up to his armpits, over his head, and on into oblivion.

Passing the bucket and beach-ball brigade, however, he realised he'd need props. It had to look like a swimming accident. A child splashed among the waves on a Lilo, giving him an idea. People were wafted out to sea on airbeds every year, weren't they? And their bodies were always washed up, in time.

Back across the promenade he blundered, toward the shops. A side street beckoned, stalls lining it like a souk, crammed with sexually explicit T-shirts, cartoon-imprinted towels, bad-taste postcards and joke-tankards displaying indecent monks or the Mannequin Pis. Hanson perused these like a visitor from another planet, and indeed was viewed as such by the stallholders—or at least by those who didn't suspect he was an inspector of some sort. Narrowing their eyes, they held back from serving him.

He stopped by a clutch of blown-up airbeds, corseted together with string: a giant banana, inflated dentures, a swollen lobster, a drooping crocodile.

'You've nothing, umm, plainer?' asked Hanson of the assistant plaintively.

'Sorry, love. Blackpool doesn't come plainer than this,' replied the copper-haired, bum-bagged, pumpkin-bosomed stallholder, who'd decided to meet the enemy full-on. 'Go on, take the false teeth, they'll give your missis a laugh—that's what people come here for.'

She jogged his elbow as she wobbled the rubbery jaws together, urging him to laugh with her. 'Ho-ho-ho,' he managed to come up with, not very convincingly.

'Here,' said Mrs Pumpkin, freeing the pink-and-white monster, 'you have this on me, love, take it for your kids,' meaning, take it and go away, leave me and my turnover out of whatever you've come to check.

'Kids?' he ventured tentatively. He was strangely touched that she should take such a personal interest in him. 'How—how did you know I had—?'

'Well-set-up feller like you, love, bound to have a family, aren't you? Wouldn't seem right if you didn't.'

'No...I suppose...' It hadn't seemed right, that's why he'd buckled down: got married, had two children, no more, the societal norm. It was what was expected... Vaguely, as if it were a childhood dream, he remembered yearning to do good works in a hot climate: live simply, barter his help for a frugal sustenance, smiles his reward—Voluntary Service Overseas or famine relief, yes, something like that. Father snorted, Mother scorned, Charlotte had kissed him at the May Ball and so the dream had crumpled.

'You all right, love? Still with us, eh?' the stallholder asked, puzzled at his reverie. Five minutes later, and slightly relieved, she watched him go away, briefcase still in hand, now containing one deflated denture-airbed, one pair of electric-blue nylon baggy swim-shorts and a plastic snorkel.

Why hadn't he bought a towel too? she wondered briefly, before swivelling back to serve someone wanting an invisible canary-on-a-leash that twittered like Tweetie-Pie.

Of course Hanson didn't need a towel, he'd be dried off in the morgue. At least he'd now look the part. The heat was becoming oppressive, he was even beginning to look forward to his final dip. He would lay down his briefcase, doff his constricting suit, don the shorts under cover of his jacket and wade in, dragging his dentures, heading for release. Impatiently he waited to cross the road to the promenade, wanting to get down on the beach and get it over with.

'Give us 50p for a cuppa tea?'

His trouser-leg was being tugged. He looked down to see a girl seated on the pavement, her hair looking as if it had been extruded from his paper shredder. She wore a cavernous jumper the colour of puddles, black leggings that bagged at the knees, riding up her scrawny calves, and mouldy boots. She looked about sixteen, the same age as his elder son, and she smelt musky.

'I only want a cuppa tea,' she repeated the last two words like a mantra. 'I haven't eaten for two days.'

A beggar, hmm? He was used to these in Manchester—they'd fester in abandoned doorways, sucking on brown plastic bottles and putting out a grimy palm when their Strongbow ran out.

'I give to charities for the homeless, not to individuals,' was his standard reply; and it was true, he could justify it if asked, but the girl was not asking.

'Fuck you then, squire,' she muttered, sizing up his bulging briefcase.

Feeling uncomfortable, he dodged the traffic to cross the road, and out of the corner of his eye he saw the puddle-coloured jumper coming after him like a reproach. He wanted to get away as quickly as possible, convinced the musky smell was growing stronger, she must be gaining on him, why hadn't he given her the wretched 50p? Oh lord, her eyes—even the whites looked dirty—bored through his suit, not scanning for labels like Charlotte's set, but X-raying for his wallet. He wouldn't be intimidated; he had to get away. He shot across the tram-tracks that ribboned the seafront, unheeding of a thunderous old tram, festooned in light bulbs, bearing down on him. He looked up, straight into its headlamps, the driver's eyes above them wide with horror as he tried to slam on the brakes. The terror froze Hanson solid. In the two seconds it took for the tram to reach him it flashed through his mind that this was the very accident he'd been looking for—quick, plausible, unexpected, far more dignified than being swept out to sea on a pair of giant dentures. Yes. He prepared to accept his fate, overcome with a sense of relief.

Blackness descended, he felt himself bowled over, steeled himself for the crush of metal on bone. It never came. He opened his eyes, found himself rolling on concrete at the side of the track. His briefcase had burst open as he hit the ground, but it had been deftly scooped up and was gone.

'She saved him,' a woman was shouting. 'Stop that girl, she saved his life, don't let her get away.'

People asked him if he was all right. With a kind of despair, he said yes, then looked up dazedly to see the girl being brought back between two hairy-chested men in shorts and very little else.

'Give it 'im back, lassie,' said one of them to her in a Scots accent. 'Give it 'im back and we'll say no more about it. You did push 'im out the way of the tram, he wouldna be here if you hadn't. P'raps he'll show his appreciation.'

And so she knelt down and produced his briefcase from under her blankety sweater, presenting it to Hanson sulkily.

'Take it,' he said, too crushed to care. 'It's no use to me any more.'

'No use to me either,' she retorted. 'Nothing sellable in it. I need money, not rubbish.' The contents—blow-up dentures, snorkel and all—displayed for her disparagement, suddenly intrigued her. 'You some kinda nutcase?'

'What if I am?'

'Welcome to the club.'

Hanson realised his briefcase had revealed him as a non-conformist, like her.

'Did I really save your life?' she asked.

'Yes, and I didn't want that either.'

'You've a nerve,' she responded with real feeling, a flicker of amusement in her eyes. He warmed to those eyes, black-ringed though they were. All his family's were an icy grey, hers a rich brown which probably matched her hair when it was washed.

People shuffled round the pair, finding

them entertaining, wondering what they'd do next.

'What's your name?' asked Hanson.

'Mandy.' A child's name, a name someone must have cooed over her cot in the days when she was bathed and fed. It fitted ill on a grungy runaway like her.

'Come on then, Mandy. Let's get away from these spectators, I'll buy you a cup of tea.'

'And the rest. Roast chicken and baked potatoes with butter, and ice-cream. Fair swap for a life.'

'Whatever you like.'

Mandy attached herself to Hanson like a stray cat.

Numbed by all that had happened, he put off setting up any more accidents and booked himself into a poky bed-sit that was billed as a holiday flatlet. Mandy would appear at the steps every morning to be fed. He'd take her for bacon and eggs or chips as she wished, and then she'd disappear again to her feral life. She'd prickle when he inquired what she did. An air of chemical substances hung around her; he couldn't leave her to fend for herself, for she might not. In a curious way he realised she was keeping him alive, for he wanted her to live.

She began to linger over her daily meal, as though she wanted to stay longer in his company. Her eyes grew brighter, and one hot day he tempted her into his room with the promise of ice-cold Coke. He'd been using the blow-up dentures as an armchair for reading, enthroned on the bed, and she giggled for the first time, her smile his reward, and then she kissed him. He glowed, realising that he loved her.

He'd told no one his real name, he'd grown a beard and sold his suit, and travelled to a far-off town to empty his bank account. Finally he cut up all the debit, credit and cash cards in the name of Hanson Gray, tore up his personal documents, and took Mandy down to the beach to make a bonfire of his old self.

'What name shall I use now?' asked Hanson, encircling her with his arms as they watched the embers die. 'I'll need to get a job soon.'

'Nigel Nutcase,' replied Mandy derisively. 'Or David Do-good.'

Hanson smiled. He had at last done good works in a hot climate. He filled up with gladness, wanting to pour it out like champagne to give her: she'd scoff if he told her, but this felt better than anything he'd ever known. Later that evening she pulled him toward the Pleasure Beach funfair, begging him to mount a carousel of galloping horses. As he twirled round and round, Mandy behind him on the saddle, clutching his waist, he realised at last what this wondrous feeling was. Peace. Nothing to strive for, nothing to prove. How many years he had wasted, struggling to be Hanson Gray.

Barely twenty feet away, at the rifle range, two middle-aged women took aim at the targets, piling up points to win fluffy toys from a selection that surrounded a large mirror at the back of the stall. One woman was a private detective, the other her client, and both were accomplished markswomen, to the stallholder's chagrin.

'I'm sorry it's turned out this way,' said the detective, accepting a second stuffed bear.

'Not as sorry as I am,' replied Charlotte, overcome with loathing for this onion-and-candy-smelling funfair with its common shrieks and garish blare. Before anyone could stop her, she swung her air rifle toward the carousel. She hadn't meant to do this, she'd only meant to give him a good dressing-down, claim her wifely desserts, but that expression of joy on his face as she watched him in the mirror hit her like a bullet. In the next second she pulled the trigger, and Hanson's world exploded. He believed it was with happiness. The pellet's shock sent him soaring away from the horse's back, still in Mandy's arms. He crashed skull-down on the carousel floor, and was no more.

So that was how it really felt to be shot, right between the eyes. Charlotte's vision cleared. Her life was over.

Eileen Dewhurst

A TOUR TOO FAR

Somewhere around her middle forties, Miss Muriel Clitheroe sublimated her unattained desire for the perfect man into a fulfilling passion for the perfect artefact.

This was a change for the better so far as Miss Clitheroe's temperament was concerned, which she herself had come to admit was really more comfortable with things than with people.

Miss Clitheroe, in fact, an only child of socially uneasy parents, had never been very good at personal relationships. It was all right in the municipal library where she spent her working life. There, her contacts with people were defined by her office, and all verbal exchanges could be limited to books. And in her lunch hour she could cross the central square from one imposing classical revival to another and browse the collection bequeathed to her native town at the turn of the century by a local philanthropist. It was still the small Lancashire town's chief glory, and Miss Clitheroe had been familiar with it for as long as she could remember. The philanthropist had had a good eye as well as a ready cheque-book, and had built up a fine collection of Chinese porcelain, nineteenth-century pictures (stronger on the Pre-Raphaelites than the Impressionists, which was all right by Miss Clitheroe), and important eighteenth-century English commodes—there was even one with written evidence of its provenance in the workshops of Thomas Chippendale.

Miss Clitheroe found her situation increasingly to her taste and dreaded retirement, but during her last working year she became aware that a second career awaited her. When the time came and she had to leave the library, her devoted study of the gallery's treasures and their history had its reward: she was able to take up a position as guide to the Pendlebury Collection.

As with her work in the library, the nature of her new appointment confined her personal contacts within reassuring boundaries: the giver and the receiver simply became the teacher and the taught.

Not so frequently, to Miss Clitheroe's one regret; her work in the gallery was by its nature intermittent, dependent on the groups who asked to be shown around. But there were always expeditions with the National Trust, or the Friends of the Museums and Art Galleries, to look forward to, and over the uneventful years she had saved a great deal of her salary. With fewer and fewer regretful moments, life was sweet.

There was no doubt, Miss Clitheroe reflected on a cold bright autumn afternoon as she briskly crossed the square towards her second workplace, that the most manageable audiences for her lecture tours were the elderly. The elderly moved when she moved, stood still when she stood still, always in a neat group close around her, politely and silently listening to what she had to tell them about her beloved furniture and porcelain and pictures. The elderly didn't go wandering off on their own being independent and then getting lost and breaking her flow when one of the uniformed attendants shepherded them back to her.

On the other hand, she had to admit

that the middle-aged tended to be the most responsive—unless there was a bossy know-all (usually, to Miss Clitheroe's regret, a woman) who argued the toss over everything she said.

Miss Clitheroe paused on the steps leading up to the pillared portico in the centre of the Portland stone façade and looked back at the neatly-laid-out municipal gardens without seeing them, suddenly reluctant to go in. The most difficult groups were the youngsters, and this afternoon she had a party of school-boys.

Preferable to schoolgirls, surprisingly. Schoolgirls, unless they were very young (Miss Clitheroe shuddered as a certain memory assailed her), were sulky and reluctant. The last time she had had schoolgirls they had peeled off bit by bit in ostentatiously bored sub-groups so that by the time she was halfway through all she had left were the two teachers and one tiresome seeker after knowledge who breathed like a panting puppy and interrupted Miss Clitheroe's every answer with another question.

Boys at least showed some enthusiasm, even though they never seemed able to keep still. Rolling around the rooms in their grey jerseys like blobs of mercury, Miss Clitheroe had once thought, a day or so after she had broken a thermometer...

Shaking herself back to duty she completed her ascent of the steps and entered the building, nodded to the attendant as she by-passed the turnstile, and went as she always did straight into the ladies' cloakroom just inside the marble-floored entrance hall.

As usual there was nothing for her to do with her appearance beyond look at it in the speckled mirror over the old-fashioned washbasins. Her French pleat was immune to all types of weather and in all temperatures her complexion remained pale and matt. In any case, her bus dropped her at the corner of the square, and it had to be a very wet day for any splashes to sully the backs of her stockings.

Miss Clitheroe made a token gesture of straightening the Victorian bar brooch linking the two points of the collar of her classic blouse, then looked up at her thin, expressionless face and experienced the brief pang of regret that still sometimes took her unawares when she was reminded that she had been good-looking, and thought of the contrast between the few men who had been available for encouragement in real life and the heroes of the romantic fiction she was ashamed that she continued to enjoy.

As usual, again, she had arrived early, and when she emerged from the cloakroom the party was only just beginning to straggle out of the coach she could see through the glass in the entrance doors. They were in uniform, more blobs of mercury, but Miss Clitheroe's experience was that uniformed children were more likely to be within the control of their teachers. Apart, of course, from the occasional Terror who appeared to be beyond discipline.

There was one of these today.

Miss Clitheroe spotted him at once, jamming the turnstile with a grubby handkerchief and looking wide-eyed and innocent at Geoff, the attendant on duty, as Geoff struggled to release it. Geoff knew what Miss Clitheroe was in for, their eyes met in a moment of understanding as the group surged between them. The presence of a young and muscular teacher fore and aft of the line didn't ease Miss Clitheroe's wariness, even when they managed to organise the boys into a group around her and impose silence as she began her introductory speech—the short version, suitable for schoolchildren.

'Good afternoon to you all, and welcome to our beautiful gallery!' Miss Clitheroe's voice, its once-Lancashire vowels now honed to a received pronunciation only a Professor Higgins would have rumbled, rose against the echo rebounding from the stone, the tiles and the stained glass that surrounded them. Later, in the smaller rooms, she could talk more intimately. 'Sir James Pendlebury knew exactly what sort of building he wanted for his treasures, and as mayor of the town and tireless worker on its behalf he had sufficient influence—and sufficient wealth'—as always, Miss Clitheroe offered her first wry smile at this point—'to be able, in 1898, to purchase the whole of the south side of Pendlebury Square. Yes!' Miss Clitheroe acknowledged a quickening of interest whether or not it was in evidence. 'Central Square was renamed in his honour, at the ceremony to mark the opening of his gallery.' One of the masters murmured approvingly into Miss Clitheroe's pause for effect. 'Although he appointed a leading local architect to design the gallery, Sir James personally supervised the building work at every stage...'

It was the Terror, of course, who had frayed the neat edge of the group, scuffing his shoes across the marble to pull a face at a Victorian statue of Apollo. And put out a hand...

'Before we start,' Miss Clitheroe said quickly, 'there is one thing we say to all our visitors: please don't touch!' She nodded towards the Terror, and one of the teachers, smiling wearily, took him by the shoulders and pushed him back into the group. As he was propelled forward the boy looked Miss Clitheroe in the eye and grinned.

A challenge. Well, she had met them before.

Nevertheless, she thought it prudent to limit herself to the minimal introduction reserved for when potential troublemakers were present, and soon had the party in the first of the larger rooms—one of her favourites, with its Pre-Raphaelite paintings and the finest of the commodes. The second of her wry smiles came the first time she used the word *commode* and explained what it *originally* meant—an eighteenth-century English cabinet in the French taste for use and decoration in drawing-rooms. It was in the centre of this gallery that the Chippendale commode was displayed, on a platform to protect its delicate gilded legs from inadvertent contact with the shoes of visitors.

The Terror's shoes were about to make deliberate contact.

'Oh, no!' Miss Clitheroe was rooted to the spot in shocked disbelief, but again one of the masters had him by the shoulders before any damage could be done.

'Sorry,' the master murmured, and to Miss Clitheroe's relief retained his grip. This time the Terror winked.

'I wonder, Miss Clitheroe...?'

Turning round, Miss Clitheroe was forced to accept that it wasn't her day. Behind her, accompanied by his tripod, lighting equipment and camera, stood the one person on the gallery staff whom she disliked, with his insolent stare and tendency to make facetious and even personal comments. Frank Cunningham, Clerk of Works. It had recently been decided that the gallery's contents should be comprehensively recorded on film and Frank Cunningham had appointed himself photographer. This wasn't the first time he and Miss Clitheroe had coincided in their official capacities, and Miss Clitheroe had usually managed to claim the field. Mr Cunningham might be a powerful NCO but in Miss Clitheroe's opinion he would never make an officer—what man would, who pronounced his name *Cooningham?*—and she had made her opinion clear.

But today she couldn't risk the delay of a confrontation. 'Very well, Mr Cunningham, if you must. I'll take my party through to the Tudor and Stuart room.'

Miss Clitheroe noted with amusement the surprise in Mr Cunningham's coarse-featured face. 'Very good of you, Miss Clitheroe.'

But the surprise had quickly faded and the eyes were once more bold and disrespectful. As she led her party away Miss Clitheroe suffered an involuntary shudder.

'The panelling in this room is Elizabethan and comes from a house in Essex...'

The Terror was still under physical control, and Miss Clitheroe relaxed into the influence of the room. How she loved it! Her eyes as she talked caressed the proportions of the court cupboard, the caning on the Charles II day-bed, the early trompe l'oeil marquetry of the cabinet that could be either Dutch or French...

The Terror had wriggled free and was bouncing on the red velvet Queen Anne sofa in the room ahead, smiling through the narrow doorway at Miss Clitheroe as he kicked his heels against the carved stretcher for the interminable seconds it took one of the masters to run through and repossess him.

Miss Clitheroe decided against including the smallest and most vulnerable rooms in her tour.

As she led the party through the others she was made steadily and more miserably aware that she had been wise. The Terror wrenched up the lid of a delicate straw marquetry box made by Napoleonic prisoners of war, tried to unscrew the finial of a George II carriage clock, and just failed to open a glass cabinet containing a wax model of the first Queen Elizabeth dressed in delicate paper quilling.

Admiring her own restraint, Miss Clitheroe merely remarked that it was a pity when visitors abused the gallery's generous policy of making its treasures accessible. The Terror gave her another dazzling smile.

The relief of shepherding the flock down to the basement tea room was enormous.

Until she noticed that the Terror was missing.

'Excuse me,' she murmured, and fled back up the stairs.

She found him in a side corridor, trying with a penknife to detach a high-relief lion from the front of a commode.

Miss Clitheroe had never in her life been so appalled. She saw red. Quite literally.

'You little devil!'

She had the thin shoulders between her hands and was shaking them.

Backwards and forwards.

'Geroff of me, tha' old cow... Ow!'

Miss Clitheroe was vaguely aware of a regular dull thudding sound accompanying the shaking, but not of the shouting and struggling growing feebler and feebler.

Backwards and forwards. Backwards and forwards...

It wasn't until the red mist cleared that Miss Clitheroe realised the thudding sound was the Terror's head striking the sharp

110

edge of tile which formed the central dado along the wall.

And that she was shaking a corpse.

She tried to tell herself it was a boy temporarily stunned but she knew that it wasn't.

The dead weight, and the eyes so fixed and wide.

Miss Clitheroe dropped the corpse to the floor and stood with clasped hands, trembling and moaning.

'Jesus Christ, Miss Clitheroe!'

'O-o-oh! Mr Cooningham!'

She was actually glad to see the Clerk of Works, to have something from the everyday break into her nightmare.

Mr Cunningham was bending down, examining the small still mound on the ground between them. Straightening up, shaking his head and again blaspheming, pointing to an enormous oak cupboard against the wall behind her. Miss Clitheroe noticed it for the first time. The very first time, she had never seen it before.

'In there!' Mr Cunningham said.

There was a large key in the cupboard lock. Mr Cunningham had to struggle with it for a few terrible seconds, then the cupboard was open, the mound scooped up like a piece of dog-dirt—Miss Clitheroe was shocked even in her horror that such an image should occur to her—and deposited inside. Mr Cunningham relocked the door and pocketed the key.

'Have you seen anyone since you left your party, Miss Clitheroe?'

'Only...' Miss Clitheroe retched. 'No!'

'Good. You came up to go to the ladies', didn't you?' At the head of the basement stairs. 'Better get back now to the tea room.'

Mr Cunningham was examining the tiles with which the Terror's head had come into contact (Miss Clitheroe could not accept as yet that she had been responsible), the floor below them.

'No visible blood, but I'll wash it over. Go back to your party, Miss Clitheroe. And pull yourself together or I shan't be able to help you.'

'Yes. Of course.' He was right, she had to pull herself together. Get back to the basement stairs without being seen and be as surprised and upset as everyone else when it was discovered the Terror was missing. She wasn't a fool, she could do it. 'Thank you, Mr Cunningham. You're—very kind.'

Under Mr Cunningham's still-disconcerting gaze Miss Clitheroe took to her heels, forcing herself to slow down as she reached the door of the ladies' room undetected and descend the stairs in her customary sedate manner. Normally she would have been hurt by evidence that she had not been missed. But today the animated chat of the boys, the relaxed faces of the masters lolling at each end of the long table, was a relief so great that for a moment she was giddy.

'Enjoying your teas? That's right!'

The masters had turned to her in surprise, a warning that she mustn't overdo it, make herself sound too affable, that she must just be her normal self.

But she was, in fact, being superhuman. She was managing to sit down for a full fifteen minutes by her watch before asking where the Terror was. 'I hope he isn't swinging on a chandelier!' she continued, and felt herself smile.

The masters' relaxation was over. They rose from the table, and after consultation at the foot of the stairs one of them went racing up.

The other came back to the table, where the giddiness had forced Miss Clitheroe to sit down again. A general restlessness was now apparent, and she and the master had difficulty restraining the boys from leaving the tea room. When the other master reappeared Miss Clitheroe also had difficulty getting up and walking across to him.

'So you haven't found him,' she said, aware of the boys crowding behind her.

'Not a sign.' The masters exchanged looks. 'But the chap on the door's admitted leaving it just now for a few moments, so the little tyke could have got out. Look...' His eyes pleaded with Miss Clitheroe. 'How if our guide comes round with one of us and points out the nooks and crannies Tony could have got into? If we don't find him then we'll have to assume he's off out somewhere.'

'Okay,' the other master said. 'And I'll get the rest of them onto the coach and we'll drive around.' His gaze swept the surging group. 'Priority number two's getting them settled.'

'You're too right. Miss, er...?'

'Clitheroe. Yes, of course. I'll lead the way.'

Miss Clitheroe's legs were only just strong enough to take her up the stairs.

She decided to get the worst over first, and led the way to the fatal corridor. Not too fast or direct, pausing en route to peer as convincingly as she could manage into the alcoves and recesses along the way.

'There's this corridor...' Miss Clitheroe peered fearfully into it, then bobbed back, involuntarily smiling. 'But you can see at a glance...'

The master came to stand beside her, and they both gazed down the uncluttered expanse of corridor, broken only by the abused commode. The cupboard had disappeared.

'Perhaps you'd better take a look in there.' With renewed energy, but remembering now that she shouldn't be smiling, Miss Clitheroe indicated the only door in the corridor wall, that of a gentlemen's cloakroom. 'Do please go and see.' She felt like the smug-looking criminals in TV crime series who open their front doors to the police and say 'Be my guest' and leave them to look round on their own because they've got rid of the evidence...

Criminals? Evidence of *what?*

Miss Clitheroe had to lean against the wall rather than faint, and told herself sternly that it still wasn't safe to start thinking.

The master came out of the cloakroom shaking his head, and shook it all round the gallery, downstairs in the shop and through the storage vaults, where they were joined by Mr Cunningham and the Assistant Curator. Miss Clitheroe had been afraid that they would come upon the cupboard somewhere else, but it was nowhere to be seen. When they eventually reached the doors the Assistant Curator questioned Geoff, who admitted, crushed, that he had answered a quick call of nature. Miss Clitheroe could have fallen on his neck.

She and the master and the Assistant Curator went outside, where the coach was just drawing up. The other master got out and told them they'd drawn a blank, but would now search more widely.

'And go to the police, I suppose,' Miss Clitheroe said.

'Yes, of course,' one of the masters responded quickly, as they looked at each other in alarm.

'We're sorry about this,' the other told the Assistant Curator, after a pause. 'But with all those dark corners down under...

116

If we don't find him in town the police'll be bound to want another look.'

'Of course, we have to expect it,' the Assistant Curator reassured him.

'Let us hope,' Miss Clitheroe observed, 'that you find the boy round the shops or in the market.'

'That'll be it,' one of the masters said heartily, and they shook hands and thanked her for the tour before getting into the coach.

Miss Clitheroe and the Assistant Curator watched it drive off and went back into the gallery, Miss Clitheroe having to keep a very tight rein on her thoughts. She told the Assistant Curator she had gone upstairs again after settling the party in the tea room. 'To the ladies' cloakroom,' she explained, dropping her eyes.

'And you saw no sign of the boy then? You'd have remembered what he looked like?'

Miss Clitheroe struggled with the hysterical laughter rising inside her. 'I'd have known a boy in school uniform on his own was in the wrong place, Mr Armitage. But I didn't see one, I'm afraid.'

'Try not to worry, Miss Clitheroe. It wasn't your fault.' The Assistant Curator wandered off, leaving Miss Clitheroe freshly shocked by how easy it was.

'Eeh, lass!' The man at the turnstile lifted his red, unhappy face from his hands.

'Don't you worry, either, Geoff,' Miss Clitheroe advised. 'He was a little devil, a born wrecker...'

She forced herself to stop. And Mr Cunningham was there, smiling at her.

'A word, Miss Clitheroe?' he suggested. 'In my office?'

Mr Cunningham's office was off the main hall. He motioned Miss Clitheroe to the chair in front of his desk and sat down behind it.

'You're a miracle worker, Mr Cunningham!'

'No, Miss Clitheroe, just quick to take advantage. That woodworm check we ran yesterday through the vaults—the cupboard was riddled. It had to be got out as quickly as possible, so it was arranged to bring it up and get it taken away the same day. It went while you were having tea. For burning.'

'Oh...' Miss Clitheroe leaned back and closed her eyes. 'But won't they open...make sure...?'

'I told 'em we'd already looked when we got it up, which we had. If they'd insisted on looking again we'd have discovered we'd mislaid the key.' Miss Clitheroe opened her eyes, and Mr Cunningham stared into them. 'But they were satisfied. Straight into the flames, they told me.'

'Mr Cunningham... Thank you.' He deserved something for his unselfish gesture. For not asking questions. 'If I could just try to explain...'

'I don't think you could, Miss Clitheroe,' Mr Cunningham said softly. 'But I saw the brat. I understand.'

'Mr Cunningham...I really can't thank you enough.'

'I think you can, Miss Clitheroe.'

'Anything,' she said, leaning towards him but aware as she spoke that she must not be too liberal.

'You see...' Mr Cunningham's voice was almost dreamy, his gaze now fixed on the ceiling. 'The reason I entered that corridor was to photograph the Mortlake tapestry across the end. Just a beautiful woven landscape. But there were two figures in it...'

Mr Cunningham brought his gaze down and fixed it on Miss Clitheroe, smiling.

Miss Clitheroe had thought the worst was over but it was only beginning. She could feel it running like a poison through her body, all the way down to her fingers and toes.

She couldn't speak, but Mr Cunningham wasn't expecting her to.

'No one will ever know about it, of course. It'll be our secret, one of the many things we shall have in common. But I shan't mention it again, because I'm going to be very kind to you. As you're going to be very kind to me. In all sorts of ways, it could be.' Mr Cunningham looked her up and down. It occurred to Miss Clitheroe that he was probably only four or five years her junior. She tried to suppress another shudder. 'You mustn't say the sort of thing you said just now to Geoff, by the way. You need looking after.'

Yes, of course she did. Mr Cunningham had to protect his investment. His investment in the private person of Muriel Maud Clitheroe. The situation was so hideously unbelievable Miss Clitheroe pinched her thigh in the sudden hope that she was dreaming and could make herself wake up. But she remained seated in front of Mr

Cunningham's desk, bathed in his terrible geniality.

'I should go home now, Muriel, lass,' he was saying gently. 'You must be worn out. Don't fret, I'll be in touch before you know.'

He led the way to the door, gripped her arm for an instant as she went out. She crossed the hall, murmured goodbye to Geoff, and went down the steps as if she was floating.

The rest of her life at the beck and call of Mr Cunningham, or the rest of her life in prison. Miss Clitheroe wondered if it would be preferable to go to the police.

Or...

The third possibility appalled her, but by the time she reached her bus stop it had grown as warm and cosy as a blanket around her trembling shoulders.

What had happened by accident could also happen by design.

Martin Edwards

ACT OF KINDNESS

'Do you know they used to call this place the Dying Dale?' asked Bryan Lillis. He waved in the direction of the valley that stretched out below their hillside garden. The impish smile on his face reminded his wife Nancy of the way he had looked when she first met him thirty-five years earlier. She was by nature serious and he'd always liked to tease her.

'Dying Dale?' She shivered slightly. A sunny March day was too rare a gift to spoil with talk of death, even in jest.

'Don't raise your eyebrows, it's true!'

'Go on, then.'

'In the seventeenth century, more people lived in Dybergh than do so today. Sheepfarmers, mostly. Then the Plague came to Dyburndale. Several people died in Dyburn down the road, but Dybergh was hit even harder. Every single family lost at least one member. Some were wiped

123

out completely. The hamlet was never the same again.'

Again Nancy could not help feeling cold. Bryan was a gentle man. He would have been hurt to think that his attempt to amuse and inform had upset her. She took refuge, as so often in the past, in gentle irony.

'I don't remember the estate agent telling us this when we were looking round.'

'Can you wonder? But never mind that. It's history. We're here and my God, we're here to stay.'

He beamed at the cottage they had bought. A simple stone dwelling from the outside, but with a spacious interior equipped with all mod cons. Their retirement home, far from the madding Manchester crowds they had fought through for so long.

Nancy had been reluctant to move. In the smart suburb where they lived, she had a circle of friends whom she had no wish to leave behind. It was different for Bryan; he was often away on business and complained from time to time that he'd lacked the time to put down roots. But there had always been another deal to clinch, another train or plane to catch.

Until he'd had his warning, she could never have imagined him slowing his pace or settling down somewhere as far away from the city's bustle as this, the remotest of the Yorkshire Dales.

Of course, in the end he had prevailed. The heart attack had been minor, nothing to worry about according to the best specialist money could buy, but enough to frighten him. A few weeks later the advertising agency in which he was a director-shareholder had received an offer too good to refuse from a larger rival keen to buy up the competition. To Nancy's amazement, he'd jumped at the chance to sell.

'No one on his deathbed ever says, "I wish I'd spent more time at the office," ' he pointed out.

She didn't care for talk of death. They were not old yet, despite the warning. Life had so much to offer and there was much she yet wanted to do. She did not feel she'd been shortchanged in her fifty-eight years—how could she, when Bryan had provided her with so many material blessings? All the same, it was inevitable that her role as homemaker, as wife and mother to two demanding children, had restricted her activities. And now Jacqui was married and living on the South Coast and Peter was working abroad for a multinational, she had an urge to spread her own wings. But that didn't mean flying to the back of beyond.

'A bungalow, perhaps,' she had suggested. 'Somewhere in mid-Cheshire might be nice. Not too far from a main-line railway station, so I can keep coming to town to do the shopping.'

'Nonsense! A clean break, that's what we need. Shake the city dust from our feet. What could be better? After all these years, at last we'll have a chance to be together more.'

He had slipped an arm round her shoulders and she had known she could not object. She was lucky, she realised, to have a husband who still cared for her despite the passage of the years. So many women she knew were less fortunate.

In choosing their new home, he had been careful to consult her. They had driven round Lakeland and North Yorkshire, investigating the possibilities. But, as it had happened, every place to which she took a fancy had some drawback or other. It might be overpriced, or too touristy, or simply somewhere Bryan described as ball-achingly dull.

Eventually, they had bought this house in Dyburndale, which Bryan had favoured from the start. He'd visited the area with his parents during his childhood and its peacefulness had stuck in his mind. On her initial visit, Nancy had been tempted to suggest that the distinction between tranquillity and tedium was a narrow one, but she had been prudent enough to keep such heresies to herself. It was enough that Bryan liked the place. And happy memories count for a lot.

She'd imagined that the absence even of a pub in Dybergh might put him off. For her part she regretted that the nearest shops were also a couple of miles away, in Dyburn. But Bryan was not to be deterred: not even the need for a few renovations had dampened his enthusiasm.

'I've spent long enough behind a desk. It will be a tonic to try my hand at do-it-yourself.'

Privately, Nancy preferred finely-crafted home fixtures and fittings to the plucky efforts of the inexperienced, but it would do Bryan good to have something to occupy himself. She suspected that his enthusiasm for Dybergh might not last long.

'I'll give it eighteen months,' she confided in her partner at the last bridge game before the move. She had still not given up hope of that Cheshire bungalow, but Bryan would have to get Dyburndale out of his system first.

And now the removal van had gone and they were left to unpack and make a start on their new life, she had to admit that Dybergh was a lovely if lonely spot. The village comprised a cluster of a dozen houses, lining a road which straggled up the hillside from Dyburn, passing over animal grids and through gates which might have been designed to discourage all but the most determined visitor. Looking down, they could see acre upon acre of fields separated by dry-stone walls and at the bottom of the valley the narrow channel of the Dyer, a pretty stream dignified by the title of river.

'Delightful, isn't it?'

A tall woman in her early sixties had come out of the house on the other side of the road. She strode up to them and extended her hand.

'Cynthia Kellett. So glad to meet you.'

Bryan began to introduce himself but their neighbour cut him short with a smile.

'Oh, don't worry, I've heard all about you. Advertising, wasn't it? In Manchester? Oh yes, I know it well, my late husband worked there in insurance for many years before we retired up here.'

She grasped Nancy's hand firmly. 'Daunting, isn't it, when you start afresh in a place like this after a lifetime of bustle? No need to worry, there are several ladies in just the same boat as you and me.'

Ridiculously, Nancy found herself experiencing a sense of awe—apprehension, even—at Cynthia Kellett's omniscient manner. Giving a nervous smile, she asked how the local grapevine had managed to work so efficiently.

'Quite simple. My niece is the estate agent who sold this place on behalf of the executors of the late Mrs Weir. You'll be glad to hear that she told me how sure she was Dybergh would suit you—Nancy, isn't it? And she's a first-class judge who knows all the ins and outs of our little community. She lives down in Dyburn at present, her husband runs the sub-post office and convenience store, but I think

129

she has an eye on finding a place here when the children are off her hands.'

She glanced over Bryan's shoulder and raised her voice.

'Miriam! Come and meet the new residents!'

Another woman, a few years younger than Nancy, had parked a Range Rover outside Cynthia Kellett's house. Nancy had the impression that she had done so out of a wish to lose no time in appraising the people who had bought Inglenook Cottage. Certainly she did not think twice before hurrying to join them.

'This is Miriam Hartley. Miriam, meet Nancy and Bryan Lillis. Miriam has the old farmhouse up at the top, where the road peters out into a track. Marvellous place, we ladies meet there every Sunday to play bridge. There are seven of us, all told, we've been one player short ever since poor Dorothy Weir passed away.'

'Was that sudden?' asked Nancy. She could not quite brush away the silly idea of this place being called Dying Dale.

'Bless you, no. Dear Dorothy was ninety-two, although she kept all her faculties right up to the end. Her heart simply gave out, she died in her sleep. Though I would not have expected anything from Dorothy other than a sensible exit. She was a remarkable woman, a widow for nigh on thirty years, an inspiration to us all. Dybergh would not be the haven it is today without her efforts to secure its character. We all owe her a great deal, don't we, Miriam?'

Nancy felt a pang of unease at the prospect of having to replace such a paragon. And she was conscious, too, that Miriam Hartley was studying both of them, and perhaps especially Bryan, with an interest she did not trouble to disguise. The nosiness of an old crone would be an irritant, no more, but Miriam was no crone. On the contrary, she had thick and glossy auburn hair—owing more to art than to nature, thought Nancy with uncharacteristic malice—and a slender figure which was fitted to perfection by a canary-coloured trouser suit of conspicuously expensive cut.

'So you're the advertising man?' she said to Bryan.

'Guilty,' he said with a disarming grin.

'You're not going to try selling us anything, I hope?'

'I've put all that in the past, I promise.'

'Good.' Her tone was decisive. 'We have

131

everything here we need, isn't that right, Cynthia?'

Cynthia Kellett nodded. 'We may seem isolated. Indeed, in some respects we are. But the sense of togetherness here is quite remarkable, you'll find, Nancy. In fact, a number of friends will be coming over to my house at nine this evening for coffee. Why don't you join us?'

Nancy made diplomatic noises about unpacking, but Cynthia waved them away.

'That's agreed, then. Splendid. Oh, I'm sorry, Bryan—if I may call you that? I should have included you in the invitation. I'm afraid I can't offer you any masculine company, or talk about rugby or politics, but please do feel free to join us nevertheless.'

'I forgot to mention,' said Miriam. 'I won't be able to come tonight. I'm expecting a telephone call from Jeremy.' She turned to Nancy and explained that her eldest son was travelling the world during his year off before university and had now, she hoped, reached Cairo after a difficult trip through Africa.

'Thanks for the suggestion,' Bryan said to Cynthia, 'but there's a good deal of work for me to be getting on with. No reason why Nancy shouldn't have a break, but I'm sure you will be better off without me.'

Cynthia Kellett gave him a pleasant smile of understanding. 'As you wish. And now, I suppose, Miriam, we had better get out of Nancy and Bryan's hair and let them carry on with their unloading.'

Miriam Hartley wished them goodbye and followed Cynthia into the house opposite. Nancy had the vaguest idea that, as she turned, Miriam cast Bryan another thoughtful glance. Sternly, Nancy told herself not to be foolish.

Squeezing the quart of their Mancunian belongings into the pint pot of Inglenook Cottage consumed her attention, as well as a good deal of her energy, for the next few hours. She was surprised how glad she was to have the opportunity to take a break in the evening by calling on Cynthia.

Surprised, too, by how pleasant that break proved to be. The other women ranged in age from early fifties to late seventies, but all were obviously on excellent terms with each other. Nancy recalled the tensions and jealousies which existed in even the most agreeable of the social groups of which she had been a member in the past and found herself impressed, almost grudgingly, by the sense of goodwill towards her which everyone seemed quite sincerely to convey.

She couldn't help asking about Miriam. 'She seems charming,' she said with care to the amiably over-weight Audrey Bentham. 'Attractive, of course, and such glamorous clothes.'

'Miriam's a delightful person,' Audrey agreed. 'And quite a stunner in her day, of course. She lost her husband not long after they moved here, but she was very brave and threw herself into all our activities. Bags of personality, and not without a penny or two, as you may have gathered. She knows what she wants out of life and she usually gets it. But there's no side to her, she's very much one of us.'

Somehow Nancy did not find this encomium quite as reassuring as Audrey Bentham might have supposed. She felt she needed to press further. 'A marvellous figure,' she agreed. 'I'm filled with envy. Does she—does she have any men friends, do you know?'

'Miriam? Oh no, I'm afraid men are in short supply here, unless you count Albert Scanlan. He's the chap you may have seen pottering about down the road. The Scanlans have lived in the village for generations, but he's the last of the line. A bit crusty, you know, but a good odd-jobman and keeps himself to himself. Very handy to have someone like that around.'

Nancy did not count Albert Scanlan and her disquiet about Miriam Hartley took the shine off what was otherwise as enjoyable an evening as she had spent in years. When she arrived back home, she found Bryan ensconced in his armchair in front of the television, sipping a glass of whisky.

'Good time?' he enquired.

'Yes, thanks. What are these?'

Bryan craned his neck to look at the table to which Nancy was pointing.

'They look like coffee cups to me, love.'

'Two cups? Have we had a visitor?'

'Oh yes, I was just about to tell you. Matter of fact, what's-her-name, Mrs Hartley, called.'

'I thought she was staying in to wait for a phone call.'

'Yes, she'd just heard from her son. Then it struck her that on our first night here we might be short of fresh milk. So she popped over to offer us a bottle. I offered her a coffee, of course, important to be sociable, but she didn't stop long.'

'I see.'

And Nancy thought she did. She resolved to keep a close eye on Mrs Miriam Hartley.

Yet during the course of the next three or four weeks, she had little or no reason to feel further concern. Bryan worked busily on a series of improvements to their home, while she took advantage of a spell of clement spring weather to tidy the garden as well as making the most of several opportunities to become involved in the life of the village.

And a very good life it was. Most of her neighbours had spent a long time in much the same way as herself, looking after a hard-working husband and coping with young children. They all had a good deal in common, even people like Glenda Wenningby and Beth Stamp, who were locals and lived in the smallest and least sophisticated of Dybergh's dwellings. Between them, Glenda and Beth helped out the others with the cleaning, yet there was no sense whatever of a social divide and, on the car trips to Lancaster and Skipton which Cynthia organised from time to time, they all chatted as equals, admiring window displays of clothes in the shops and feeling sorry for all those people who lived in traffic-burdened towns so much busier and noisier than their own peaceful oasis. Miriam was a lively participant in these events and Nancy found herself grudgingly acknowledging that there was some truth in Audrey Bentham's words of admiration. Miriam even shared with Nancy and Cynthia a love for the theatre and on one fine April night they travelled as far as Manchester to see a performance of *An Inspector Calls,* treating themselves to a thoroughly pleasant overnight stay in one of the better central hotels so as to avoid the need for a long return journey in the dark.

Nancy had almost forgotten about the name of the Dying Dale when Bryan had another warning.

It happened one Sunday. He had been digging in the garden and when he came in for a restorative cup of tea in late afternoon, he complained of tiredness.

'Are you all right? Your face is so grey.'

'Tell you the truth, love, I'm not sure. In fact, my chest doesn't feel right. It's as though there's a band strapped across it.'

Nancy trembled, but tried to keep her voice calm. 'Is it the same feeling as—as last time?'

'Do you know—I think it might be.'

She summoned the doctor at once. Their local GP was a no-nonsense woman of forty-five called Anna Rothwell who lived in Dyburn. She had no hesitation in calling for an ambulance to take Bryan along the winding country lanes to hospital. Afraid to contemplate what might happen, Nancy chewed at the smooth edges of her fingernails and waited outside his ward for news. Eventually a nurse came to offer reassurance. It was going to be all right. Bryan had, she confirmed, simply had another warning.

When he was allowed back home, Anna Rothwell came to see them again. She lectured him about the perils of over-exertion and he meekly promised that he had learned his lesson. He was not as young as he had been.

The doctor took Nancy on one side. 'It's been a nasty experience for both of you, I realise. But you should understand that, with any luck, Bryan will keep going for many years yet. Naturally, he may be a little more limited. Keep an eye on this breathlessness he mentioned and don't let him walk too far. But I don't see any reason for him to become an invalid. It's simply a question of recognising his limitations.'

Nancy had felt sick with relief when she had learned her husband was not going to die. Since then she'd had to restrain herself from mollycoddling him, for Bryan was apt to become irritable when she fussed. But something in Anna Rothwell's tone chilled her. She sensed the doctor was trying to break news gently. Their future would be strictly circumscribed.

As if reading her thoughts, Anna Rothwell said kindly, 'Don't look so glum. There are plenty of possibilities for you to lead an interesting life, even in a place as small as Dybergh. Perhaps especially in a place like Dybergh, with people as marvellous as Cynthia around.'

'She's one of your patients as well, I suppose?'

'And a very good friend. She's often urging me to make my own home up here. I must admit—sometimes I'm tempted. I envy the lifestyle here, the close circle of companionship. But I won't be moving yet awhile, I think. Perhaps in another few years.'

Afterwards, Nancy came to the conclusion that Anna Rothwell had been right. Although Bryan needed to take things easy, she spent more and more time with the other women in the village. There always seemed to be something going on. An embroidery competition held by the Women's Institute in Dyburn to raise money for charity, a jumble sale, a trip to the less-frequented northern lakes. As things turned out, Bryan tended to stay at home while she gallivanted. He did not begrudge her freedom. On the contrary, he said more than once how happy he was that she had taken to life in the Dales.

There was only one of the Dybergh ladies whom Nancy continued to regard with a degree of caution. Miriam Hartley had reacted generously as soon as she'd heard of Bryan's warning. She was an excellent cook—many years ago, before marrying a prosperous actuary, she had taught domestic science at a school in Leeds—and she often insisted on bringing round cakes or scones she had made. Nancy always made her welcome, but the enthusiasm with which her husband greeted these visits never failed to disturb her. And Miriam had a habit of flattering Bryan subtly, comparing his successes in the world of commerce with her own limited achievements as a home-maker. By implication, she seemed to bracket herself with Nancy as a little woman, subservient to the male and content to be so.

Nancy had no time for feminism, which she equated with left-wing politics and thus with the kind of policies on income tax which seemed specially tailored to hurt the comfortably-off, such as Bryan and herself. Yet she resented the thought that she was in some way inferior to her husband, because she had not gone out and made money. Her priorities had been different, but the more she thought about them, the more she regarded them as being at least as important. Once or twice she almost succumbed to the urge to say as much to Miriam and to point out that while Bryan was far from active these days, she still felt in the prime of life. Anna Rothwell had been right, thought Nancy. Just because he isn't fully fit, that doesn't mean I should consider myself debarred from having fun.

Was it unfair to suspect that, in her different way, Miriam too was having fun—by making up to Bryan? Nancy could see through the false modesty; she could see it was a mistake to underestimate Miriam Hartley. Yet she told herself that the woman surely meant no harm. Indeed, from time to time she did Nancy little kindnesses which were all the more considerate because they were unexpected and unsolicited.

'We all pull together in this village,' Miriam said when Nancy thanked her for one of those friendly gestures. Nancy had mentioned to Cynthia that morning that she had woken up with a strained neck and half an hour later Miriam was knocking at her door, pointing out that the warmth of the June sun made it necessary to water the begonias and busy Lizzies Nancy had recently planted out.

'I've brought my own watering-can, to show I mean business. Can't have you making that strain any worse and Bryan still needs to take things easy.'

Even on such occasions, though, when she felt genuine gratitude towards Miriam, she could not help wondering if there were an ulterior motive. That sneaking thought made her feel ashamed of herself, but it persisted.

For Bryan was still an attractive man. True, he was not as strong as in the past, but Nancy knew his smile could still melt the knees of an impressionable woman. His easy manner was equally appealing; one had to live with him to be aware of the moments of tetchiness and self-interest which made him all too human.

He could be weak, too. Once, in conversation, Cynthia had mentioned Audrey's late husband with a sad shake of the head.

'Pleasant enough, my dear, but he did have a roving eye. Not that he did much about it in his later years, naturally, but one always had that uncomfortable sensation in his presence that one was being—well, *measured up.*' She laughed. 'And found wanting, I suspect. Ah well, he was not a bad man in his way, I suppose. It did take Audrey a little while to recover from the blow of his death, although now, as you know, she's as right as rain and can think back to the happy times they shared together. Any past infidelities are forgotten.'

Patting her on the hand, Cynthia said, 'You are luckier than you realise, my dear. Few men in my experience are as faithful as your Bryan.'

Nancy said nothing. She felt herself colouring and, perhaps in vain, hoped that Cynthia would not notice. The remark had roused from their slumber painful memories of Janine Spencer.

Janine had been Bryan's personal assistant for three or four years, more than a decade ago. The high-pressured nature of the advertising world made late-night working the norm and Nancy had taken little notice when her husband had needed to spend more time than ever at the office. A big biscuit contract, a presentation to a multinational, a series of television commercials about furniture polish, all his explanations had seemed to her plausible.

If anything, he was more attentive to her than ever in the brief times he had at home. He started bringing her flowers and taking her out for meals at expensive restaurants more regularly than before. Admittedly, he was less inclined to ardour in the marital bed, but Nancy put that down to exhaustion, and since her own appetites were modest, the lack of physical relations—as she termed it in her own mind—did not unduly trouble her.

The truth came out, as it so often does in such cases, by the merest chance. Picking up the bedroom telephone extension when a call came through one Saturday with Bryan working in his study, Nancy overheard part of a conversation which made everything clear before she slammed down the phone and threw herself onto the divan, sobbing without control. She wept for a week, and at the breakfast and dinner table she confined herself to muttered monosyllables. Bryan must have realised at once that she knew, yet she felt unable to confront him directly with his treachery. Something within her always shirked the harshest realities.

Before long he mentioned, in the most casual way, that his PA had resigned. Someone in London had made her an offer she could not refuse. Nancy wished Janine had possessed the self-discipline at least to turn down whatever offer Bryan had made, but she understood the message she was intended to receive. Bryan was sorry, as husbands usually are. She could believe he had not meant to cause her suffering. Janine may even have been the predator, with Bryan simply lacking the strength to resist. Inch by inch, Nancy's relationship with Bryan began to creep back towards normality.

Six months later, while Bryan was away in Milan, something occurred which somehow set a seal on the whole sorry business. A young man named Gregory called round at their smart detached home. He was out of work and trying to make a go of offering his services as a gardener. Nancy took pity on his fresh-faced enthusiasm and let him cut the thick holly hedge. Afterwards she offered him tea in the kitchen and they talked for a while. He had recently split up with his girlfriend and when he spoke of her, his eyes misted. She took pity on him and held his hand. It did not seem wrong to take him to her bed.

There was never any prospect of a repetition, she made that clear. In her own mind she thought of herself not so much as having gained revenge on Bryan for his own indiscretion, but rather as having helped a fellow human being to cope with a bad time. There was nothing more to it than that. Whenever in later years she recalled that pleasant interlude on her own crisp sheets—and she could not help herself thinking of it every now and then—she told herself it had simply been an act of kindness.

If Cynthia had any inkling of Nancy's

reservations about Bryan's fidelity, she gave no sign of it—except, just possibly, in the way she seized every opportunity to sing Miriam's praises.

'I admire her very much,' she once said. 'An extraordinarily courageous woman. So many people in life recognise what must be done—yet how few actually have the guts to do it?'

Nancy did not enquire about the ways in which Miriam might have demonstrated her valour—or, as she had begun to think of it, her ruthless determination. She felt frustrated that even Cynthia, a woman of discernment whose opinion she had come to value and respect, should have fallen under Miriam's spell as much as Audrey—and, even worse, Bryan.

Her husband alarmed her one summer evening. They were lying on the loungers in the back garden, watching the sun as it sank in the west. Miriam had just left. She'd come bearing gifts, two fat bags of the first of her crop of this year's tomatoes.

'Fine woman, that, you know,' he remarked. 'Heart of gold. I reckon she's the one decent friend we've made since we came here.'

'What do you mean?' Nancy was astonished. 'We have lots of friends. There's Audrey, there's Cynthia...'

'Yes, yes, I know you have your own little group. But frankly, love, I do find it rather dull sometimes when you're out with the girls and I'm stuck here with the telly. There's not another fellow worth talking to in the village, let alone the chance of a jar or two at the local.'

Since his second warning, he had hardly driven their car and they had only visited the pub in Dyburn once. Nancy always seemed to have so many other things to do.

'There's Albert Scanlan. You can have a natter to him any time.'

Bryan's face indicated what he thought of Albert Scanlan. 'That old idiot? He obviously doesn't think I have any right to have come here in the first place. And he can be damned rude too. The other day we were passing the time of day. I may have made my thoughts about Dybergh rather undiplomatically clear. He gave me that stupid gap-toothed grin of his and said he reckoned I'd soon be off anyway. The devil of it is, I think he may be proved right.'

Nancy was aghast. 'I don't understand. I thought you loved it here.'

'So did I, but that was before I came. To be perfectly honest, I reckon we ought to up sticks right now and move back somewhere nearer to civilisation.'

'We can't do that! I've put so much effort into building a new life here. And I like it. I really like it!'

As she uttered the words, she realised their truth. In a short time she had in every sense made herself at home in Dybergh. The Cheshire bungalow seemed now like the fantasy lovers she had had as a schoolgirl: quite inappropriate and hopelessly unappealing when considered in the cold light of day.

The vehemence of her reaction took Bryan aback. He patted her hand and assumed a conciliatory tone.

'Well, there's no reason to make any hasty decisions. I'll give it some more thought and perhaps we'll talk about it again.'

The subject was dropped but for the rest of the evening Nancy felt a sense of misery. She knew Bryan of old. He would let ideas churn in his mind for a long time before giving tongue to them. For him to have spoken so bluntly must mean that he had already made his decision. Sooner or later they would be leaving the village.

Next morning she found herself confiding in Cynthia. As ever, her friend was not only sympathetic but practical.

'I suppose I can see his point of view,' she conceded. 'Albert Scanlan is hardly an ideal companion for someone as intelligent as Bryan. Albert is an old fool, of course. Fancy him trying to discourage your husband from making an effort to blend in with the community. I shall have a sharp word with him. It's really not fair, when it's bound to be hard for a man like Bryan to adjust to a different way of life. It's inevitable that for a successful businessman who has been used to being the centre of attention, Dybergh must come as something of a blow to the self-esteem.'

'Miriam gives him plenty of attention,' said Nancy. Her own unvarnished bitterness startled her, but in her present mood she did not care. Cynthia was a decent woman and absolutely trustworthy: there was no need to present a false front to her.

'Now, dear, you mustn't take Miriam

150

amiss. She is still a thoroughly attractive woman, I'll grant you, and vivacious as well. I wish I had her energy and drive. But believe me, her heart is in the right place. What concerns me, if you like, is that you ought also to be in your right place. And I'm absolutely sure that is here with us, in Dybergh.'

Nancy shed a tear. 'I feel so at home in the village. And now it looks as if it is all going to come to an end.'

'I'm sure something will be worked out. But let's not upset ourselves without too much cause. How are you fixed for cheese and wine here this evening?'

The conversation switched to happier topics and an hour later Nancy left, feeling as invigorated as she always did after spending any time with Cynthia.

Shortly before lunch Miriam popped round unexpectedly. She was wearing jeans and her lovely hair was wrapped in a scarf. Even in gardening clothes she somehow contrived to give an impression of elegance. Yet something about her made Nancy feel uneasy. Had she not told herself it was absurd, she would not only have felt intimidated by the woman, but also frightened by her.

Bryan, of course, brightened as soon as she walked through the door. 'Don't apologise, please. Always good to see you. How's the work going?'

Miriam had recently embarked on a thorough overhaul of the farmhouse. No new building, she had explained, just an attempt to smarten the place up. Albert Scanlan had been recruited to lend a hand and she'd been tidying the garden.

'Slowly, but I'm making progress. I just wondered—do you have a ladder I can borrow?'

'Why yes, of course. Don't you remember I did a little pointing just before I had that spot of bother with my heart?'

'Oh, that's right, it had quite slipped my mind. How providential!'

Miriam averted her eyes as she spoke and in that instant Nancy knew that she was not telling the truth.

'What do you need it for, may I ask?'

'Quite a small job, Bryan. The gutters need unblocking and I want to have a crack at them once I get the afternoon's chores out of the way.'

'Is Albert clearing them for you?'

'As a matter of fact, he isn't. He's had a couple of dizzy spells lately, I understand. Nothing serious, but I don't think it would be wise to ask him to climb in the circumstances. So I thought I'd better have a go myself.'

'I'll lend you a hand,' Bryan said.

Miriam smiled shyly. It struck Nancy as a special talent for such a brazen woman to feign diffidence with such conviction.

'I really didn't mean to...'

'Of course you didn't, but I'm offering and you're accepting. Yes, yes, the matter's settled. When do you want me to come over?'

'Well—would half seven this evening be too late?'

'Not at all, not at all. We'll have finished eating by then. Nancy is going to a do at Mrs Kellett's.'

'Cheese and wine,' said Nancy, controlling her emotions with difficulty. 'But surely you will be there, Miriam?'

'Actually,' said Miriam, 'I explained to Cynthia a few minutes ago that I would have to give it a miss. A shame, but I have so much to do at the moment.'

'I see,' said Nancy, and once again she was sure she did.

During lunch she responded to Bryan's attempts to chat with vague affirmative

153

grunts. Outwardly calm, she was wrestling with a dilemma which seemed to her to be more acute than any she had had to face in the past. For his part, Bryan was nervously talkative and too clumsily solicitous for her liking.

She knew he was looking forward to his visit to Miriam's. Like a schoolboy anticipating a secret treat, he was half-fearful, half-excited. At last he would have the chance to start an affair with a woman he had coveted for months. And by the time the meal was over, Nancy had decided that she had no option but to let him have his fun.

It filled her with a cold anger, the prospect of sharing her husband. Yet she could see no other solution. The choice might have been proposed by the devil. But she felt an aching despair at the idea of having to leave the village and her friends. If she went away, she told herself, she would have nothing. Nothing at all. In contrast, she knew that at least she was strong enough to survive betrayal by Bryan. It had happened once in the past—perhaps more often, for all she knew. She had to confront stark truths. Bryan needed a powerful incentive to stay in Dybergh and only Miriam could supply it.

'Shall we go for a run in the car this afternoon?' he asked eagerly.

She shook her head. 'I need to lie down for a little while.'

'You're not sickening for something?' He could not hide the alarm in his tone and Nancy realised that any concern for her wellbeing was outweighed by dismay at the prospect of being obliged to sit with her this evening instead of cleaning Miriam's gutters.

What a bloody euphemism! She couldn't help uttering a harsh bark of laughter.

'No, no, I'm not sick at all.'

Except of you, she was tempted to add.

She spent most of the afternoon fully clothed on the bed. Staring sightlessly at the ceiling, she went over and over the same old ground until her head started to spin and she feared she might really be ill after all. Every time, though, the answer was the same. She now cared more for life in Dybergh than for her marriage.

They ate a light tea together. Bryan clucked about her poor appetite and kept asking if she felt all right. She bit her tongue on a hundred acid retorts and promised brusquely that she was fine. Perhaps she might have suffered a slight touch of the sun, nothing more.

'Are you going to Cynthia's then?'

When she nodded, he could not conceal his relief. 'Well, if you're sure. But I'm positive myself it's a good idea. Better by far to be up and about, get the old cogs moving. You know what my old mum used to say: "They die in bed." '

'Yes,' she said grimly and went upstairs to change. When she came down again he kissed her and said how lovely she looked.

'I've just remembered,' he said with a show of elaborate unconcern. 'I did promise Miriam this morning that I'd give her a hand with clearing her gutters. A bit of a bore, but I don't like breaking my word. I don't mind doing a neighbour a small act of kindness. Any idea what sort of time you'll be back?'

'Quite late, I expect.'

'No hurry, no hurry. A job like that may take me some time and I expect a woman on her own may have one or two other small tasks around the house she would welcome a hand with whilst I'm there.'

'I'm sure she will,' said Nancy. 'Goodbye.'

She walked briskly out of the front door without waiting for his customary peck on the cheek. As she crossed the road to Cynthia's, she was already starting to regret her complaisance. But it was too late now. The bridge had been crossed.

Thankfully, it did not take long for the lively companionship of Cynthia, Audrey and the others—Anna Rothwell, the doctor, and Cynthia's niece, the estate agent, were among those there—to drag her mind away from what might be about to happen at Miriam's farmhouse. The wine tasted wonderful and when Nancy found her glass being refilled at regular intervals she did not utter her usual polite protest. Looking around at the other ladies of Dybergh, she knew she was among friends.

Later, with the little party still in full swing, Nancy and Cynthia were alone together in the kitchen. Nancy's head was swimming but she felt suddenly free from care.

'There's something I wanted to tell you,' she said. 'Bryan went round to Miriam's tonight.'

Cynthia put a hand on her shoulder. 'I

know, Nancy, I know.'

It seemed important to Nancy to seek words of comfort. 'You do understand, don't you?'

'Better perhaps than you realise, my dear.'

Cynthia's smile was not only calm but eternally wise. Feeling rather confused, Nancy wrinkled her brow.

'I'm not sure I...'

Cynthia gestured towards two chairs. 'Why don't we sit down, dear? It's been a long day.'

'Thank—thank you. It seems so...'

Cynthia pressed on Nancy's shoulder again. 'You must be very brave, my love.'

Tears began to fill Nancy's eyes. 'It's just that...'

'Hush, dear. Listen to me. You have so many happy years ahead of you. With me and Audrey and all your other friends in Dybergh.'

'But Bryan...'

'Bryan's a fine man and in his way I don't for a minute doubt he was a good husband. And that is how you should always think of him. The time for recriminations is past. But how dreadful it would be—either in Dybergh or elsewhere—to watch him growing frailer with every passing year. You would hate it and so would he. It's so much better to have just the happy memories.'

'I don't...'

'You see, at his age, climbing up and down ladders is bound to be dangerous. It is so very easy for accidents to occur. Miriam couldn't be blamed if something did happen.'

Nancy stared at her friend. 'Miriam—Miriam fancies him.'

Cynthia shook her head. 'Oh, no. I told you before, dear. She is one of us. And so very brave and strong. I would trust her with my life. She has helped so many of us over the years. Please don't ever reproach either her or yourself. I'm sure Anna will confirm later, whatever grief you feel when the bad news comes, you must cling to this one truth—it was all for the best.'

And as the sense of the words slowly sank in, bringing with them a strange contentment, a single thought came to the surface of Nancy's mind. She wasn't shutting her eyes or her heart to a wicked deed. Not at all, she could never do that. She was simply participating in an act of kindness.

Roger Forsdyke

VIDEO NASTY

Before dawn, Friday 18th December. The heating had not yet come on and the chill that met my arm as I reached for the bedside phone foretold a hard winter to come.

'There's a seven-year-old been murdered in Scarborough. You're on the team—report there by 9.30.'

An hour later I was front-seat passenger in an unliveried Ford Escort, driven by a fellow detective constable who never missed an opportunity to demonstrate the prowess he had developed as a patrol-car driver. Blue light permanently illuminating some part of his psyche, we arrived at the seaside station that was to house the enquiry for the next weeks, a cold half-hour before we needed.

The first briefing gave sketchy details of the crime. Seven-year-old girl left alone the previous evening had been found dead by her mother upon her return from her night's carousing. Little sign of any violence or disruption in the one-bedroom flat where they lived by themselves. Just a small girl who died, alone because her mother had failed to find a baby-sitter whilst she pursued her regular round of lads and lager. First reports indicated that the girl had been strangled, but we would learn more after the post mortem. The HOLMES [Home Office Large Major Enquiry System] team had worked through the night to set up the computer links with the mainframe at headquarters that would organise and keep track of the hundreds of enquiries and many thousands of interrelated pieces of information that would come our way.

We were thrust into the peculiarities of winter life in a seaside town. Here was bedsit land, seedy guest-houses that took in homeless people funded by the welfare state during the winter months, to subsidise the holiday trade. Most people came in the summer—and enjoyed their break. Some enjoyed themselves and came back year after year. Others came, stayed and never left. A few of the enquiry teams were there for nearly two weeks before they interviewed anyone born and bred in the vicinity. We raised the clear-up rate for ordinary crime in the area by three hundred per cent. The local intelligence officer had to take on an assistant to help process the mountain of information on local crime and criminals produced by the enquiry teams. But the murder? No positive leads or information in the first few days always prompts a rapidly-developing sense of concern. Murder is the one crime you cannot be seen to fail to detect. Fear of not cracking a murder enquiry is the detective's writer's block. And then there's the money. The days of contingency funds are long past and murder enquiries—whatever their beneficial side-effects—are too expensive to maintain indefinitely. Especially where there is no concrete progress being made.

Nobody had seen anything untoward. Yes, mum liked her lager and had a string of boyfriends, mostly one-night stands, but they were only ordinary lads—and none who would harm a seven-year-old. Following up the list of sexual conquests took the enquiry teams all over the north of England. A holiday camp was being refurbished during the closed season and had drawn labour from far and wide.

It seemed that Angela had conducted a one-woman winter-welcome wagon for the lads from the north.

Angela originally came from Darlington, had met Carrie's father (whichever he had been) in Scarborough and liked the place so much she'd just stayed on.

Tim Hodgson's family had also liked the place, but being more commercially-minded, had bought a large property and set about turning it into a guest-house. Tim had been twelve when Angela moved to Scarborough and had Carrie. And, as one of her many acquaintances, was amongst those first to be interviewed. The youngest of four children, he was a quiet, introverted lad with few friends, but known to many locals as one of the crowd of youngsters who hung around the bus station and latterly the Sahara Nightclub; little enough business, but just enough to warrant its staying open all year round. The DJ, who supplemented his dole money three nights a week at the club, described Tim as 'a sandwich short of a picnic.'

The results of the post mortem were equally concise. Cause of death, manual strangulation, possible vagal inhibition, it may only have needed a modicum of pressure for thirty seconds or so... Worse for us, the crime seemed without motive. Nothing appeared to be missing from the flat and Carrie had not been interfered with in any sexual way.

HOLMES, developed after the disastrous but almost inevitable mismanagement of the myriad items of information in the Yorkshire Ripper enquiries, will not solve any crime. It will collate and cross-reference every single name, location and time, thus ensuring that a complete and comprehensive jigsaw may be built up, presenting the investigating officers with the wherewithal to get on with detecting. The enquiry teams were issued with TIE actions—documents printed by the computer with instructions to Trace, Interview and Eliminate suspects, raised automatically every time a name was mentioned.

Tim was eventually interviewed four times. First, because Angela said that she knew him and that he had visited the flat on a couple of occasions. The second time because his name cropped up as being present when another interviewee's alibi needed corroboration. The third time because a friend had placed him at the top of Angela's road at about the right time on the night in question. He turned out to possess a similarly low IQ to Tim and had got the date wrong. The fourth time because we were getting desperate and there was roughly an hour's gap in his verifiable movements, the night Carrie had died.

Experienced detectives are supposed to develop a sixth sense, to get "hunches". I got nothing from Tim, despite having interviewed him three times out of the four. Having been promoted during the enquiry to the heady heights of acting detective sergeant, I was eager to make my mark, but all I got from Tim was a peculiar absence of any feeling, a complete lack of emotion over the fact that his friend's little girl had been murdered.

'Doesn't it concern you that there may be a murderer loose in the community?'

'Yeah, I suppose,' he replied vacuously. I put it down to him being thick.

His father had carried his economic theories to an extreme. Though Tim was yet only nineteen, he was unlikely ever to find gainful employment, so his dad had moved him into a bedsit in another part of the rambling property and charged him rent. That way they could claim the welfare benefits from such an arrangement. On the night of the murder, Tim had eaten dinner with the family in the large guest-house dining-room, watched television with them until about 8.30, then adjourned to his bedsit room for half an hour to get changed before going to the Sahara club. The DJ said he'd clearly seen Tim arrive in the almost-empty club sometime after 9 pm. Allowing for travelling time, that meant we now had a gap in his verifiable movements of roughly twenty minutes. Not bad going really. Could you account for every moment of the evening two weeks ago last Thursday?

Christmas came and went, a joyless time for the murder team, although we were welcomed in degrees varying from a large whisky to 'Why don't you all just fuck off and leave us alone?'—especially when visiting the same premises for the fourth and fifth time. The snow arrived and cut us off from our own loved ones. One of our comforts was "Ginger" Rogers' café. Normally closed for the winter season, he opened up especially for us and kept the inner men (and women) going with his splendid home cooking. The very antithesis of his famous namesake—bluff, balding and looking as though he over-indulged in his own cooking—he did us proud. I have no doubt that he made a fortune out of his unexpected windfall from the police authority, but he earned every penny of it. Soon learning the policeman's penchant for maximising every opportunity—getting something for nothing—he would allow a midday meal of soup, roll and butter without sight of a meal ticket, then fillet steak and chips or whatever delicacies the menu ran to would be yours in exchange for two tickets in the evening.

'Just let us know, so's I can stock the larder up, lads.'

Four weeks into the enquiry, we did not need the depressing weather to cast gloom over it. We had not so much run into a brick wall, as we had just plodded ourselves to a lumbering, grinding halt.

Scratching his head at the daily morning meeting, the detective chief superintendent in charge of the enquiry announced that we would be running a "project" on likely subjects. He couldn't very well use the term suspects, as there weren't any. Did anybody have any suggestions?

I hesitated to put forward Tim's name,

but the chief said to me, 'What about this Hodgson? I see you have written on this TIE action, "We have alibied this young man as much as we can, but I'm still not a hundred per cent happy with him." What's that mean?'

On the spot, I had to think quickly. What did I mean? What could I say that would justify someone being brought in for questioning, when in all probability he had done nothing apart from failing to be as bright as he might be?

'I'm not absolutely sure, sir,' I stammered. 'It's just that when I talked to him, there just seemed such a lack of response...his friend's daughter being murdered...I asked him if he was concerned about there being a killer loose in the community. He seemed absolutely unconcerned about anything...I put it down to him being thick.'

Because of my assessment, or perhaps even in spite of it, Tim and three others were targeted. Their movements were traced, scrutinised minutely and verified using HOLMES to assist with the accuracy of all details. Eventually, Tim was asked if he would be prepared to assist the police with their enquiries. Surprisingly, he agreed and had been in custody, giving the interviewing officers his best impression of hapless, hopeless, helpless humanity for a couple of hours, when I was sitting in the cosy condensation of Ginger's Family Grill, listening to the bosses on the next table.

'Nothing, eh? Well, go back and give it to him with both barrels. We've got nothing on him, so we've nothing to lose. Another ten minutes or so and we'll have to let him go anyway.'

We finished our evening meal wondering what we could do next to find whoever had been responsible for ending this young life so prematurely.

We wandered back to the station, cold toes and the biting wind reminding me forcibly why I preferred CID to patrolling the beat. Inside the station, I didn't need any sixth sense to know something had happened. The DCI in charge of interviewing Hodgson came towards me along the corridor.

'What? What?' I demanded.

'He's coughed it!'

'Who, Hodgson? You're joking! What happened?'

He thrust papers into my hand and I read the contemporaneous notes of interview as he machine-gunned the incredible circumstances at me.

They had come back and said to him, 'Come on, Tim, stop fucking us about. We know you did it, you know you did it, and you know we know you did it.' As one last desperate stab in the cold winter darkness, they added, 'We've got a bloody witness, for Christ's sake. How's that going to look in court, you lying all this time and our witness saying he saw you come out of the flat?'

There was a long silence. 'Someone saw me coming out of the flat?'

'Yep.'

'Don't believe you.'

The detectives could not believe what they were hearing, either. 'Well, that's up to you, Tim. You know the truth and I think we're getting to it now, aren't we?'

'Where's this witness, then?'

So close and yet so far. 'One thing at a time, Tim. Tell us what happened first, then we can talk about our witness.'

'I want to see him, then I might tell you about it.'

Now what? There was no witness, but Tim would not be budged. Literal-minded as he was, they soon realised that he would not believe in the existence of this "witness" without seeing him in the flesh. The DCI took a desperate gamble. He said, 'All right, Tim, but I shall have to go and find him.' He turned his back so that Hodgson should not see his lips. 'Keep him talking,' he mouthed urgently as he left the room.

As he wandered around the night-darkened corridors of the station, desperately trying to figure a way out of his predicament, he was spotted by one of the investigation team leaders, a detective inspector he'd known since training school.

'What's up, boss?'

The DCI explained.

'He doesn't know me, I'll be your witness.'

The DCI was a gambling man. He knew that if he let Hodgson go, he would lose everything. If he allowed the DI to be his "witness", he was in for a battle in court—if it ever got as far as that.

'OK,' he sighed. 'Just go into the room, point at him and say—as convincingly as you can—"That's him, that's the one," then beat it. All right?'

Hodgson talked, but characteristically

without a lot of detail or feeling. Yes, he had watched television with his family—they'd hired a film from the local video library. The sort where thousands of rounds of ammunition are fired and nobody gets hit, the fist fights last ten minutes or more and all the punches sound like someone pulverising a melon with a heavy mallet. He'd gone to his room to get changed for the Sahara club, but suddenly remembered he'd lent Angela a video-tape the week before. It was time to retrieve it. Carrie had answered the door to him, but mummy had said she could watch the film before she let Tim have it back, and she had not yet done so. When Tim had insisted on taking the video away, she'd thrown a tantrum and had hung onto his clothing, attempting to stop him. Her neck was the nearest part of her to get hold of... He'd seen them do it in the films and he'd only held onto her for a little while, honest...

The defence painted a picture of a simple, immature lad, unduly influenced by the violence in the film he had watched just before going to retrieve his video. And PACE [The Police and Criminal Evidence Act 1984] dictates that the court may exclude "evidence unfairly gained". Much was made at Hodgson's trial of the non-existent witness; the jury was sent out and a trial within a trial was held on this point of law. But Angela had remembered the video when prompted, and forensic tests matched fibres taken from Hodgson's pullover to those found on Carrie's dress. He was sentenced to twelve years.

For all its summer size, Scarborough is a small town and the Hodgsons were forced to move out and conduct their business elsewhere. And Carrie? Perhaps her innocence is better preserved where she is, wherever that may be.

Reginald Hill

WHERE THE SNOW LAY DINTED

Dalziel awoke. He knew nothing, remembered nothing, and felt neither the desire nor the will to activate cognition.

He lay unmoving and might have so continued for an indefinite period had not a physical sensation finally forced itself upon his embryonic consciousness.

His bollocks were cold.

Time to make contact with the waking world. Nothing rash, minimum risk. He opened his left eye just sufficiently to admit light in the smallest measure known to man, which is a single scotch in an English pub.

Jesus wept!

Light poured in, white and blinding as if someone had indeed poured a glass of whisky onto his eyeball. He squeezed the eyelid shut and lay still until the dancing white patina had faded from his retina.

Sight no good, so try the other senses...

Touch...cold, he'd already established that...

Sound...voices, gently murmuring...

Smell...antiseptic...

Taste...BLOOD!

Oh God, I'm being operated on and the anaesthetic hasn't took!

'Nobody move!' he bellowed, sitting bolt upright and opening both eyes wide.

In a huge dressing-table mirror he saw a naked fat man with a split lip sitting up in a four-poster bed. On a bedside table stood a half-empty bottle of whisky and a half-full bottle of TCP. Through a tall open window drifted a chilling draught, a blinding white light, and a murmur of voices.

He rolled off the bed onto the floor, landing on a spoor of damp clothes which ran from the doorway to the bedside. After a while he pushed himself to his knees. When his head didn't fall off, he rose fully upright, took three uncertain steps towards the window and, catching hold of the pelmet to maintain verticality, he looked out. And knew at last where, and when, and why he was.

He was in the Hirtledale Arms Hotel on the Yorkshire Moors, it was Boxing Day morning, and it had snowed hard during the night.

It was a scene to touch even the done-over heart of a hung-over cop. The sky was delft blue and the still-low rays of the morning sun were gilding the horizoned hills, lending the curves and hollows the sensuous quality of female limbs in repose. Where the foothills gave way to pasture-land, the varicosed lines formed by dry-stone walls were all that marked one field from another. Small trees and bushes sagged beneath the weight of their temporary blossom, while beech and oak and elm stood upright as judges in their wigs of white. About a mile away, the small village of Hirtledale had all but vanished under the sealing snow, but nearer still the fairytale turrets of Hirtledale Castle floated like something imagined by Walt Disney over the icing-sugared battlements.

Dalziel let his gaze drift down to the square of perfect lawn which was the pride and joy of Giles Hartley-Pulman, the hotel's owner. At its centre stood a bronze statue of little St Agnes clutching a lamb, saved from dereliction in Rome (according to the hotel brochure) by a nineteenth-century Lord Hirtledale, and planted here when the hotel building had still been the castle's dower house.

The perfect lawn was now of course a blanket of perfect white, and this seemed to be the focus of attention of the several guests standing on the terrace immediately below Dalziel's window, whose soft conversation he had mistaken for the blasé chit-chat of heartless surgeons.

So what was so interesting? wondered Dalziel.

He returned his attention to the lawn and as his eyes adjusted to the dazzling light, he saw that its surface was not perfect after all.

From the feet of the statue ran a set of small human footprints with alongside them another set of even smaller animal hoofprints. The trail swung in a wide circle round the lawn, though always staying well clear of its edges, before returning to the base of the statue.

'Bugger me,' said Andy Dalziel.

His exclamation drew the attention of the watchers below to his presence. They looked up at him with expressions ranging from the amused to the amazed. Among them, he spotted Peter and Ellie Pascoe who maintained the neutral faces of people

178

who'd seen it all before. If so, they were seeing it all again, for it suddenly occurred to Dalziel that he was stark naked.

Time for retreat. Any road, miracles shouldn't be taken on an empty stomach.

He belched gently, gave a little wave, and called, 'See you at breakfast, I'm fair clemmed.'

As he showered and shaved, memory struggled back into his mind like the sea up a long shallow beach.

At low-tide level, things were pretty clear. This time last week, he'd had no plans for Christmas and didn't give a toss. Then Peter Pascoe had let slip that he was planning to spend the break at the Hirtledale Arms, and suddenly Dalziel realised how much he'd been relying on the usual Boxing Day invitation to lunch with the Pascoes.

He must have let it show. Or perhaps Pascoe just felt guilty, because he'd started explaining.

'Not my cup of tea, really, but Ellie's mum, well, you know she's not long widowed and she needs a change of scene, and it takes the pressure off Ellie...' Then, with the expansive generosity of one who knew the hotel had long been booked solid, he'd added, 'Look, why not join us? We'd all love to see you there.'

And God, who is a Yorkshireman, had grinned, nipped a guest in the appendix and made sure news of the cancellation reached the hotel five minutes before Dalziel rang.

When he heard the price quoted by Giles Hartley-Pulman (who immediately in Dalziel-speak became Giles Partly-Human), his Scottish/Yorkshire blood curdled. Then he'd asked himself, 'What are you saving for? a cashmere winding-sheet and a platinum coffin?' and booked. His reward had been the discovery that one of the things the inclusive price included was wine and liqueurs with Christmas Dinner. Somewhere between the turkey and the truffles he had a vague recollection of calculating that profligacy had turned into profit. And he thought he recalled starting on the liqueurs in alphabetical order, but now they sat like an oil slick on the tide of memory, turning it sluggish and opaque well short of high water. What he needed was some mental menstruum and he knew just the formula. First take a precise inch of the Macallan in a tooth glass and toss it straight down to avoid contact with your cut lip. Then add half a pound of streaky bacon, a black pudding, several eggs and a potato scone, and chew gently.

He descended to the dining-room to complete the cure.

As he entered, a voice cried, 'Andy, good morning. Now the Great Detective is among us, the riddle of the perambulating statue will be solved in a trice. Or would you rather we all assembled in the Library later?'

This was Freddie Gilmour, a young man who was something in the City and had been Christmassing at Hirtledale for many years with half-a-dozen like-minded friends. They had adopted Dalziel in a way which Peter Pascoe found offensively patronising. But Dalziel's huge frame was lead-lined, and this imperviousness, plus his prodigious feats of consumerism, had brought these devout free-marketeers to a wondering respect.

'Nay, Fred,' he said. 'I only solve real mysteries. Like if you put your hand in your pocket and found some of your own money there.'

Followed by a gust of laughter, he crossed the room and joined the Pascoes.

' 'Morning,' he said.

He couldn't have behaved too badly last night because both Ellie and her mother gave him a welcoming smile, though the former's began to fade as little Rosie Pascoe piped up eagerly, 'Uncle Andy, did you see? The statue went for a walk last night and took her little lamb with her.'

'I don't think so, dear,' said her mother who, though having nothing against flights of imagination, was a natural enemy of anything smacking of superstitious credulity. 'I'm sure there's some other explanation.'

'No, they went for a walk, you can see the footprints in the snow. Isn't that right, Uncle Andy? Because anything can happen at Christmas.'

Dalziel looked from mother to daughter. The same dark, serious, unblinking gaze, the same expression of expectant certitude.

Pascoe was observing him with a faint grin which said, 'Get out of this one!'

'Aye, owt can. That doesn't say it will, but.'

Good try, but not good enough.

'But this *has* happened, hasn't it?' insisted the girl. 'You can see the prints.'

'That's right,' agreed the Fat Man.

'What I can't see is anyone to serve me breakfast.'

'I get the impression there's some sort of crisis in the kitchen,' said Pascoe.

'If there's not, there soon will be,' said Dalziel, glad of an excuse to escape Ellie's threatening glare.

He rose, went to the kitchen door, pushed it open and bellowed, 'SHOP!'

Giles Hartley-Pulman, deep in confabulation with his chef and three young waitresses, jumped six inches in the air. His lean ascetic face was creased with concern, but oddly when he identified the source of the sound, it relaxed ever so slightly.

There had been a moment last night when he would gladly have given half his kingdom for the privilege of never seeing Dalziel again. This had been when he bravely but foolishly attempted to slow if not stem the Fat Man's consumption of claret. To the applause of the other guests, Dalziel had flourished the menu, stabbing with a huge finger at the words *Wine and Liqueurs ad lib*, and saying, 'Here in Yorkshire we've got a word for a man who's not good as his word! We'll try another bottle of the '83.'

A good hotelier knows when to withdraw. He also knows how to get even if the chance offers, and now Hartley-Pulman advanced saying, 'Superintendent Dalziel, thank heaven. There's been a burglary. I was about to phone the police but of course with you on the spot, it seems a shame to drag someone out in these conditions...and I should hate for the Press to get involved, asking impertinent questions about my guests...'

Meaning, I'd rather not have uniformed plods all over the place, but if I do, I'll make sure the world knows you were pissed the far side of oblivion last night!

Dalziel considered. Hirtledale was on the northernmost fringe of his Mid Yorkshire patch so he certainly had jurisdiction, if he cared to assert it. On the other hand, he didn't care for Partly-Human imagining he could threaten him.

Postponing decision, he said, 'What's been stolen?'

'Well,' said Hartley-Pulman, savouring the moment. 'It's mainly...your breakfast.'

And in the dining-room conversation ceased as a great cry of pain and loss exploded out of the kitchen.

Five minutes later, Peter Pascoe was

summoned to join his boss. It didn't take long to put him in the picture.

'Partly-Human's making a list,' Dalziel concluded. 'You talk to the staff, lad. Use your boyish charm.'

'Yes, sir,' said Pascoe, looking unhappily at the chef who was breaking a bowlful of eggs into a pan. He didn't want to be involved in this, but if he was... 'Sir, shouldn't we seal the kitchen in case Forensic...?'

'Stuff Forensic,' said Dalziel. 'There's nowt left but eggs and I need to keep me strength up.'

Sighing, Pascoe went in search of the waitresses.

Fifteen minutes later he returned to find Dalziel wiping the pattern off a plate with a slice of bread.

'You've got that aren't-I-clever look,' said the Fat Man.

'We've got a name,' said Pascoe. 'Remember little Billy Bream?'

'In the frame for the Millhouse break-in, but CPS got their knickers in a twist. Still, it gave him a scare and he dropped out of sight.'

'Hirtledale was where he dropped to. His old gran lives there. And Milly Staines, the waitress with the squint, she reckons she saw him hanging around here last night.'

'Grand. Owt else?'

'Maybe. Patty Strang, the pretty blonde, says she glanced out of her window just as the snow was starting and saw someone down the drive. No description except it was too big for little Billy and moving very slowly.'

'Even Billy 'ud move slow carrying this lot,' said Dalziel, producing a list.

Pascoe whistled. As well as twelve pounds of sausage, fifteen pounds of bacon, forty kidneys, thirty kippers, twenty-five black puddings and a kilo of salt, a dozen bottles of champagne had gone.

'One thing's certain, he must have left some tracks.'

'Let's take a look,' said Dalziel.

Close to the building the snow was already churned up, but a few yards down the drive they spotted two lines of footprints, one approaching, one moving away.

'How's your tracking, Pocahontas?' said Dalziel. 'Get your wellies and let's see where these lead us.'

Before they left Pascoe had a quick word

with Ellie, who rolled her eyes in not-altogether-mock rage and said, 'Trouble follows the fat bastard but I don't see that's any reason why you should.'

'We're just going to look at the tracks in the snow,' protested Pascoe.

'Yeah? With a bit of luck he might catch pneumonia. If he does, my sympathy's with the bacilli!'

Freddie and the Free Marketeers must have been earwigging on this exchange for, as Pascoe joined Dalziel outside the kitchen, they appeared in the doorway and struck up a rousing chorus of Good King Wenceslas.

'Twits,' muttered Pascoe. 'Wouldn't surprise me if they had something to do with this.'

'Wouldn't displease you, you mean,' said Dalziel, acknowledging the carollers with a friendly two-fingered wave. 'Where's your festive spirit, lad?' And joining in their song at the line *Mark my footsteps good my page*, he strode off up the drive.

As Pascoe floundered behind already feeling the cold strike through his soles, the carol's words fell with heavy irony on his tingling ears. *Heat was in the very sod That the saint had printed.* No chance! You needed a saint for that and all he'd got was the very sod!

Where the drive joined the road, the prints turned towards the village and were joined by another outward set.

'Accomplice,' guessed Dalziel. 'Stayed here to watch.'

'Or someone who'd set out before the snow started laying,' Pascoe contradicted sourly.

But as they walked on and he began to warm up, the enchanted silence of the snow began to work its magic on his mood. This was what Christmas was all about, not the gluttonous consumerism of the telly ads but a brief interval in which all the filth and flaws of human existence were cloaked in a mantle of purest white.

They were approaching the gothic archway marking the entrance to the castle estate. They heard the sound of a hunting horn and a merry chatter of distant voices.

'Must be the Boxing Day Meet,' said Dalziel. 'I could just sup a stirrup cup. Come on!'

He hurried forward, clearly with every intention of turning into the castle grounds and inserting himself among the huntsmen. But his haste was almost his undoing, for as he reached the gate there was a drumming of hooves mingled with shouts and laughter, and next moment a posse of red-coated riders erupted in front of them and galloped across the road into a wood. Pascoe, still in his master's steps, was protected from the worst of the spume of slush thrown up behind them, but Dalziel took the full brunt.

'Fuck me,' he said, coming to a halt. 'Rigid!'

He looked, thought Pascoe, like a snowman on a Christmas card, lacking only the carrot nose and old pipe to complete the picture. It was a thought he kept to himself.

Another horseman came through the archway, moving at a more decorous pace. This was a much older man, grey hair showing beneath his black cap. He came to a halt in front of Dalziel and examined him for a moment. What might have been a glint of amusement touched his bright blue eyes but didn't extend to his narrow patrician face as he said courteously, 'Sorry about that. Impetuous youth. I'll speak to them.'

'Aye, but will the buggers listen?' said Dalziel, brushing the snow away.

'Eventually, once they've ridden off all their festive excesses. No excuse, of course, but if we recall our own younger days and the tricks we got up to, perhaps we can forgive.'

This appeal seemed to strike a chord in Dalziel who said, 'Aye, well, I'll not die of a bit of snow. Daresay some on 'em enjoyed themselves so much last night, they didn't even get to bed.'

'They were certainly still carousing when I went up,' said the horseman. 'I'd better get after them before they find a frozen pond to ride across. Again my apologies. And Merry Christmas to you both.'

He touched his riding-crop to his cap and cantered on.

'Know who that was?' said Dalziel. 'Lord Hirtledale himself.'

'Well, roll on the revolution,' said Pascoe. 'Never thought you were a fore-lock-tugger, sir.'

'Long time since I had one of those,' said Dalziel equably. 'Thought you'd have been all for his lordship. Doesn't he chair that Bosnian relief gang your missus collects for? Cost me a fiver last time she rattled her can!'

'I don't see how that entitles him to

prance around the countryside, slaughtering foxes.'

'Nay, lad, you'd best put that one to the Pope next time you write. Too deep for me. I just hunt villains. Tally-ho!'

They had no difficulty in refinding the trail beyond the hoofprints, but when they reached the cobbles of the village High Street, it vanished completely.

'What now?' asked Pascoe.

Dalziel didn't answer straight away but thrust his great head forward and moved it slowly this way and that, like an old bear checking out the scents of the forest on waking from hibernation.

Then, showing his teeth in a hungry smile, he said, 'I reckon I'll follow my nose up here. You sniff around further along.'

He vanished down the side of a tiny grey cottage, leaving Pascoe to continue up the street, still scanning the trodden snow in search of the vanished spoor. But the combination of cobbled surface and the fact that people had clearly been out and about in the village made it an impossible task. Only on the doorsteps of some of the cottages fronting the street did the snow lay even enough to take a good print, and all you got here were the perfect circles left by milk bottles.

He turned to cross the street to see if he had any better luck on the other side. And halted abruptly as a puzzling thought came into his mind.

Surely even out here in the country where some trace of old-fashioned standards of service still remained, there was unlikely to be a milk delivery on Boxing Day?

Behind him a door opened. Something hard and cylindrical rammed into his spine, making him squeak with pain. And a harsh Yorkshire voice grated, 'Stand still, mister, and state thy business. Now!'

Dalziel meanwhile was pushing open a kitchen door, his nostrils flaring wide.

He found himself looking into the surprised eyes of a slightly-built young man sitting at a scarred oak table, topping up a pint pot with Veuve Clicquot. In front of him was a huge plate piled high with the delicious freight of the full English breakfast.

' 'Morning, Billy,' said the Fat Man cheerfully. 'Cansta spare a sausage?'

Ten minutes later he emerged, chewing pensively. Looking down the street he spotted Peter Pascoe sitting on the low wall running round the churchyard, cradling a large plastic carrier bag.

'You look knackered,' said Dalziel as he approached. 'Should take more exercise.'

'Fails my heart I know not how,' said Pascoe. 'What are you eating?'

'Kidney. Billy Bream's back there stuffing his face and washing it all down with bubbly.'

'So why's he not here in handcuffs?' asked Pascoe without much passion.

'He says he found it all on his gran's doorstep this morning when he got back from the hotel.'

'And what had he been doing at the hotel that kept him all night?'

'You recall yon bonny waitress, Patty Strang? That's what he says he was doing at the hotel that kept him all night.'

'And you believe him?'

'Well, she looks a healthy young animal,' said Dalziel. 'Still, I admit that normally I'd have had him in for questioning so quick he'd have got indigestion. But when I opened my mouth to give him the caution, I found meself putting another sausage in. Peter, I think maybe I took a knock on the head last night and it's left me concussed. I've started imagining some very strange things. Tell me to get a grip on myself, then pop back in there and arrest Billy Bream, and I'll give you a big wet kiss.'

Pascoe smiled wanly and said, 'Sorry, sir, not even for such an inducement. You see, I've been having a strange encounter of my own too. With Miss Drusilla Earnshaw of this parish, age 83, vegetarian and devout Methodist, who poked her walking-stick in my back and didn't take it away till she'd seen my warrant and my library card. Then she told me a very strange story indeed.'

'I don't think I want to hear it,' said Dalziel.

'I don't imagine you do,' said Pascoe. 'Seems she was woken by a noise outside her cottage not long after midnight. She got up, took hold of her stick and flung open her front door. A man was crouching on the step.'

'Description?' said Dalziel desperately.

'Her eyes are bad. Big, broad and brutish, is the best she can do. But her hearing's fine. To her question, "Who are you?" he replied, "Never fret yourself, luv. It's only Good King Wenceslas." Upon which, she hit him in the mouth with her stick and slammed the door. When she opened it again this morning, she found these on her step.'

He opened the carrier to reveal a bottle of Veuve Clicquot, five sausages and a kipper. Dalziel looked at them, shivered, and touched his wounded lip as the tide of memory finally broke clear of the slick of liqueurs and ran clear and high and oh, so very cold.

He let his gaze rise to meet Pascoe's. And spoke.

'Well, here it is at last, lad. Your big moment. Ring the Chief Constable, alert the Home Office, call out the SAS and get yourself put in charge of a nationwide hunt for a well-built man with a cut lip and a bedroom floor covered with damp clothes who might be staying at the Hirtledale Arms Hotel. Could be the making of you.'

'No thanks,' said Pascoe, standing upright with sudden decision. 'I'm made already, I reckon. But here's what I do suggest. You go back to the hotel, get in your car and head for town. I'll say you've been called away on an urgent case. But first I'll go round the village and collect as much of the stuff as I can find. I'll tell Partly-Human that we lost the trail but are ninety per cent sure it was some local lads, having a bit of a joke...'

Dalziel was shaking his head.

'Nay, lad. Good try but it won't work. Local lads means yobs and poachers to the likes of Partly-Human. Vermin. He really would want to call in the SAS to flush 'em out.'

'So what *do* you suggest?' demanded Pascoe, exasperated.

'Well, first off, I'm not going to take advantage of your loyalty to get me off the hook. But I'm touched, lad. Deeply touched.'

His voice broke and he gave a choking cough.

'Please,' said Pascoe. 'No need...'

'Nay, I'm right. Bit of kidney got stuck, that's all. No, there are times when a man's got to face up to consequences. What is it I'm always telling you?'

Pascoe thought. None of the things that Dalziel was always telling him, such as he should eat more red meat, or that a university degree was what any convict could get between jerking off and sewing mailbags, seemed to apply.

'Can't think, sir,' he said. 'What is it you're always telling me?'

'Speak the truth and the truth will set you free!'

Pascoe couldn't believe his ears.

'You've never told me that in your life!' he cried. 'Besides, in this instance, it's rubbish. The truth will lock you up. You've got too many enemies, starting with Partly-Human...'

'Peter, you always think the worst of people,' remonstrated Dalziel. 'There's good in everyone, especially this time of year. Remember the carol.'

Seeking the tune, he began to intone, *'Wherefore Christian men be sure, Wealth or rank possessing...'*

'You won't have any rank,' insisted Pascoe. 'And precious little wealth. Andy, it's your career...'

But Dalziel was away down the street, the words now bursting out in a thunderous baritone.

'Ye who now do bless the poor Shall yourselves find blessing!'

Fifteen minutes after his return, he emerged from Hartley-Pulman's office looking solemn. Pascoe, waiting anxiously, cried, 'What did he say? What did you tell him?'

'I told him the truth,' said the Fat Man. 'And it's OK, lad. Like the decent chap he is, he listened, he understood, he forgave and now he's starting to forget. And I'm off down to the kitchen. All this confessing don't half make you hungry! And it's a shame to waste yon stuff you rescued from the old lady.'

He walked away smiling. He loved Pascoe dearly, but it did his heart good to see those intelligent sensitive features gobsmacked from time to time. Not that he hadn't been touched by the lad's willingness to cover up for him. But why tell lies when the truth was good enough? And in his dealing with Partly-Human he'd spoken nowt but gospel truth.

Of course what most folk forget is, there are four versions of the Gospel.

He'd said, man to man, 'I followed them tracks as far as the castle where I came across Lord Hirtledale and some of his young guests. High-spirited lads, but no harm in them. His lordship and I spoke briefly—man with a mind like that doesn't need things spelt out—and he apologised sincerely for any inconvenience his young friends may have caused. He said...but I reckon a chap like you doesn't need things spelt out either. Suffice to say, if you can see your way to keeping this business under your bonnet, you'd be highly obligating someone not a million miles away. No names, no pack drill. In fact the only name you need bother with is mine, 'cos that's the one that'll be on the cheque covering your losses. And I'll tell you, I'll be proud to sign it. What do you say? Draw a line under this lot? It won't be forgotten, I promise.'

Partly-Human was looking as if the Michelin guide had just awarded him three stars.

'Well, naturally, in those circumstances, I'm only too happy to oblige. And I must say I'm pleasurably surprised by your part in this, Superintendent.'

'Andy,' said Dalziel. 'Well, it 'ud be a sad world if them as are born to rule it couldn't sow a few wild oats. Tell you what, I bet his lordship 'ud be really chuffed if half the damages went to his Bosnian Relief Fund, eh, Giles?'

And Partly-Human to his credit hardly blanched as he said, 'I think that's a lovely idea, Andy.'

Driving home the next day, Dalziel grinned

at the memory. All right, it had cost him, but he'd really enjoyed his break.

Best of all, though, had been the delight on Rosie's face, not to mention the dismay on her mother's, as they'd all stood on the terrace together before they left and examined the mysterious footprints still visible on the lawn.

'You see, the statue did walk, mum,' insisted the little girl. 'Because it's Christmas. Isn't that right, Uncle Andy?'

'That's right,' said Dalziel, winking broadly at Ellie. 'Everyone gets what they want at Christmas, that's what it's all about.'

Everyone who had an Uncle Andy, anyway. It was funny, all these clever buggers like Pascoe, and not one of them had thought to speculate why the kitchen thief should have included a kilo of salt in his swag. But the salt had been the first and principal object of the raid. The Wenceslas idea had been an afterthought.

He'd trotted round the still snow-free lawn, marking out the trail of footsteps and hoofprints in salt. On the rest of the frost-hard surface the big flakes had soon started to settle, but for a while those that hit the salt melted away. And when the white coverlet was complete, the spoor of prints remained to baffle the adults and delight the little girl.

Andrew Dalziel threw back his head and laughed long and loud, and God, who is a Yorkshireman, looked fondly down on him and laughed too.

Rosie Pascoe, drowsy by her gran's side in the back of her dad's car, was also looking back on Christmas with much pleasure. Of course, any time spent in the close company of adults was bound to have its baffling elements. Like did her mum and dad *really* like Uncle Andy or not? *She* liked him, because he was funny, and kind, and never worried about being rude. Also, because he was a bit sad sometimes.

She recalled Christmas night when she couldn't get to sleep because of all the day's excitements. Finally she'd got up and looked out of the window. There on the lawn, she'd seen him, Uncle Andy, lumbering around like an old dancing bear with the snowflakes whirling like moths round his great grey head. He'd been pouring something onto the grass, she didn't know what. But she didn't doubt next morning that it had something to do with the statue's supposed footprints.

Now, why Uncle Andy should want people to think the statue had walked, she didn't know. It was silly really. Statues couldn't walk, everyone knew that. But it was what he wanted, and that was enough for her to give him her total uncritical support.

Everyone gets what they want at Christmas...even Uncle Andy...

She fell asleep with her head on her grandmother's lap.

Margaret Lewis

A BEND IN TIME

The snow had taken her by surprise. Gillian and her mother had passed the evening pleasantly if not excitingly, tucked into a corner of the cosy restaurant, fire blazing in the inglenook. Parental birthdays had to be noticed and her mother expected a certain amount of fuss.

As they opened the heavy oak door, huge flakes of snow swirled around the entrance. Gillian packed her mother into her car, which fortunately was parked nearby, and attempted to scrape snow from the windows. As fast as she cleared, a new layer obscured the glass. They lurched off down the hill towards her mother's small bungalow near the river. Durham was a series of plunging slopes and it did not take much to bring traffic to a halt during a snowstorm, but tonight most sensible people seemed to have stayed at home and the roads were almost deserted.

A golden blur was all that could be seen of the flood-lit cathedral and castle, usually so dominant above the town.

Her mother hovered anxiously on the doorstep.

'Won't you stay tonight, dear, instead of going off into the wilds? It does seem to be a very bad night.'

She was tempted. But it was a little late to ring the neighbour now and make arrangements for the dog and cat.

'I've always got home before, mother, in all the years I've lived out there. If I can't make it, I'll come back into town. I'll put my boots on, just in case.'

Her navy suede court shoes were already stained and leaking and she was glad to push her cold feet into her old sheepskin boots that lived permanently in the back of the car. She waved cheerfully and set off once more. Gliding insecurely in the rutted snow, she turned westwards towards the tiny hamlet, perched on a hill, where she had lived for the last six years.

Snow did not alarm her, just the opposite in fact. She was exhilarated and challenged by the driving conditions and the transformation of a familiar daily trip into a contest of will between her and the relentless, all-engulfing snow. The car passed through the last village on the ridge before the open moorland. The tiny market square was deserted, its picturesque butter cross in the centre decoratively burdened with snow. Even the pub seemed to have closed early; everyone must have sunk their last pints and retired to the domestic hearth.

As Gillian left the lights of the village behind her, what in Durham had been lazy, swirling snowflakes falling gently on the cathedral tower became hissing, horizontal lines. Sculptured drifts were forming along the dry-stone walls and the road, here and there blown clear of snow, was drifting up where farm gateways allowed the wind to sweep through. The old, humpy milestones were already nearly buried. She thought of stories of stagecoaches lost for days on the northern moors, and even of present-day motorists who found, to their surprise, that the natural world still wielded considerable powers.

The car was in third gear and she kept up a good pace even though the wheels were barely gripping and occasionally deep snow sent the vehicle sideways like a toboggan. She knew every inch of the road, having commuted to work in all weathers, and she knew that the sharp right-angled bend at the disused chapel was the likeliest place to run into a major drift. If she could get beyond that, her cottage was only a mile away, up a steady gradient with a useful line of thorn hedges to break the wind. As the road continued westward along the ridge to the Pennines, black and white snow poles would still mark it out when walls and hedges had disappeared, guiding the traveller on, post by post, until the next stone village emerged from its craggy landscape.

A copse of pine trees on the left warned her that the bend was approaching. It was a wild and desolate spot at the best of times but now, leaning forward and peering desperately into the beam of the headlights, she felt a sense of unreality that was beginning to be alarming. She accelerated as much as she dared and pulled the car around the corner, almost crashing broadside into what looked like an overturned vehicle, barely distinguishable under a heavy layer of snow.

Gillian's car spun around out of control as she automatically hit the brakes and she glided gently into the ditch. She hung over the tightened seat belt for a few moments, catching her breath. Her head had crashed into the side window but she was all right. She had avoided the other car, and no damage was done. From here she could easily walk home in twenty minutes. Was there any point in leaving the lights on? Surely no one else would come this way until the snowploughs arrived in the morning. And even then, Sunday was always a slow day for digging out the roads. Feeling slightly dizzy, she tied a scarf over her head, picked up her bag and pushed open the door.

Immediately she was out into a swirling roar of wind and snow. The pine trees behind her howled and thrummed. The door was torn from her hand and flung back on its hinges. It was certainly the worst blizzard she had ever experienced, the sort that village old-timers talked about in the local pub—"Why, ye could walk up the roof and look down the chimneys, man. Them was real snowstorms in them days."

As she turned, staggering into the gale, she wondered for a moment about the other car. No one could be in it, surely? Perhaps she should check. The wind buffeted her mercilessly and she narrowed her eyes against the intense cold. The overturned vehicle looked distinctly odd. More like a farm cart than a car. As she drew closer, the outline emerged from its heavy blanket of white snow. More like a stagecoach than a farm cart. Beneath her warm coat, she shivered.

Suddenly the wind changed direction and the snow lessened its fierce, horizontal drive. From the door of the disused chapel a path of light stretched towards her, warm and golden in the snow.

Common sense told her to set off as fast as possible towards the village. But the desire to see inside the chapel was overpowering. It was impossible to turn away. Slowly, her head throbbing, she followed the path of light into the chapel, through a door, now open, that had never been open before.

'It's a very curious death,' mused Chief Inspector Armstrong to his sergeant. 'How on earth did she get into a building that's normally padlocked, with a gash like that on her head? And if it wasn't an accident, who would be lurking out here on a night like last night?'

They stood watching Gillian's car being winched out of the ditch and towed away for examination. The road had been ploughed now although a particularly bad patch at that corner had delayed their getting through until after midday. The first police patrol had found Gillian's car, no problems. But while making a cursory search around the vicinity, just in case the driver had been overcome in the blizzard, they had heard the creaking of the chapel door blowing in the wind. Gillian was lying spread-eagled on the stone floor, her eyes frozen open, with a huge gash in her head.

The young constable had just managed to stagger outside and radio for help. He'd seen bodies before, but not like that, not without knowing they were there. The Chief Inspector took his report and sent him off duty. He wasn't going to be much help to the investigation in his present state.

Armstrong looked at the footprints leading up to the chapel door. Only one set approached and none went away. The snow had ended soon after midnight so Gillian's trail, although slightly feathered by the wind, was still quite clear. There was no evidence that he could see of any vehicle but her own.

Bob Armstrong had lived all his life in Weardale. He strolled around the corner, hunching into his sheepskin jacket, and looked down the valley where mile upon mile of silent white fields unfolded, punctuated by stark black thorn trees and an occasional stone wall. From this high point on the ridge an undulating blanket of snow had transformed the landscape, softening its scars and revealing sensuous folds in the valley sides. Apart from the wind, hissing as it sharpened the edges of the drifts, there was complete stillness for miles around.

He knew exactly where he was standing: on the spot of Tom McIvor's gibbet. McIvor had been a highwayman, and he was hanged at the scene of his crime. His wife had sat beneath his chained figure day after day, raining curses on everyone who passed by. Everyone around here knew about Tom McIvor's corner.

Ridiculous. He pushed such thoughts to the back of his mind. Either Ms Cochrane had been injured when she came off the road or she had been attacked by someone in the chapel. A tramp? Or one of those weird travellers, perhaps? One thing was sure, the queue of witnesses would be short and sweet.

He went back into the freezing chapel. The tin roof was flapping and crashing in the wind and icy draughts were funnelled through gaps in the walls. The building was old, but had been used as a barn for as long as he could remember. It had probably fallen into disrepair centuries ago, after Thomas Cromwell had cut his ruthless swathe through the north of England.

Gillian was being zipped into her plastic bag and carried away. No one was anxious to linger in this icy weather, with more snow imminent in the lowering grey sky. He stood, deep in thought, trying to recall something else about Tom McIvor. Ah, yes. He remembered now. McIvor had caused the coach he robbed to overturn by the simple expedient of digging a hole in the road. In the accident a young woman had been badly hurt. She was carried into the chapel and later died.

Armstrong had another look around the stone-flagged floor, using his torch in the fading light. Apart from an old spade leaning against the corner behind a withered bale of straw, the chapel was completely empty. He strolled over to have a look at the spade. The sort of thing you'd find in a farming museum. When he picked it up, the handle disintegrated, crumbling away into powder. No one could have disturbed it for years. Yet clearly to be seen around the edge of the metal was a ring of fresh blood. He dropped it with a crash, his hands full of sawdust.

A murder weapon? Or a figment of his imagination? Outside, scudding dark clouds were hurtling across the sky, bringing another blizzard in from the west. The light was weakening by the minute. He called to Sergeant Gregory, who had already started the car engine and was distinctly reluctant to get out into the icy wind again.

Armstrong held out the remains of the spade.

'Do you see anything on this metal?'

Gregory looked closely. 'Not at first sight, sir,' he replied cautiously. 'Would you like it examined by Forensic?' He produced a plastic bag and Armstrong dropped the spade in. He could see for himself that the rim of blood was not there.

'I'd like a detailed examination of this

place and the car as soon as the crews are mobile again. Padlock the door and seal it. Although I can't imagine many passers-by out here for a few days.'

He stood looking over to the little milestone and the hump behind it that marked the spot of Tom McIvor's gibbet. Snow was swooping down across the moors, erasing the roads and the bridle-ways. The B5219 would have to be ploughed out again, and perhaps this time the operator driver could avoid making such a mess of the road surface at that corner. Beneath the broken asphalt, the outline of a huge pothole was fast disappearing under the suffocating snow.

Peter Lewis

BORROWER OF THE NIGHT

A SERIAL MYSTERY

It was centuries—well, years and years anyway—since Perdita had been anywhere within long-range spitting distance of the North-East. Until now, there'd been no compelling reason for her to return, and after moving to London she kept her distance. Until now, with SOS after SOS coming from Belinda as well as some important exhibition work she had to get round to sooner or later at the Robinson Library in Newcastle.

Perdita still remained in touch with a few people up there. Christmas cards, birthday cards, holiday postcards, the occasional letter, even the odd phone call. With Belinda it was different, since she descended on Perdita as often as money, time, the twins and Bernard would allow for a theatregoing binge together. "Capital punishment", Belinda called it, quoting Dylan Thomas, but in her case the punishment was mostly financial. Perdita never returned these visits although she had a standing invitation to do so. Once in London she'd wanted to put the North-East, especially Durham, as far out of mind as it was out of sight. Impossible, but she tried.

With her doctoral thesis far from complete, Perdita had been fortunate to obtain a post as junior curator of manuscripts in the British Library in London. Very fortunate, she insisted, at someone else's very unfortunate, tragic expense. She was the second choice, but the historian appointed, a man working temporarily at the Shakespeare Institute in Stratford, died in a bizarre car crash shortly before he was to take up the position. She'd met him on the interview day and found him arrogant and patronising, but one shouldn't think ill of the dead unless one has to, she told herself. Especially someone who died like that, mysteriously, ending up in the Avon not far from the Shakespeare Memorial Theatre during a performance of *The Tempest*. Perdita knew the place well, having made several visits with Belinda.

Even before his funeral, Perdita was offered the job on condition she could begin almost at once, and she did.

How many years was it since she'd left Durham? Since that farewell dinner party with Belinda, Catriona and Mairi? And the last of the few nights she'd spent with Gavin? Perdita had lost track, perhaps didn't want to remember, and had to tunnel into her memory to work it out. Was it in...? Or...? Everything had been so messy at the time, what with working in the Scottish libraries and hardly ever being in Durham. The date she was absolutely certain of was her graduation ceremony since it coincided with her birthday, and her best present was the one she earned herself, a first. No other student in her department got one. Nobody else in her circle of friends got within long-range spitting distance of one. She worked bloody hard for it, but unlike some of the professional virgins and workaholics who always did the full day shift with her in the library, she played fairly hard too. Did some acting, which she enjoyed, although not nearly as much as Belinda, who was in everything when she wasn't in bed with Bernard. Drank a good bit every Friday and Saturday night in the best North-East tradition, and sometimes other nights too. And she couldn't deny the occasional joint. Very relaxing after the daily endeavours with her books.

But she didn't sex hard with either men or women, even though she was studenting in the wake of the pill-popping Sexual Revolution—so-called, she would add, being an historian quick to contest established labels and particularly hostile to instant journalistic slogans. For her the reality never matched the persuasive propaganda. Like the time she'd been drinking heavily with Belinda and Bernard and they urged her to join them in an every-which-way threesome described in an advanced manual of experimental sex they were perusing and laughing over together, only to find that while she was getting ready in the bathroom the other two had started without her and fallen heavily asleep on the job, leaving her very much to her own resources. Sobering, it was, and since there was nothing in the manual to cover eventualities like this, she slipped away quietly, leaving the two-backed beast snoring away through its two noses.

Perhaps if she had devoted herself to the

quest for the modern Grail of the perfect and indefinitely sustained multiple orgasm, the way Belinda seemed to do when she wasn't on stage, Perdita wouldn't have walked in triumph on her twenty-first birthday from St John's College past the cathedral to collect her first in the great hall of the castle with a handshake and abundant congratulations from the chancellor, accompanied by a fanfare of hurrays and cheers as well as loud, rather than the usual polite, applause. A female Tamburlaine entering Persepolis, one of her year murmured. Dr Faustus in maiden's weeds, according to another. Even her friends said it had gone to her head. And why not, she thought, once in my life? That day she really did hold her head high after burying it in books—bloody boring and wrong-headed, too, some of them, many of them—for a couple of years. That day was a magical experience.

Members of staff from her department, with whom Perdita had frequently crossed swords, queued up to shake her hand as though it had suddenly acquired talismanic properties. In classroom encounters she had become increasingly aggressive in challenging orthodoxies with her radical feminist and Foucault-inspired theories. Pretty well everything her lecturers and tutors said, she had concluded, was based on a set of unexamined and unwarranted assumptions, which she wanted to explode.

'There's only one thing worse than a Scottish Catholic, and that's a lapsed Scottish Catholic,' one of her lecturers said about her to a colleague, who replied, 'apart, that is, from a lapsed Scottish Jesuit,' and in the department she acquired the nickname of "the Jesuit", even "the Jesuitess" to the less politically correct among them. But however strident and contentious she proved to be, treating "liberal" and "humanist" as among the dirtiest words in the language, she couldn't be accused of being uninterested or predictable or lacking in intellectual rigour, and in her examination answers she maintained perfect control and icy rationality. She made damned sure that they couldn't penalise her for polemical rant. She wasn't going to give them that satisfaction. Oh, no. She was determined to beat them at their own game. All the handshakes were a grudging acknowledgement that she had succeeded. Indeed she was their star student. Since her application for a three-year postgraduate award was bound to be successful, they were keen for her to stay on to do her PhD in Durham. And she did.

She shouldn't have, but she did. Her research topic was never in much doubt. She wanted to deconstruct the history of the witch mania of the seventeenth century and rewrite it from a feminist perspective. "Witches" had been denied a voice so she would provide one for them. Her fascination with this subject had begun when she was chosen to play the part of the cunning, mendacious, hysterical and lustful servant-girl Abigail in a production of Arthur Miller's *The Crucible* at her school. Perfect type-casting, claimed her classmates. They'd said the same when she acted Prospero in an all-girl version of *The Tempest* only months before, and she did enjoy having magic powers and being in control of everything, on stage at least. This was the role that triggered her interest in white magic and black magic, but at a time when she had decided to read History the play didn't seize her imagination as much as Miller's.

Until *The Crucible* she had known nothing about the Salem witch trials in

1692, on which the play was based, but during the long rehearsal period she read everything she could find. Obsessed, her History teacher said. And obsessed she certainly became, about how the greatest wave of witch hunts coincided with what was held to be the High Renaissance and the burgeoning Enlightenment. Frenzied irrationalism and its diametric opposite seemed to go hand-in hand. And why not, since in her parents' lifetime unprecedented scientific and technological triumphs accompanied the Final Solution of the Jewish Problem in Nazi Germany? While not long after the Second World War, which was supposed to put an end to fascism once and for all, Senator Joe McCarthy's manic crusade against anyone even the palest shade of pink, like Miller himself, took place in the Land of the Free.

If Perdita had found a suitable supervisor for her PhD elsewhere, she would have left Durham without a moment's hesitation, but she didn't. She tried quite hard. Wrote around. Even phoned around. But one strong possibility in Glasgow had just accepted the offer of a chair in Australia. Another was taking up a fellowship for a year in California. She managed to meet a third in Edinburgh, but it was animosity at first sight. A fourth, in Aberdeen, claimed to be a full-frontal feminist of the new wave, but Perdita doubted whether she had yet caught up with Mary Wollstonecraft, let alone the suffragettes. To her surprise, the devils she knew, in Durham, turned out to be no worse than ones she didn't. British historians, even the Marxists, were a deeply conservative lot. Paris might have been very different, but that was out of the question with her award.

In the end, fatigue and inertia got the better of her. She stayed put. And Durham certainly was not without its advantages. Among the Special Collections in the Palace Green Library was an abundance of seventeenth-century material, and being on the main railway line between King's Cross and Waverley, Durham was strategically placed for her necessary forays to both London and the east coast of Scotland, where she would have to spend periods of time researching in the British Library, the National Library in Edinburgh, and Aberdeen University Library.

The transformation from being an under-graduate to a research student proved to be greater than she anticipated. If she had gone to another university, she would have made a fresh start and the change would not have been so startling, but Durham was abruptly different. The idyll was over, and even Perdita, for all her criticisms, had found something idyllic in her three years there. She may not have succumbed totally to the Durham magic, but neither had she proved resistant to its spell. Now, however, most of the people she knew had left. Only a handful remained, some to do teacher training, like Belinda and Bernard, and some because they were still in the grip of the spell and couldn't bear to leave the city yet. Unlike her, virtually all of these were settling into steady relationships, making their nests. Having had more than her fill of college life, she moved out of St John's to a large bed-sit in one of the terrace houses at the bottom of The Avenue, and discovered loneliness. The loneliness of the long-distance researcher, she called it.

Her "flat"—the hyperbole was her land-lord's, not hers—was central, convenient, and within walking distance of everywhere, but apart from the library there no longer seemed much incentive for going out.

She even missed the muted, nodding-acquaintance camaraderie of the professional virgins and workaholics who had shared the out-of-the-way study area she used in the library, where they all had their favourite seats, like Karl Marx in the Reading Room of the British Museum. For her research she needed to work in the Special Collections, where she hardly saw anyone except the librarians who helped her occasionally. There were very few humanities PhD students around, and none with interests close to hers. Being a postgraduate was turning out to be a sentence of solitary confinement. She was becoming an anchoress, though not by choice as in the Middle Ages.

There was a poem by John Donne she remembered about two lovers finding the room they occupy together "an everywhere", their bed expanding to become a universe. For Perdita, on the other hand, Durham had suddenly diminished and shrunk to become something akin to a prison cell. Previously Durham hadn't seemed such a circumscribed world but now she realised just how small a provincial city it was, the massive Norman cathedral, sitting high in the saddle on the peninsula formed by the great U-bend of the River Wear, out of all proportion to what lay at its feet. Durham was famous for its cathedral, its university and its high-security prison. There was a famous cynical description of Durham as the city of three prisons: the prison itself, the university, and the cathedral. The first, it was said, imprisoned the body; the second, the mind; and the third, the soul. Perdita was beginning to think that it wasn't so much cynical as accurate.

If she hadn't felt so isolated, she might not have contrived a totally improbable affair with the current Northern Arts Literary Fellow, who acted as writer-in-residence to both Durham and Newcastle Universities. The fellowship was a prestigious post for a young, relatively unknown Glaswegian writer, and Gavin was aiming to finish one novel and write a good chunk of another during his two-year stint. He was an outspoken gay with a long-term partner he'd met in Norwich while doing some teaching on the MA course in Creative Writing at UEA. Colm still lived on the Norfolk coast near Blakeney, a bugger of a place to get to from Newcastle without a car, Gavin once complained to Perdita, but worth it. For the buggering, she assumed.

Knowing him to be a fellow-Scot, Perdita had called on him one day in his Durham office to show him a couple of fictional pieces she was writing as a by-product of her current research into Scottish "witches", since she was the type of historian who stressed the constructed fictionality of all historical discourse. She'd read his two published novels and his collection of stories and been struck by the sensitivity with which he treated his female characters, young and old. Perhaps he had a thing about his mum, the way gays were alleged to have. Perdita also recognised that only someone whose entire childhood had been as saturated in north-of-the-border Catholicism as her own could have written the way he did. They had some things in common, she felt, although their social backgrounds were so different. If some students were to be believed, Gavin didn't suffer women gladly and made sardonic personal remarks, but according to others his initial abrasiveness was no more than protective irony, an easily penetrated defence mechanism. It was the mask he wore as a Glaswegian from a working-class family with strong socialist principles to confront the well-heeled and public-school Sassenach students of which Durham had more than its fair share.

She didn't introduce herself properly at first, but when she did tell him her name, he burst out laughing. 'That's a good one,' he said, 'Perdita Wycherley, indeed. And you a wee Highland lassie from Aberdeen or Inverness or somewhere up there, to judge from your accent. Are you sure that's not the *nom de plume* you made up for your literary lucubrations?'

And she told him that, believe it or not, it was her real name. Her mother started life as Sinclair, had become Urquhart, and was now MacLeod, but after the death of her first husband she had been married, briefly and disastrously, to an Englishman called Wycherley. Perdita didn't let on that her dead father had been a member of the aristocracy and that she herself could use the courtesy title of "Lady", something that a couple of the History staff liked to remind her of when she was being outrageously unladylike.

Gavin went on: 'There's a crime novel by Ross Macdonald called *The Wycherly Woman*. Do you know it?' She shook her head. 'You should read it. But that's "LY" not "LEY" like the dramatist. How do you spell your name? With the "E" or without?'

'With, like the dramatist,' she said, 'a remote ancestor.' As soon as she said this, she knew it was a mistake.

'Ancestors, eh? People like me don't often have the privilege of meeting anyone with ancestors. What's it like having ancestors? Famous ones, at that. Well, I suppose it guarantees the authenticity of your name. I knew there was something very theatrical about you the moment you came in. You can't deny it, can you? Perdita Wycherley! Could be a character in a Restoration version of *The Winter's Tale*. Or the name of Shakespeare's Country Wife. So which is it, witch-hunting Wycherley? I wouldn't put it past you to have sisters called Viola and Miranda.'

If he'd been straight, she would probably have said something extremely abusive, shown him a couple of fingers, aimed a kick at his balls and slammed the door, but he wasn't and she didn't. He was testing her, she felt, inviting her to be homophobic, since he knew she knew he was gay, but she refused. Instead she discriminated positively in his favour. Perhaps she shouldn't have, but she did. 'My sister's called Ophelia,' she said, 'and my other one's Desdemona, and my other one's Cordelia, and then there's Portia, and...do you want me to go on?'

'Touché,' he replied, and they both dropped their guard. Somehow or other, by the end of their first session, they had clicked. After that, she dropped in regularly on the one day of the week he spent in Durham, and they usually had a sandwich and a pint together at lunchtime in one of the pubs or hotels near the English Department. By the time he discovered she was entitled to be called "Lady", he was amused by her guile in concealing it from him, and he didn't take the piss as much as she expected.

At first she imagined he was as lonely as herself, and he might have been if he'd lived in Durham rather than Newcastle, but she soon learned that she'd got it hopelessly wrong. Compared with her fairly uneventful and totally chaste life—not through choice, she insisted—his was a non-stop social round. Sexual round too, she suspected.

'I go down as often as I can,' he told

her. 'To Norfolk, I mean. And Colm comes up as often as he can. To Newcastle, I mean.' He liked teasing her with *double entendres*, keeping her at arm's length, yet he could also be extremely frank with her about homosexual marriages and how they had to accommodate one-night stands and short-term liaisons. No, he wasn't lonely, she concluded, not outwardly anyway since in Newcastle, a much more anonymous city than gossipy Durham where everyone knew everything about everyone else, the opportunities for flings and one-night stands were legion. But if it wasn't loneliness that bonded them, and it couldn't be sex, what did? Obsessions, she decided. They were both obsessed. What seventeenth-century witches were to her, serial killers had become to him. And as they swopped obsessions, they realised that these had more in common than they expected.

Gavin's first two novels, set in the Glaswegian sub-culture he knew at first hand, involved violent death, murder as well as suicide, but much more like Dostoevsky, he claimed, than English detective novelists. He was interested in a society in which words like "good", "evil", "right", "wrong", "just", "unjust" and even "crime" had become devoid of meaning. One of the characters in the novel he was completing was a female multiple killer and he had been reading widely in relevant psycho-pathological studies. The next novel would also feature a woman murderer, but this time a revenge killer. Each of his novels had vague parallels with a Jacobean tragedy, his most recent one with *The White Devil*, the one in progress with *The Changeling*, while his first, which made his name, was actually called *'Tis Pity He's a Virgin*.

Like Gavin, Perdita was fascinated by the tragedies of the Jacobean and Caroline dramatists, in her case because their treatment of women, especially defiant and transgressive ones, shed light on seventeenth-century constructions of womanhood and femininity, and therefore indirectly on witches. But it was the psychology of the inevitably male witch-finders she was concentrating on at that moment, and what Gavin had to tell her about serial killers was extremely relevant. Witch-finders were hunter-killers too. The upholders of justice and the representatives of law and order were the real villains. They, not their

232

victims, were the demonic and inhuman ones with far more power than the witches were alleged to possess.

One day he asked her if she'd like to see a play about serial killers coming to the Gulbenkian Studio Theatre on the Newcastle campus. Serial killers of a kind, he added, out of necessity not for the fun or love of it. Guess which play? She couldn't. It was a new touring production of the Scottish Play. Much ado, Gavin observed, about the treatise on witchcraft by James I, whom he called James VI. She didn't need to be told. James' *Doemonologie* was a text she knew inside out, and *Macbeth* was the Shakespeare play she knew best since it was so pertinent to her research. She appreciated the invitation. Theatre outings with Belinda and other friends to Newcastle, especially the Theatre Royal, had been a regular feature of her undergraduate years, but she didn't much like going on her own. Now she looked forward to going to the theatre for the first time in months.

According to the posters outside the Gulbenkian, the production was "adventurous and daring", "a post-Freudian,

Lacanian interpretation", "a sexually challenging *Macbeth* about the Dark Anima of the female psyche". After the first minute Gavin, who'd knocked back a couple of whiskies with some of his thesp and lesb friends in the theatre bar while waiting for Perdita, whispered in her ear, 'I don't think I'm going to like this.' The three nubile young actresses playing the witches were contorting and spread-eagling their bodies around the stage in a recklessly uninhibited dance, dressed, if that were the right word, in a few tartan ribbons tied around their necks and waists, and with large coloured beads woven into their pubic hair. This certainly gave new meaning to Macbeth's words about their "beards" and their "wild attire" when he first meets them. From their seats in the middle of the front row, Gavin and Perdita could see more than the most optimistic of the dirty-mac brigade would expect in a strip show. A gynaecologist having a night out could be excused for thinking he was still with his livelier patients in the clinic.

'It's like visiting Fingal's Cave,' Gavin muttered to her. 'Not exactly Scottish country dancing, is it? Unless it's the witch version. These sisters really are weird,

234

but not quite in the sense Shakespeare intended, forsooth.' Perdita wasn't sure whether his negative responses were to the highly aggressive female nudity—it was near-nudity really, but so near that the near didn't count—or the novelty of the conception, or indeed to both. Perhaps Gavin wouldn't have minded if there'd been some tight-bummed, well-endowed young men decked out in a ribbon or two to compensate for the witches. But then perhaps she wouldn't have, either.

No such luck, however. An over-exposed Lady Macbeth made the most of her "Come to my woman's breasts" and "I have given suck" speeches to provide a Page-Three-Girl display of her nurturing equipment. A couple of times when her ladyship bore down on the front row, Perdita noticed Gavin flinch and duck as though he thought he were about to be involved in an unusual form of audience participation as she provided a physical demonstration of her words.

During the interval Gavin insisted on strong fortification for the ordeal ahead. Scotch. What else? And plenty of it. Two doubles each for starters. 'We need them,' he said, 'need to down our spirits to keep our spirits up. What a cow! Did you see her udders? What's Lady Mac going to be like in the sleepwalking scene if she can't keep her top on when she's sane? Do all Ladies carry on like this? You should know.'

'But she's possessed, or yearning to be possessed,' said Perdita, wondering whether the rapidly downed whiskies had made him forget he was talking to someone also with udders—not admittedly anything like those—rather than to his gay friends, who responded to women's bodies so very differently from the way men were supposed to. Since meeting Gavin she had become interested in the gay world after recognising that something linked gays and the women accused of being witches. Both were outsiders posing a threat to patriarchal norms and power. Both had been horribly done to death in the past. The biography of Joe Orton, *Prick Up Your Ears*, had been a revelation to her, and unlike a number of the women students Gavin had recommended it to, she'd understood the punning title immediately. To save money, she'd recently read it in daily instalments in remote corners of the higgledy-piggledy university bookshop. In the past one of her male friends might have "borrowed" it for her, since they did that kind of thing, arguing that because books had become too expensive for students, the only justification for the university bookshop was to provide them free of charge.

After the whiskies on an empty stomach Perdita felt so light-headed she didn't bother to protest at Gavin's misogynistic comments about the female flesh being thrust hither and thither— Lacanianly if the pretentious note in the programme about the Dark Anima were to be believed. She'd never known Gavin like this before, but women's naked bodies did funny things to men, and perhaps gays were no different from heteros except that it was a different funny thing.

'What does this whizz-kiddess from the National theatre think she's up to?' he asked. The producer was a young woman not much older than Perdita who had made her name with a revolutionary feminist interpretation of *The Taming of the Shrew,* of all things, so the ostentatious physicality of her *Macbeth* was certainly not exploitative. On the contrary, it was disturbing rather than erotic. Even the studenty Gulbenkian audience, so different from the Theatre Royal crowd, was disturbed. Gavin's behaviour indicated that, in spite of the precautionary whiskies, something was getting through to him.

Perdita was trying to identify the layers of anti-patriarchal subversion she found in the production. By rubbing the audience's noses in women's more private parts, almost literally in Gavin's case, the producer was demystifying women while simultaneously celebrating their power. Something like that. It was the same kind of thing that Perdita and Belinda had attempted, with much less success, in the satirical two-woman show they'd put together for the Edinburgh Fringe when undergraduates, *Country Girls* (what else for a Wycherley?), a feminist romp which caused a minor sensation and attracted the photographic attention of the press because of what they did in some anti-porn sketches when prancing around in tarty underwear or even just stockings and suspenders. It wasn't Scottish country dancing. For all the wrong reasons they played night after night to a packed church hall. They set out to disturb but miscalculated. The takings, however, were very much better than expected.

After the interval, which ended for Gavin with more fortification hurriedly gulped down, there were further surprises before Lady Macbeth's sleepwalking scene. The killing of Macduff's family usually ends with Lady Macduff rushing out pursued by the murderers after they have stabbed her son, but not this time. Definitely not. The audience wasn't going to get away any more scot-free than Lady Macduff herself. Not with a merely symbolic rape of Scotland. After ripping most of her clothes off, the gang of killers subjected Lady Macduff to such a realistic sexual assault only a few feet from them that Perdita had to thump Gavin hard when he stage-whispered tipsily, 'Somebody call the police for God's sake. They're gang-raping and buggering the poor bitch.'

After that even the sleepwalking scene was an anti-climax. Her ladyship's waiting woman speaks of her throwing her night-gown upon herself, but this Lady Macbeth needed to improve her aim. The gown ended up on the floor. Attention was focused on her candle, which she moved caressingly and suggestively in front of her thighs. Perdita felt apprehensive, especially when Lady Macbeth exclaimed, 'Yet here's a spot' and 'Out, damned spot!' Where was the candle going to end up? Surely she wasn't going to, was she? 'To bed, to bed,' she said, blowing out the candle and moving it dangerously near, 'there's knocking at the gate.' Was she? But no. Her ladyship may have had a host of sexual problems but she wasn't going to solve them that way. Instead she smashed the candle against a sharp metal rail and stamped on the broken pieces savagely. Gavin was squirming with his legs tightly crossed, Perdita noticed.

A few scenes of mayhem and carnage remained, including Macduff's presentation of Macbeth's severed head looking so authentic at a distance of three feet that Perdita and Gavin were amazed when the actor who played Macbeth joined the rest of the cast for the applause with his head still apparently in place. Some of the surgeons in the RVI and the other Newcastle hospitals were world-famous for transplants among other things, but even so. Sewing things back together normally took time.

Afterwards they joined the thesps and lesbs in the theatre bar for a more leisurely drink than the down-the-hatch interval whiskies. Perdita and Gavin strongly disagreed about the production. For him, it was perverse, garish, excessive. 'Of course it was,' she said, 'but quite deliberately so. That's the point.' The entire production, she maintained, concentrated on the power of female sexuality so terrifying yet hypnotic to men. The witches embodied this, Lady Macbeth embodied this, even Lady Macduff embodied this, so that the nasty rape scene made sense since it was a concerted male attempt to kill her sexually before actually killing her. The men in the play like Macbeth and Banquo were bewitched and controlled by this force, which they resented but couldn't resist. This was partly what the witch thing at the time was all about, she explained. Shakespeare knew more than a thing or two about women and sex—about men and sex too. The modern dominatrix was a kind of witch, casting her spells over her victims or clients or punters, wasn't she? Why else did so many men pay her good money to tie them up, tie them down, spank, cane, whip, punish and humiliate them? With the lesbs siding with her, the discussion became a gender confrontation, with Perdita accusing Gavin of a deep-seated fear of castration.

Hadn't the candle crushing incident got to him? He admitted it had.

Perdita enjoyed this opportunity for a good argument and discussion since it no longer happened in Durham, and she lost track of time. Afterwards she wondered whether this had been accidentally on purpose. When she did look at her watch she realised she had virtually no hope of catching the last train to Durham. One of the thesps with a car offered to whizz her down to the railway station, but he had difficulty getting to his feet, so she declined politely. She did make a dash for it on the Metro with Gavin in tow, just in case the train was late leaving, but it wasn't. In her experience, this one never was. The driver was every bit as eager as his passengers to get home for the night.

'Well, what now?' he asked. 'You'd better stay with me.' And she did. She hoo'd and haa'd a bit. But she did. As she knew she would ever since she'd looked at her watch. Maybe even earlier, during the performance. Had she been subconsciously hatching a plot even while the Macbeths were reaping what they'd sown? Was she intent on borrowing him for the night? Put like that, she thought, made it sound like one of Macbeth's lines, but then, as with *Hamlet,* there was a long tradition of pillaging the Scottish play for quotable phrases, especially by authors for titles, sometimes the same one: "sleep no more", "the seeds of time", "something wicked this way comes", "light thickens", "sound and fury". She couldn't immediately think of others but there must be plenty.

'As you can see,' he said, letting her into his palatial university flat, 'I'm not short of space. Acres of it.' And there were. He offered her the choice of the large bedroom with an equally large bed—queen-size, she thought—or the enormous living room on a put-u-up couch. Completely alone with him for the first time that evening, Perdita felt liberated rather than randy. What had got into her? Apart from too much alcohol? It was as though she were possessed. In the play Lady Macbeth asks to to be possessed by demons so that she can commit murder. Murder was the last thing on Perdita's agenda, but some mischievous sprite or other had certainly taken possession of her. Was it the Dark Anima the programme notes went on about? She ignored his attempt to deal with the sleeping arrangements, and treating the

243

room as her stage she launched into an impromptu performance. She took off every stitch of clothing and did an imitation of the weird sisters' dance, circling around him, rubbing against him, the way they'd done with Macbeth. As Gavin had said, it wasn't Scottish country dancing. More like Scottish country foreplay.

'Put some music on,' she said.

'What? "The Witches' Sabbath"? "Bewitched, bothered and bewildered"?'

'Something Spanish. Something with balls to it. Manuel de Falla. *Love the Magician.*' She may have been a bit drunk, but she knew very well that she would never speak like that normally. Sexist talk that was. What was up with her?

The nearest thing he could find was Miles Davis' *Sketches of Spain.* A bit tame, the balls on the small and floppy side, but she didn't complain. She didn't want to seduce him exactly. She certainly didn't want to "cure" him, the way some women apparently wanted to "cure" gays by showing them the love of a good woman, or some such baloney. That would be a case of "Physician, cure thyself", since her own sexuality was a bit wobbly, and both at school and later she had succumbed to the occasional "pash" for another girl or woman. She didn't even want to punish Gavin for his remarks about udders and cows and kiddesses. Rather she was demonstrating her thesis, proving her point about domination. It was not unlike a couple of sessions she had had with the man supervising her PhD when he challenged her vigorously and she made fierce counterattacks, nearly making an exhibition of herself in the process but hanging onto her cool by her fingertips. Then she'd been dead sober. This time she was anything but, and she was making a spectacular exhibition of herself, as in that Edinburgh show *Country Girls*. Soon the unaccustomed exertions made her tired and breathless—she needed more exercise than turning pages, she decided—and she led him by the hand into the bedroom.

'Who do you think you are? The Wife of Bath? Lady Mac?' he asked.

'Lady Per, actually. Do you know what they called me at school? Lady Purr of Purring Pussy. And as for the sleeping arrangements,' she said, pushing him on the bed and tearing at his clothes, 'we'll both sleep here, but not before...'

And they did. It. Well not really It, if

what you mean by It is It. More like a sort of It. What she wanted. Which a woman could have done just as well. But what the hell. She sat on him, pressing her lips to his. He didn't seem to mind, didn't appear to feel used or abused or soiled or raped. The last thing she fancied was going at It hammer and tongs—no "wham, bam, thank you, man" for her.

'Lie back and think of Colm,' she said, 'or Scotland or even Fingal's Cave.'

'I don't have to think about it,' he replied. 'I'm looking at it.' She shut him up by smothering him with it.

It—their It—took no time at all since she'd worked herself up and was so exhausted she was ready to drop but had to establish her hegemony over him first. She was Dr Faustus in the nude, Tamburlaine entering Persepolis. She was flying without any visible means of support. Without even a broomstick, she thought. They fell asleep back to back, forming a two-fronted beast that snored the night away through two noses.

Not long after the rape of Lady Macduff and what Gavin himself called his "bewitching, bothering and bewildering" at the hands and not only the hands of Perdita, her friend Mairi was raped in earnest. Mairi had been in Perdita's year in St John's and was one of the stayers-on in Durham, where she worked in the university bookshop, turning a blind eye to Perdita's unconventional reading habits. Perdita had thought of her as one of the professional virgins, but after graduating, Mairi became infatuated with a trainee journalist called Max—grossly engrossed, Perdita called them, like Belinda and Bernard—and then gradually disinfatuated. The relationship, Mairi decided, had run its course and had no future. It had been good for her and she was grateful, but it had served its purpose. It was over, finished. Only Max refused to accept this. It was partly his possessiveness that had alienated her. She tried to talk it over with him, explaining that there was no one else—she made a real effort, she really did—but he wouldn't believe her. She was his and he didn't want to give her up. He phoned her at work as well as at home, and when she had the number changed and went ex-directory after a siege lasting a couple of weeks, he used his journalistic tricks to obtain the new one. He didn't bother her in the shop, thank God, since he'd always had a thing about keeping their relationship very special and private, almost secret. Sometimes, however, he hung around outside her flat after ringing and ringing the bell, knocking and knocking the door. He was an absolute pain, but she felt pestered, not threatened, and didn't want to cause him trouble by calling the police or complaining to the newspaper he worked for. What could they have done anyway? She assumed her tactics would work. And just when she thought they had, she learned the hard, brutal way that they hadn't.

One evening after work she went all the way down the Bailey to deliver some urgent packages to the various colleges on the Durham peninsula. She didn't notice Max but he must have followed her because he was waiting for her when she came out of her last port of call, St Cuthbert's, near the river. He wanted to talk, somewhere quiet, and he led her through the archway at the end of the Bailey to the river-bank paths. She wasn't afraid of him. Perhaps she should have been, but she wasn't, since he'd never shown violence towards her. A bit rough in bed, but she took that with the smooth.

Weren't all men like that? How was she to know, an ex-professional virgin like her? But with the place so deserted and shadowy, with all the trees and bushes, she did feel a bit anxious. Term had recently ended so there were no students going to and fro across Prebends' Bridge, and as it was almost dark there were no people around at all. Women were advised not to walk alone there after dusk since it was notorious for flashers. One had been in the news recently, but he flashed the wrong students, two members of the women's hockey team. They returned in force, laid a trap, and gave him such a drubbing that he didn't have much to flash with when they'd finished with him.

Max wanted one more chance, he told Mairi as he led her off the path to the edge of the river, but she said there was no point, and then he set about her, punching and kicking her, and when she began to scream he hit her in the face, knocking her almost unconscious. She fell heavily, banging the back of her head on the ground. She would have fought hard if she could, kicked him where she knew damn well where to kick the bastards, but she was totally incapable of putting up any resistance when he set about her clothes. He didn't even have to gag her before he raped her, turned her over, and raped her that way too, pushing her face hard into the grass to muffle any cries of pain. Then left her.

When she came to, Mairi heard people passing nearby but she didn't want to call for help. She was too confused to know what she wanted. Except to get home. It wasn't that far. She'd give it a go, even though she was in a state of severe shock. But how would she manage, the mess she was in? She couldn't see herself—fortunately—but her skirt was badly torn and there was blood from her nose and lips all down her front. When she got to her feet, she found her shoes and her bag, stuffed what remained of her tights and pants into it, and started back along the Bailey, making slow progress. She didn't want any Samaritans and didn't meet anyone at all until she was almost back at the bookshop, where she intended to tidy herself up since she had a key, but then the Samaritans did descend on her.

'I'm all right really,' she said. 'It's nothing much. I just had a bad fall.'

But even as she spoke she knew her voice betrayed her. She could hardly talk.

'Fell from the top of the cathedral tower, by the look of you,' came the reply. 'You're badly hurt. Stay here with my wife while I get some help.' She sat down in a doorway and waited for the ambulance.

The story she told the hospital and later the police was that after leaving St Cuthbert's she'd just gone through the archway for a moment to look at the river when she'd been grabbed from behind, hit on the head, and then assaulted, although she didn't know much about that, being out for the count. She had barely glimpsed the man, only enough to know that she didn't know him, and couldn't offer a helpful description. Asked why she had staggered all the way down the Bailey when she could have gone for help to St Cuthbert's or St John's or one of the other colleges, she said that she was too concussed to think straight. She'd just walked.

It was on that walk she'd decided not to shop Max. She had felt love for him in the past, still owed him a lot, and didn't want to ruin his life. She knew that this was the wrong decision, a betrayal of the solidarity

251

women should display towards male abuse. It would infuriate her most feminist friend, Perdita, and she hoped to hell that Perdita wouldn't shop Max herself since she would guess correctly and wouldn't believe this fiction for a millisecond. What did lend credibility to Mairi's fiction as far as the police were concerned was the recent spate of flashing activity near Prebends' Bridge. Her attacker might have been a flasher wanting to try something more adventurous than flashing, and suspicion focused on the man who had suffered at the sticks of the hockey team. Could this have been his revenge? If the police had grilled a couple of Mairi's friends, they would probably have discovered enough about Max to finger him, but they had no reason to, since she insisted the rapist was a complete stranger.

When she did have a long talk with Perdita, who took her home from Dryburn Hospital in a taxi, Mairi expected Perdita to cast a spell on her, turn her into stone or a pillar of salt, and perhaps she would have done if Mairi's bruised, battered appearance hadn't demanded great sympathy.

'If someone did that to me,' said Perdita

'I'd have him hanging from a meat hook by his prick for twenty-five hours a day. I might even do it on your behalf. But if that's the way you want to play it, do so. When you're better, though, you'll get a lecture from me, as you bloody well know.'

Perdita wasn't surprised that Mairi couldn't face the police investigation and pressing charges and giving evidence in court and the media interest and everything. Mairi was like many women before her, but not like Perdita, who would have put him through the mincer with her bare hands after he'd spent sufficient time on the meat hook.

'As long as you leave me out of it, you can do what you like. Let him stew for a while. There's no need to conjure anything up,' Mairi told her.

'He needs to be seen,' Perdita said. 'He needs to be seen to. Stewing's too good for him.'

Perdita went to see Max.

At the inquest the only witness of any significance was the train driver, and even his evidence concerning the vital part was hopelessly vague. He was just approaching Durham station from the south, he explained, had come out of the deep cutting at Neville's Cross and was on the railway viaduct high over the city when he saw a shape lurch from the side of the track in front of the engine. He knew he'd hit something or somebody but didn't know what. Everything happened too quickly for him to see properly. It was so unexpected, up there of all places; the visibility was poor since the light had almost gone, not to mention a bit of mist about; and he was travelling as fast as was allowed on the sweeping curve of the viaduct. His was a through train to Newcastle that didn't stop at Durham, which was virtually deserted, as it often was when no stopping train was expected for some time. Durham was that type of station. On top of a hill next to a not-much-visited park at the edge of the city, it had nothing to offer except the occasional train. Questioned about the shape, he couldn't swear that it was only one figure. Most probably, but it might have been two. He found it impossible to say whether the figure he hit had fallen or jumped. It was even conceivable that the figure had been pushed if there had been more than one.

He was more definite about someone

he'd glimpsed standing in Wharton Park very near the railway track and apparently looking across the viaduct in the direction of the dramatically floodlit cathedral and castle on the peninsula. Probably a woman, but it might have been a man. Probably dressed in a black cape or loose coat with a hat or a hood. Looked very eerie and sinister in the thin mist, he said, but no doubt only someone walking a dog even though he hadn't noticed a dog. He had been concentrating on braking, not observing the scenery. When he walked back down the line with a member of the station staff, they found a corpse, if the heap of minced meat could be called a corpse. The autopsy established the presence of alcohol in the minced meat, but not excessive quantities.

The police asked the mysterious woman—or man—in Wharton Park to come forward since she—or he—must have seen something, but she—or he—didn't. With no suspicious circumstances, no evidence of foul play, suicide had to be seriously considered. Yet there was no suicide note or indication that the victim had ever thought of taking his own life. On the contrary. His traineeship with the paper was going well. A couple of colleagues observed that he'd seemed on edge recently—and why not, thought Perdita, since he didn't know that Mairi was going to conceal his identity from the police—but they put this down to pressure of work. This was all to the good, Perdita told Mairi, since a pre-suicidal confession of rape would have placed Mairi in a very awkward position with the police.

Could Max's death have been an accident? At first sight this, too, seemed unlikely, but teenagers from Neville's Cross had been walking the viaduct for a dare, and there had been reports and warnings about their dangerous behaviour. Choosing a time when he wouldn't be observed, had he been seeing for himself, in the interests of journalism, what this dare entailed? Or had he succumbed to an irresistible impulse to walk the viaduct just for the hell of it, as people did from time to time? To walk it because it was there? Predictably an Open verdict was recorded.

If Max had not been a journalist, the mystery surrounding his death would probably have been sensationalised by the local press and media, but he was one of their own and they handled the story discreetly just in case something nasty might emerge to tarnish them. Not quite a conspiracy of silence about the man who, according to Perdita, had taken the high railroad out of Durham, but one of tact. They made up for this reticence some months later when a sex scandal involving a Durham clergyman and, among others, the young daughter of one of Perdita's acquaintances reached its bizarre apotheosis in the larger of the two mediaeval buildings the unidentified woman—if it was a woman—was looking towards when the train driver saw her—him?—at the time of Max's death. This story had everything, and because of the worldwide fame of the cathedral, which the bishop subsequently had to reconsecrate, there was international as well as national and local coverage of it.

Perdita was reading her daily instalment of a new book by Angela Carter in the bookshop with Mairi turning a blind eye, when they both noticed one of the part-time assistants, Catriona, snuffling and crying after a man they both knew by sight had spoken to her. Catriona was older than they were, married with two children but separated from her academic husband, David. She and Mairi had become friendly—sharing their loneliness, thought Perdita, who also had plenty to share—and through Mairi, Perdita was getting to know her as well. Three Scots together, but not three weird sisters, Perdita hoped. Catriona followed Mairi's example of condoning Perdita's treatment of the bookshop as a reading room. With lunchtime imminent, Mairi and Perdita persuaded Catriona, still very upset, to have a bite with them somewhere quiet, so they strolled across Elvet Bridge to the Royal County Hotel.

Comfortably seated in a corner of an empty section of the lounge, Catriona blubbed out a story she had plainly been suppressing with difficulty for a while. It concerned her older child, Jaynne. The name was Catriona's choice, after a favourite aunt, but David insisted on the "y" and two "n"s since his daughter had to be different—not any old Jane. Jaynne, it sounded to Perdita, was as precocious as the spelling suggested. Very tall for her years and looking older than she was, she liked to associate with children more mature than herself. She had joined a youth club attached to the parish church not far from home, even though she was really too young. Catriona hadn't been at all keen, but after reassurances from the curate's wife, Ursula Upfield, who was officially in charge, she thought Jaynne would be safe. She wasn't. Anything but.

Catriona sensed that something was bothering Jaynne but didn't catch on straight away how much her daughter was concealing. When Jaynne finally blurted out some wild stuff about the curate himself, Roderick Upfield, turning up to arrange "communion games" and "private confirmation classes" for a few of the younger girls, Catriona at first thought she was fabricating early pubescent fantasies. Jaynne was imaginative and fanciful as well as physically advanced for someone her age. Catriona couldn't believe that the pleasant young married man from the local church was some kind of weirdo. This was Durham, for God's sake. The Church of England, which she had joined when she married. Rod Upfield seemed steady, reliable, supportive. She knew that Jaynne was going through a difficult time, as she herself was, after the marital break-up and David's departure to live with his recently divorced departmental administrator—his bimbo, to Catriona. Jaynne must be projecting her confused feelings about her father onto other men.

Once alerted, however, Catriona became aware of some gossip about Rod "having an eye for the girls"—meaning "girls", not "young women". As a precaution Catriona put a temporary ban on Jaynne participating in the club. To her surprise Jaynne didn't resent this, even welcomed it, and liberated from its pressures she told her mother what Rod had done, and not only with her. How he touched and stroked and fondled and probed her body. It was part of growing up, he said, indeed it was helping her to grow up, to discover herself. Jaynne felt spellbound, in his power, under his control, and he threatened her subtly, put the fear of—well, not God exactly—of Roderick Upfield into her so that she would never ever talk about their special games, their private communions. She promised him—on the Bible or the Book of Common Prayer? wondered Perdita—to keep their secret to herself.

Having made this discovery, Catriona told Mairi and Perdita she didn't know how to handle it. What was she to do?

She desperately wanted to act and at the same time felt paralysed, and her paralysis fed her torment. Rod Upfield had to be exposed and stopped, but the prospect of subjecting her daughter to police questioning and possible court appearances appalled her since Jaynne was on a knife edge as it was. Here we go again, thought Perdita. In some ways it was remarkably similar to Mairi's reaction to her rape, although this time there was no residue of affection for the perpetrator. The reason why Catriona'd broken down in the bookshop was that Rod Upfield had spoken to her, not only about books he wanted—that was bad enough—but also about Jaynne whom he hadn't seen recently. Until then Catriona hadn't set eyes on him since Jaynne's confession to her and hoped she never would again.

Perdita was going to say, 'Here's another one for the meat hook, if it's not too short to get a meat hook into it,' but stopped herself in time, since it was best not to say anything that reminded Mairi of Max. Perhaps crucifying was more appropriate for Rod Upfield. She didn't say that either, not wanting to risk offending Catriona, a practising Anglican who worshipped regularly at the cathedral but whose faith was in disarray after Jaynne's revelations. Perdita had been less surprised. After several years in Anglican Durham, she had reached the conclusion that however much practising Anglicans did, they never quite made it to being Christians.

As a lapsed Scottish Jesuitess, Perdita was unable to reconcile all that meek-and-mild lack of emotion, Tory-Party-at-prayer gentility, and never-cause-anyone-any-offence politeness of Anglicans with the violence and cruelty and barbarity and destructiveness with which Henry VIII created his Church. If a head of state behaved like that today, the White House would be threatening to send in the Marines, the CIA would be plotting to destabilise the regime, the United Nations would have voted for mandatory sanctions, and civil-liberty groups would be advocating a crimes-against-humanity trial. How could such a passionate beginning produce such a passionless Church, even a Passion-less Church to judge from the way academic theologians—or were they heretics?—were subverting and deconstructing the found-ations. Heretics, like witches, used to be burned at the stake. Perhaps a few well-roasted and toasted Anglican theologians would put some fire into the bellies of the faithful. Perhaps. But would anyone notice if all the members of the Durham Theology Department together with the entire cathedral establishment were torched in the middle of Palace Green outside the cathedral? Perdita thought not.

When it was time for Mairi and Catriona to return to work, Perdita said, 'Roderick Upfield needs to be seen. He needs to be seen to.'

Perdita went to see Rod Upfield.

His body was found one morning lying in a cruciform position on the high altar of the cathedral. Near his outstretched right hand was a cut-throat razor which on this occasion had been used for the purpose its name indicated. There was a good deal of congealed blood on the altar. Nothing redemptive about this stuff. It all came from Rod Upfield, not the Lamb of God. The forensic report indicated that his prints were on the razor but were not the only ones. The pathologist who conducted the post mortem concluded that the large gash to the throat was consistent with a self-inflicted wound by a right-handed person like Rod Upfield, but it could just as well have been made by another person standing at the end of the altar. The body had not been moved after death so Rod either slashed himself or was slashed while on the altar. It was difficult to explain why he would have done so on his own, unless it was a ritualistic self-sacrifice to expunge a terrible guilt, in which case some form of explanation would be expected, but none had come to light. It was just as difficult to imagine him climbing onto the altar and lying down in order to be ritually slaughtered by someone else. Unless he had been drugged or hypnotised or under some form of mind-control. Spellbound or bewitched, ventured one of the policemen involved in the investigation.

Whether or not on his own, Rod Upfield must have entered the cathedral fairly late on the evening before he was found, at a time when the area is extremely quiet. A member of the staff had seen him on his own in the cloisters but had thought nothing of it since he was a frequent visitor to the cathedral precincts, where a couple of his clergy friends resided. The only stranger seen in the vicinity that evening was probably a young woman but it might have been a man. It was hard to tell the difference in bright sunlight these days, complained the verger, let alone at a distance at that time of day. The figure was possibly wearing an academic gown, but then it might have been a black cape or even a cassock if it were a man. Despite police appeals, this person did not come forward.

What eventually swayed the inquest to bring in a verdict of Suicide was the evidence that began to filter through slowly about Rod Upfield's paedophilia. Even Catriona didn't want to be accused of speaking ill of the dead, much to the annoyance of Perdita, who argued that it was much less inhibiting than when speaking ill of the living. Yet it took only a couple of small revelations to bring the national press to Durham determined to follow every scent, and they did. They really did. No stone unturned. If there had been any thoughts of a cover-up they were doomed. When it came to the intoxicating cocktail of sex, religion and violent death, the tabloids and not only the tabloids hadn't had it so good for a long time. They'd done poofter-priests who cottaged around. Now they were after paedo-priests. Was Rod Upfield the tip of an ice-berg? The public assumption was that Rod Upfield couldn't live with his conscience. Only a few people, like Perdita after she'd been to see him, knew that he'd managed to live with his conscience quite comfortably for years and that at the time of his death he was not under real threat of exposure, except by Perdita. And what did she know? What could she prove? What could she do? What, indeed?

When the journalistic hue and cry caught up with Catriona and even Mairi, Perdita decided it was high time she pursued her research in Scotland. She had been asked to write an article on some famous Scottish "witches", especially Isobel Gowdie, and this provided a good excuse for a quick exit from Durham. A few years later when the young Scottish composer James MacMillan's orchestral piece *The Confession of Isobel Gowdie* was rapturously received at the Proms, Perdita wondered whether she might have provided part of the stimulus for such a passionately Catholic work. At the time she left Durham she made up her mind to get a job as quickly as possible, and she soon struck lucky with the British Library—as soon as the man initially appointed had been struck unlucky in that puzzling road accident. Perdita hadn't looked back since, especially not to Durham. She even began to develop a fetish about not revisiting Durham. She consulted her PhD supervisor by letter and phone, and even her viva took place in London at the request of the external examiner from UCL, who had broken his leg after falling down a flight of stairs in the North Library in the British Museum. Conveniently for Perdita. It felt as though he'd been pushed, he said, but since there was no one around, he must have imagined this. Perdita didn't even travel to Durham to receive her doctorate, but obtained it *in absentia*. Putting in another appearance on Palace Green in a black gown would have been an anti-climax, and she timed a necessary work visit to archives in Paris to coincide with the Durham Congregation.

In London her career went from good to better. The elegantly written and jargon-free book she produced from her rather stodgy thesis helped, since it attracted widespread rather than merely academic attention. She didn't want her book-of-the-thesis to suffer the usual fate of a tiny print-run, a handful of reviews by academics in journals nobody read, and a lonely life on university library shelves, infrequently consulted and seldom read. Her witch book, dealing with the victimisation of women by men and also with ideas about demonology, the supernatural and the occult, struck a chord at the time it was published. It appealed to the common as well as the uncommon reader: feminists, cultural materialists, new historicists, even voyeurs of torture, suffering and excruciatingly painful deaths. A paperback followed, and its success led to a commission for a more popular book on the subject, which achieved almost cult status. Perdita was soon in demand. She endured tedious journalistic puns of the "Which Wycherley?" sort. There were interviews here, there and everywhere. *Woman's Hour, Kaleidoscope,* a book programme on TV. She did a talk for Radio 3 and was the major contributor to a BBC *Timewatch* programme inspired by her book.

And now after centuries—well years and years anyway—she really was going back to the North-East. Not just within long-range spitting distance of it, but there itself. Belinda's urgent distress signals reached Perdita when she was faced with a professional visit to Newcastle. She had to meet the librarians putting together a major exhibition based on an archive in the Robinson Library at Newcastle University. It was going on national tour, including London, before the British Council took it abroad for an international airing. Since it was a long-term project, Perdita could have gone at any time and had been putting it off as long as possible, but she quickly arranged a visit after receiving Belinda's Maydays, something completely new in their long friendship.

Belinda was never one to complain, although she had plenty to complain about these days, so she must be really desperate, totally at her wits' end. If the situation had been normal, Perdita would at long last have accepted the open invitation to stay with Belinda and Bernard, but it wasn't. Instead she booked in at the new Copthorne Hotel on the Quayside. She didn't fancy driving all that way on her own, and she decided against the train, fairly fast though it was, because she didn't want to pass through Durham again and look down on the city from the railway viaduct. Her private superstition. So she flew to Newcastle.

Staying at the Copthorne, Perdita was astonished at the transformation and improvement of the whole area of Newcastle under the famous bridges since she'd last been there. It brought back memories of Gavin and the unforgettable night of naked witches, long knives, whisky galore, Fingal's Cave and It after the Scottish Play. She occasionally met him in London when he was down to see his agent or publisher, but now that he was living in Glasgow again it didn't happen often. And It didn't happen at all. Not with Gavin anyway. Not in the age of AIDS.

Belinda was Perdita's only close university friend who'd stayed in the North-East. Even Mairi had finally departed and was now managing a Waterstone's in Kent. Belinda was a Northerner but from the other side, industrial West Cumbria. When she and Bernard finished their PGCEs at Durham, they both obtained teaching posts on Tyneside, but they split up for a time after their student romance. Belinda began in a North Shields comp, which provided her if not the kids with a comprehensive education, and then went up-market to a prestigious independent girls' school in Newcastle, only minutes from where she lived. There she didn't expect to learn about the finer points of burglary, car theft and ram-raiding. She was right. Regular forays south for "capital punishment" became part of her life style, and by staying with Perdita she could afford enough theatre visits to satisfy even her. Perdita enjoyed the theatre as much as ever, although she'd given up acting, but Belinda was different. It was in her blood and she couldn't get enough. She'd joined the People's Theatre in Newcastle, was on the boards as often as possible, and produced plays at school. Perdita's diagnosis was that she had the theatrical equivalent of nymphomania.

After a couple of frenzied but short-lived affairs with actors, Belinda ended up back with Bernard, whom she'd kept in touch with despite his fairly indiscriminate philandering. The old romance was over but they settled down as a couple for a while, giving each other space. It was when they were drifting apart again that Belinda became pregnant. Bernard had never been keen on children and put all the blame on her, unfairly, for not taking adequate contraceptive precautions. He even accused her of deliberately trying for a pregnancy in order to pin him down. How could he be sure that it was his? He told her to terminate it. Abortion on his demand. She refused. Just as he was coming round to the idea of a baby, she learned that she was bearing twins, and he had another fit. This too was her fault, part of her conspiracy against him. There was a history of twins in her family, but why did it have to happen to her? He agreed to marry her, but only after the birth in case she miscarried or the twins were stillborn. She should never have accepted his terms, Perdita insisted, a modern woman like Belinda. How could she do it? But she did, humiliating as it was. She felt trapped, but she also believed that in time the children would produce the necessary cement and that something of the old romance would return. They didn't. It didn't.

Belinda kept her job but relied on a succession of local girls and au pairs, some of whom, she was convinced, slept with Bernard, although where he committed his adulteries she didn't know. In a friend's house? In the car? In the open on the Town Moor? Or the heavily wooded Jesmond

Dene, where she often found condoms and discarded underwear on her Sunday afternoon walks? Periodically there were ructions, but Belinda was too tired most of the time to care where Bernard was in-putting, as she called it. Not her very often any more. They co-existed. It suited Bernard since his affairs were short-term without any commitment to a continuing relationship. Neither separation nor divorce were on his immediate agenda. But when she let her hair, and more, down and allowed herself to be seduced by one of her actor friends, Bernard turned against her savagely. Sauce for the gander was one thing. Sauce for the goose, quite another.

Unfortunately for Belinda, she had technically condoned his numerous infidelities and had no incontrovertible evidence against him anyway. His against her, on the other hand, was too, too solid. Beginner's luck didn't apply to adultery. Her first extra-marital affair and she'd been caught in the act. There were eye-witnesses. Bernard informed Belinda that he was considering sueing for divorce and would ask for the custody of the twins since she was an unfit mother. If there'd been a bottle of barbiturates or a cut-throat

273

razor handy, she would have reached for it. Instead she reached for the phone. Perdita. Perdita was tough, independent, a born man-fighter. Belinda's other women friends would have calmed her down, been understanding, said all the right, sensible things. She didn't want that. Didn't want compassionate drivel or soppy, sloppy liberalism. If she didn't kill herself she wanted to fight, fight, fight. But how? She didn't know how. Perhaps Perdita would. Perhaps Perdita and Belinda together—the old *Country Girls* team—could come up with something. When Belinda met Perdita in the Copthorne for a leisurely dinner, she told her the whole story of her marriage. This time Belinda didn't hide anything as she'd done in the past. She used to defend Bernard to Perdita to some extent. But no longer.

'He really needs seeing to, doesn't he?' said Perdita.

'If it's not too late. You know how stubborn he can be. Once he's fixed on something.'

'Almost as bad as me, you mean, for getting my own way.'

'Almost.' Belinda managed a smile. 'But this time he does intend to crucify me. He wants to destroy me. Ruin me in the eyes of the school. He wants me in my box, in my grave.'

'I didn't come all this way for nothing. Certainly not to bury you. And not just for the library business either. You do want me to see Bernard, don't you? Talk to him? See if I can bring him round? There must be a way.'

'It's just that he's so determined now that he probably won't listen to a word you say. I doubt if he'll agree to meet you, even for old times' sake.'

'I'll have a go. We'll have to try everything. Pull out all the stops. I haven't broken my staff or drowned my books yet, you know.'

Belinda managed a laugh.

During Perdita's long phone call to Bernard, he made it abundantly clear that he wasn't going to budge. He was convinced he had Belinda over a barrel. He didn't want to see Perdita and told her to mind her own business. Wasn't it business that had brought her to Newcastle? Why didn't she get on with it? Didn't she have enough to do as it was? She kept trying, but he refused to speak to her again, let alone see her. So she gave up. Admitted defeat. An unusual experience for her, who was used to winning a few, then winning another few, and then a few more. But as the man said, she had other things to do in Newcastle, and she did them. It was the end of the road.

When she read the report in *The Independent* of the accident in which Bernard died, his car ending up in the Tyne one evening, it struck her as uncannily like the description, years and years—it seemed like centuries—earlier, of the crash that had killed the man from the Shakespeare Institute whose career she had somehow appropriated. Neither involved another vehicle but both involved a river. Was it possible that the same journalist had written both? That would be a coincidence, wouldn't it?

Val McDermid

HEARTBURN

Everybody remarked on how calm I was on Bonfire Night. 'Considering her husband's just run off with another woman, she's very calm,' I overheard Joan Winstanley from the newsagent's say as I persuaded people to buy the bonfire toffee. But it seemed to me that Derek's departure was no reason to miss the annual cricket-club firework party. Besides, I've been in charge of the toffee-selling now for more years than I care to remember, and I'd be reluctant to hand it over to someone else.

So I put a brave face on it and turned up as usual at Mrs Fletcher's at half past five to pick up the toffee, neatly bagged up in quarter-pound lots. I don't know how she does it, given that the pieces are all such irregular shapes and sizes, but the bags all contain the correct weight. I know, because the second year I was in charge of the toffee, I surreptitiously took the bags home and weighed them. I wasn't prepared to be responsible for selling short weight.

Of course, the jungle drums had been beating. Oswaldtwistle is a small town, after all. Strange to think that's what drew Derek and me here all those years ago, willing refugees from the inner-city problems of Manchester. Anyway, Mrs Fletcher greeted me with, 'I hear he's gone off.'

Shamefaced, I nodded. 'He did finish building the bonfire before he left,' I added timidly.

'She's always been no better than she should be, that Janice Duckworth. Of course, your Derek's not the first she's led astray. Though she's never actually gone off with any of them before. That does surprise me. Always liked having her cake and eating it, has Janice.'

I tried to ignore Mrs Fletcher's remarks, but they burned inside me like the scarlet and yellow flames of the makeshift bonfire I'd already passed on the churned-up mud of the rec at the end of her street. I grabbed the toffee ungraciously, and got out as soon as I could.

I drove through the narrow terraced streets rather too fast, something I'm not particularly given to. All around me, the crump and flash of fireworks gave a shocking life to the evening. Rocket trails showered their sparks across the sky like a sudden rash of comets, all predicting the end of the world. Except that the end of my world had come the night before.

Constructing the bonfire had always taken a lot of Derek's time in the weeks leading up to the cricket-club fireworks party. As a civil engineer, he prided himself on its elaborate design and execution. The secret, he told me so often I could recite it from memory, the secret is to build from the middle outwards.

To achieve the perfect bonfire, according to Derek, it was necessary first to construct what looked like a little hut at the heart of the fire. Derek usually made this from planks the thickness of floorboards. The first couple of years I accompanied him, so I speak from the experience of having seen it as well as having heard the lecture on countless occasions. To me, Derek's central structure looked like nothing so much as a primitive outside lavatory.

Round the "hut", Derek would then build an elaborate construction of wood,

279

cardboard, chipboard, old furniture and anything else that seemed combustible. But the key to his success was that he left a tunnel through the shell of the bonfire that led to the hut.

The night before the bonfire was lit, late in the evening, after all the local hooligans could reasonably be expected to be abed, Derek would enter the tunnel, crawl to the heart of his construction and fill the hut with a mixture of old newspapers and petrol-soaked rags in plastic bags.

Then he would crawl out, back-filling the tunnel behind him with more highly-flammable materials. The point at which the tunnel ended, on the perimeter of the bonfire, was where it had to be lit for maximum effect, burning high and bright for hours.

There are doubtless those who think it highly irresponsible to leave the bonfire in so vulnerable a condition overnight, but the cricket club is pretty secure, with a high fence that no one would dream of trying to scale, since it's overlooked by the police station. Besides, because the bonfire was the responsibility of adults, it never became a target for the kind of childish gang rivalry that leads to bonfires being set alight in advance of the scheduled event.

Anyway, this year as usual, Derek went off the night before the fireworks party to put the finishing touches to his monument, carrying the flask of hot coffee laced with brandy which I always provided to help combat the raw November weather. When he hadn't come home by midnight, naturally I was concerned. My first thought was that he'd had some sort of problem with the bonfire. Perhaps a heavy piece of wood had fallen on him, pinning him to the ground. I drove down to the cricket ground, but it was deserted. The bonfire was finished, though. I checked.

I went home and paced the floor for a while, then I rang the police. Sergeant Mills was very sympathetic, understanding that Derek was not a man to stay out till the small hours except when attending one of those masculine events that involve consuming huge amounts of alcohol and telling the sort of stories we women are supposed to be too sensitive to hear. If he'd been invited back to a fellow member of the fireworks party committee's home for a nightcap, he would have rung me to let me know. He knows how I worry if he's more than a few minutes later than he's told me he'd be. But of course, there was nothing the police could do. Derek is a grown man, after all, and the law allows grown men to stay out all night, if they so desire.

I called Sergeant Mills again the following morning, explaining that there seemed to be no reason to worry, at least not for the police, since, on searching Derek's office for clues, I had uncovered several notes from Janice Duckworth, indicating that they were having an affair and that she wanted them to run away together. It appeared that Derek had been using the bonfire-building as an excuse for seeing more of Janice. I had rung Janice's home, and ascertained from her husband Vic that she too had not returned home from an evening out, supposedly with the girls.

The case seemed cut and dried, as far as Sergeant Mills was concerned. It was humiliating and galling for me, of course, but these things do happen, especially, the sergeant seemed to hint, where middle-aged men and younger blondes are concerned.

I sold out more quickly than usual this year. I suspect the nosey parkers were seeking me out "to see how I was taking it" rather than waiting for me to come round to them. Seven o'clock rolled round, and the bonfire was duly lit. It was a particularly spectacular effort this year. Though I grudge admitting it, no one built a bonfire quite like Derek.

I don't suppose he thought when he was building this year's that it would be a funeral pyre for him and Janice Duckworth. He really should have thought of somewhere more romantic for their assignations than a makeshift wooden hut in the middle of a bonfire.

Kay Mitchell

INTIMATE VOICES

A few days after the funeral Avril Swale began to talk to her mother—which was comforting in a way because they'd never had much to say to each other before that. Mrs Swale had never encouraged her daughter to talk back, democracy not being a part of her nature, which explained why a lot of people expected Avril to go to pieces after Mrs Swale was laid six feet deep in Pontefract cemetery. Surprisingly that didn't appear to happen, even though freedom had come at the most awkward time of Avril's life. On the surface at least things went on as they always had, Avril went to work at the library every day, still dressed soberly because that's what her mother would have expected, and put on an appearance of calm acceptance.

To solicitous colleagues she simply said brightly, 'Life goes on,' and each evening continued to set two places at the table, although now she often called in at Tesco on the way home to buy a bottle of wine, and had changed her diet dramatically from plain cooking to Italian or Chinese. In doing that Avril felt quite daring, but as she told her mother—she chatted to her a lot now there was no girdle of sarcasm holding her tongue—there was no longer any need to worry about its being indigestible.

Faintly the words, 'Foreign rubbish,' seemed to float across from her mother's empty chair and Avril giggled as she drank the last dregs of Chablis.

It wasn't long before the conversations took on an appearance of two-way exercises, especially at times when Avril woke in the night gripped by a menopausal sweat. On those occasions she would throw back the bedcovers and strip off her nightdress to stand naked near the open window until it had passed, often mourning out loud that she had no daughter of her own to offer comfort and support.

The sad lack of fecundity had been entirely her mother's fault.

Any one of the small succession of young men who had courted Avril years ago would have made a good father, but her mother had given them short shrift. 'Seeing off the dogs,' she had called it brutally, reinforcing each dismissal by telling her daughter she should keep herself clean instead of thinking about *sex*—dropping her voice on the last word. In her whole life the closest Avril had come to carnal knowledge had been through reading D H Lawrence, when certain passages in *The Rainbow* had caused strange bodily sensations that she had been afraid to discuss.

And now...? Well, it was too late of course. She blamed her mother for that, berating her out loud for the wasted years, and before long heard her mother answer back that it had all been for Avril's own good. From that point on a regular dialogue developed between them, and Avril found that having someone tell her what to do again was a definite comfort, especially now her mother could no longer reinforce advice with physical presence.

It was because death's gate hadn't mellowed her mother's habit of intolerance that Avril stood firm against her neighbour. The width of her drive was greater than his by almost a yard, and he needed to encroach by six inches to build a garage wide enough to take his car. Avril would have let him do that, six inches being neither here nor there, but her mother was adamant. "Give him an inch and he'll take a full yard," she heard her mother say, and the garage stayed unbuilt.

The neighbour was resentful and not a nice man to cross. Soon after that Avril had her first obscene telephone call. She was too shocked to do anything but hold the receiver frozen in her hand. The voice told her things that even D H Lawrence had never written about, and when she finally managed to break out of her shock and hang up, the telephone rang again almost immediately.

'I've got your number,' the voice said, and laughed unpleasantly.

She couldn't tell her mother about that! Her mother would say the whole thing was Avril's fault, that she had encouraged him to talk dirty even though she hadn't, and Avril couldn't stand the thought of going down that road again.

She kept it to herself until Saturday, then told her friend Dorothy about it when they went shopping together. Over a cup of coffee in a small café on Beastfair, Dorothy insisted on having every word the caller had said repeated to her. Avril felt herself flush hotly and become flustered as she recounted it all. It was *so* embarrassing, but Dorothy didn't seem at all disturbed because, as she told Avril, being a Samaritan she had been taught how to react to such pathetic men.

What she omitted to say was that on the only occasion such a call had come through to her, she had slammed down the receiver without listening at all.

The next call came after Avril's tomcat sprayed the neighbour's mint. He threw a tin of beans at it and missed. Later, when his wife went out to visit her sister, he rang Avril. This time, having listened to Dorothy's advice, she talked back to him and his eyes boggled. See his doctor? See *his* doctor? Speechless with anger he hung up.

Avril finished off the half-bottle of indifferent wine opened at dinner, and went to bed feeling fuzzy-headed. In the small hours she woke, sweating heavily, and thought again about discussing the whole thing with her mother—then decided it would be safer to talk about buying new loose covers instead. As she stood akimbo in the cool breeze from the window the thought drifted into her mind that somewhere out there was a man who desired her, who wanted to do strange and disturbing things to her body.

Later that morning she rang Dorothy, and found herself invited over to lunch so that she could tell her friend all about it. She began to do that as soon as she arrived, but Dorothy shushed her, saying, 'Later, Avril dear, when Gerald's gone off to play golf.' During lunch, Avril threw covert glances at Gerald's portly figure and wondered if he had ever done those shameful things she'd heard about to Dorothy.

The following week, in a magazine article, Avril read that the best way to treat obscene telephone calls was simply to hang up. She considered that and dismissed it, because in a strange way she had begun to enjoy the thought of them. On her way past the wine shelves at Tesco's she chose a litre bottle of wine instead of her usual half.

The neighbour bought a new Sierra in bright blue and a scratch appeared on it overnight. He raged at his wife. 'Six bloody inches. I ask you. Six bloody inches! That's all I asked.'

His wife, having wanted a Montego, refused to be sympathetic. She snapped, 'Probably she'll move away somewhere smaller now her mother's gone. If she sells up you'll just have to be a bit quick and move the fence over.'

The thought came from nowhere that if he really scared the frigid cow she'd be glad to go.

Avril was shocked when the next telephone call came. It was different from the rest. Now she was threatened with things that were not nice at all. She wept a little. He wanted to kill her.

When Dorothy heard about it she said perhaps, after all, it would be best to go to the police, but Avril couldn't stand the thought of that.

At three in the morning, sponging herself with cold water in the bathroom, she finally told her mother all about it. Her mother said she was wicked for having listened to the man at all. That was pretty much what Avril had expected her to say. The next day Avril took wine in her flask instead of coffee when she went to work, and bought another bottle of the stuff on the way home.

It was almost midnight when the

telephone rang again, and her thoughts were so clogged it took a few seconds for his words to sink in. *He knew where she lived. He was coming now—to kill her.*

With his terrible laugh ringing in her ears she telephoned Dorothy and told her what he'd said. 'Call the police,' Dorothy advised, frightened herself now. 'Call them right away. This minute.' But Avril put the phone down and talked to her mother instead.

Dorothy looked at the silent receiver and decided if Avril wouldn't tell the police, then she would. It was the very least she could do.

Avril meanwhile sat on the edge of her bed and sang to herself quietly. When the telephone rang again her mother said not to answer it, but she disobeyed. The voice whispered intimately, 'I'm almost there now. Are you waiting for me?' Avril put the receiver down.

Her mother said, 'It's dog eat dog, kill or be killed. Do unto others before they do unto you,' and she led Avril into the kitchen and put the biggest carving knife into her hand.

Crouching uncomfortably in the darkened hall, with the front door unlocked and partly open, Avril waited for him to come. When he did, it didn't seem in the least surprising that he should be surrounded by a blue light, or that he should knock before he came in.

Stephen Murray

WILFRED'S LAST DO

T'works outing to seaside in August
Is our favourite annual do.
T'gaffer shuts mill for the day, like
And we all go along—the whole crew.

The outing committee chose Scarborough
    this year:
We'd a train to ourselves for the day;
T'lasses all sat on their own in best
    hats
And the lads talked of soccer all t'way.

Our Wilfred were there, and our Thelma,
And Leonard and William and Art,
And that well-known Don Juan, Bob
    Bagshaw
Who'd a lump of mill grit for a heart.

Now, Wilfred were courting young Daisy
    Muldoon
A peach of an Irish colleen;

295

She lived down our way and they'd always
   been sweet
Since she first winked her eye at him out
   in the street
And now she were just on eighteen.

A right handsome lass is young Daisy,
Far too lively for Wilfred, said folk;
With a mischievous eye, black curls,
   dimpled cheeks
And a grin always ripe for a joke.

Well, 'twas just gone midday when we
   got there;
We were hungry and raring for fun;
So we all ran straight down to the sea front
   and sat
Eating pie, peas and chips in the sun.

Then some of the lads who'd a football
Set goals up and marked out the sand,
And t'gaffers as weren't up to running
   around
Strolled along to pick holes in the band.

As for t'women, the old ones got deckchairs
And settled to knitting and talk,
While t'lasses put heads in a huddle and
   said

They were all going off for a walk.

Well, 'twas overly hot to play soccer
And after each side had scored twice
Our Wilfred said, 'Lads, that's me done
    for!
I'm going in search of an ice.'

Said I, 'I'll come with you.' 'No, ta,' said
    our Wilf.
But I picked up my shirt all the same,
And I said as we looked back from t'prom,
'Now, that's queer:
Bob Bagshaw's not playing in t'game.

'He was there at start, for he scored the
    first goal:
A flashy one, just like the man;
But I haven't seen him since half-time,
    and that's odd.
I wonder where he can have gone?'

'Bob Bagshaw?' said Wilf. 'Nay, don't
    waste time on him.
He's up to no good, I'll be bound.
There's a kiosk ahead and we'll get that
    ice cream:
I'm right frazzled with running around.'

We stood in the queue for a cornet
And strolled on, each licking our ice;
Then we leant against railings and gazed
    out to sea
And Wilfred said, 'Eh, this is nice!'

We came across lasses by t'funfair.
They'd been having a whale of a day
What with swingboats and dipper and
    eyeing the lads
And all of 'em nattering away.

Now they'd stretched out on sand to get
    sun-tanned.
'Twere a sight for a lad, I tell you!
With their skirts halfway up and their tops
    halfway down
There were all sorts of good things on
    view.

But our Wilfred seemed rather distracted,
And when I said, 'Wilf, let's stay here!'
He answered, 'Just let me find Daisy.
She's miserable when I'm not near.'

'Where's Daisy Muldoon?' he asked lasses;
'Has ter seen 'er?' our Wilfred exclaimed.
'Nay, she slipped off to go to the lavvy,'
    said one,

'And I don't think she's ever returned.'

'Ay up, Wilfred!' I said, with a grin on
  my face,
'That's another we've lost—that makes
  two!
First Bob Bagshaw goes off from the soccer
  and then
Your young Daisy gets locked in the
  loo.'

At that Wilfred looked rather thoughtful
Like a lad that's remembered too late
That in among chips that he'd eaten for
  lunch
There'd been one that he shouldn't have
  ate.

Said I, 'Never fear! She'll have gone for
  a stroll.
Nowt to worry about, Wilfred, trust me.
And what if Bob Bagshaw had disappeared
  too?
Tha knows she thinks only of thee!

'Let's stop here awhile, and look at the
  sights—
And I don't mean the sand and the
  sea!'

Answered Wilf as he mounted the steps to
the prom,
'Please thisen, but tha'll stay without me.'

With a last look at lasses I ran after
Wilf;
When I caught up his face were quite
black.
We searched the whole front all the way
to the Spa
But of Daisy Muldoon not a wrack.

'Now I'll tell you what,' I told Wilfred;
'She's happen gone back on the sand.
Or there's that many folk on the prom and
the front
We might have missed her by the band.

'There's the answer, you trust me—no
need to get fraught;
Why, I dare say she's looking for you!
Daisy'd not get mixed up with Bob
Bagshaw—
I'm sure she would always be true.'

Well, we hurried on back to the bandstand.
By now Wilf were getting quite warm;
And though I said, 'Nay, no point thinking
the worst!'

I could see we were in for a storm.

The kiosk were right by the bandstand.
Said I, 'Wilf, it's my turn to buy.'
But he cried, 'Sod ice cream! I don't
    want one!'
And suddenly neither did I.

T'gaffers looked up when they heard that;
They could see there were something not
    right.
But Wilfred marched past them with never
    a word
And the knuckles he clenched were quite
    white.

'Twas along by the lighthouse we found
    them at last,
Far away from the crowds and the din
Where the cliffs and the rocks made a nice
    private spot
For a lad and a lass to lie in.

It were Daisy's bright laugh that gave
    them away
And I saw as we crept up behind
She'd her skirt round her thighs like the
    other girls had—
But a tan weren't the thing on her mind.

'Now, Wilfred, don't jump to conclusions,'
   I warned;
'There's lots of folks lying on t'sand.'
'Aye, an' I suppose that's a cornet he's
   sucking,' he cried,
'An' that's Scarborough rock in her hand!'

'Don't kill him, though, Wilf, don't do
   that!' I implored.
'Won't I, though!' answered Wilf with
   a cry.
'What else should a man do with vermin?'
And he raised a great rock up on high.

On the train going home we were all right
   subdued;
We hadn't the heart for a song.
There weren't many jokes nor much larking
   around
And the journey seemed terribly long.

Now I'm taking another excursion:
Not to seaside this time, just to York;
To say my farewell to our Wilf in the
   gaol;
To have a last brotherly talk.

He's coming to end of his stay there.

He says it's quite comfy, but then
They make a fair effort, considering,
To brighten up lives of condemned men.

For that's what our Wilfred is come to.
No more outings to Scarborough for him.
Just one short excursion tomorrow,
One last funfair ride—one last swing.

As for Daisy Muldoon, who's a game
    lass,
She were rather cast down just at first;
But I showed her as how it were all for
    the best
And she quickly got over the worst.

We've fixed for the honeymoon in Black-
    pool—
Well, Scarborough didn't feel quite right,
What with having been there once already
    this year
And seen what there is of the sights.

Committee meets next week to ponder
Where to fix on for next year's works do;
But somehow I don't think they'll ever
    get votes
To go back to Scarborough—do you?

Alan Sewart

THE OLD FOLKS' HOMES MURDER (COLNE) 1970

On 16th June 1970, about 11 am, the body of Carrie Sibson, a widow aged 80, was found in the bedroom of her home at 12 St Stephen's Way, Colne. She had been murdered.

St Stephen's Way is a modern concept in housing, situated off Byron Road, Colne, and consisting of three linked terraces of small bungalows running along three sides of a square. Access to the small estate is from Byron Road—the fourth side—along a series of flagged paths which cross a communal grass court. The units comprise living-room, bedroom, kitchen, bathroom and coal store. Each unit has only one door and all doors face out across the communal court. The bungalows were custom-built for elderly people and, in 1970, many of the residents were in their seventies or eighties.

Carrie Sibson had been born at Colne on 19th May 1890. Her husband Thomas had been well known in the town as a wine and spirit merchant until his death. There were no children of the marriage and Carrie had no surviving relatives other than distant cousins, so she lived alone in her bungalow. No 12 is situated in one corner of the square and the front window commands a view across the whole of St Stephen's Way.

Carrie was very agile for her age and was often seen walking round the town, sometimes covering long distances. Her sight was failing, causing her to move carefully and deliberately, but her hearing was good, which helped to compensate. Her few friends lived in other parts of Colne, and although she was on good speaking terms with her close neighbours she did not seem able to mix more closely. As a result, Carrie Sibson had earned the reputation of being "religious", "eccentric" and "independent". But people did notice her, and when enquiries began on Tuesday 16th June, it was not difficult to trace most of her movements on the previous day.

Annie Gowling, 71 years old, a retired weaver of 4 St Stephen's Way, saw Carrie hurrying past her home at 3 pm. Maggie Dyson, 83 years old, a housewife of 1 St Stephen's Way, saw her passing her window at about 6 pm. Shortly after 6 pm she called on an acquaintance, Beatrice Varley, 70 years old, of 90 Oak Street, Colne, which is several hundred yards away. At 6.30 pm she called on Pastor Robinson at her local church to deliver a charity collecting-box for which she was responsible, and finally, about 7.30 pm, Mrs Varley saw her walking back towards her home. Apart from her killer, Mrs Varley was the last person to see Carrie Sibson alive. But during the next few hours there were other happenings on the old folks' estate, and all of them would be seen to have some relevance at a later stage.

Mrs Elizabeth Turner, aged 80, lived two doors away at 10 St Stephen's Way. About 10.45 pm on Monday 15th June, she heard a knock on her door. She was not expecting a caller and was timid about opening her door, so she stood inside the door and shouted, 'Who's there?' She heard a man's voice shout back to her, 'Do you know a Mrs Heseltine who lives round here?' Mrs Turner shouted, 'No.' Being too slow-moving to reach the window she did not see the man, but she heard him walk away.

During the next half-hour or so, the same sort of thing was to happen to two other elderly residents. About 11.15 pm it was the turn of Annie Gowling. When the knock came to her door she opened it and saw a man standing there. He asked her if she knew of a Mrs Webb, or Webster, living in the area. She had never heard of such a person and told the man so. He did not approach her and she closed the door on him. The man was wearing some sort of hat that threw shadow on his face, so Mrs Gowling was not able to give a useful description.

It can only have been a few minutes later when a knock sounded on Mrs Maggie Dyson's door. She kept her door shut but asked, 'Who's there?' and heard a man's voice reply in a local accent, 'Do you know a Sidney [or he might have said Cyril] Heseltine living in this district?' She told the man that she knew no such person and he went away.

Mrs Rose Muriel Bell, 70 years old, was not a resident of St Stephen's Way, but from her house at 59 Ellesmere Avenue she could look across to the front of Carrie Sibson's. She knew that Mrs Sibson was in the habit of going to bed early—sometimes as early as 7 pm—so she was quite surprised on the evening of 15th June to notice that lights were showing from both windows of 12 St Stephen's Way at something like 11.20 pm. But the curtains were drawn across the windows so she assumed Mrs Sibson was just having a late evening.

Next morning, about 10 am, Mrs Turner and Caroline Atkinson, 80 years old, of 11 St Stephen's Way, each noticed that the curtains were still covering the windows at No 12, so they came together to compare observations. Plucking up courage they went together and knocked on Mrs Sibson's door, but there was no reply. Worried but uncertain what to do, they kept a watch on the house for some time, until two elderly men joined them and they were able to pass on their worries about Carrie. The men were Ernest Williams, 82 years old, of 17 St Stephen's Way and Henry Smith, 70 years old, of 98 Oak Street. The sprightly Mr Smith, still young enough to be a man of action, managed to free a catch on the kitchen window. He opened the window and climbed through, closely followed by another comparative youngster who had just arrived, Thomas Hind, aged 73, of No 65 in nearby Ellesmere Avenue.

Both men went through into the living-room. They noticed a certain amount of disorder but no more than might have been expected in the home of an elderly person. Smith crossed over to the bedroom door, which was closed, and tried to open it. At first it would not budge but he managed to release it by degrees, to find that a rug had been doubled up behind it. When he got into the room it was quite dark, owing to the curtains being closed. He switched on the light and then saw the shape of a body, lying on the bed entirely covered with bedclothes.

Death is the most common human tragedy of all, and amongst the elderly it does not bring surprise. Smith and Hind expected to find Carrie Sibson dead and must have supposed the cause would turn out to be a natural one. Noticing a red cushion and a white pillow over the head of the body they carefully removed them, only to find that blankets and a green eiderdown still covered the woman's head. They lifted the bedclothes away. Perhaps now they began to be uncertain, but their reactions have not been recorded.

Mrs Sibson's body was lying three-quarters prone on its left side, facing the far wall. Her nightdress and cardigan were drawn up over her shoulders, leaving the lower part of her body naked. Both hands were out of sight beneath the body. The only incongruous item was a partly-used pack of butter which lay on the body and neither man knew what to make of that. Smith took hold of one arm and ran his hand towards the hidden wrist with the aim of feeling for a pulse, but the arm felt very cold and stiff and he abandoned the test as hopeless. They agreed with each other that the old woman was dead. Thomas Hind took up guard position at the door of the bungalow and Henry Smith went to summon the police.

The first official to arrive was Police Constable 4392 Potts. Smith showed him the body and, because he knew the dead woman by sight and name, was able to identify her to the constable. At this stage, PC Potts was dealing with what seemed to be a routine matter and he knew how to handle death. He made a superficial examination of the body and saw no marks of violence, so he enquired the name of Mrs Sibson's doctor and sent for him to attend. Afterwards, looking round the bungalow, he noticed some untidiness, with drawers and cupboards standing open and some of the contents disturbed. He left the packet of butter on the body—but he must have wondered about it.

Dr Alfred Kenneth Cooper arrived at 1.10 pm, having been delayed on his rounds. When he examined the body he found rigor mortis well established and from this he calculated that Carrie Sibson had been dead for between twelve and fifteen hours. The doctor listened carefully to Henry Smith's description of the scene as it had been when he first entered and how the bedclothes, the cushion and the pillow had been lying in relation to the body. This was enough to make him suspicious, and when he was shown the disturbance in the bungalow and the packet of butter lying on the body he decided it would not be proper to issue a death certificate.

Only one construction could be placed on the doctor's decision. PC Potts was obliged to inform his station that what had begun as an ordinary "sudden death" might now be something quite different.

Had he been aware of it, the difference was more obvious than it seemed.

Hind and Smith had missed a very important detail; so had PC Potts; and when Dr Cooper made his examination of the body, he missed it too. *Carrie Sibson's wrists were tied tightly together beneath her body: so tightly that the flesh of her wrists and hands had become terribly distorted.* The ligature consisted of a piece of red curtain material joined with one of her stockings.

In fairness they can hardly be blamed for the oversight. Hind and Smith were just good citizens with no personal responsibility. If anything, they investigated the scene more deeply than perhaps they ought, and when Smith hunted for a pulse he must have come very close to making the discovery. PC Potts was torn between the duty to investigate and the standing instruction to leave well alone. In sending for the doctor he absolved himself from the need to handle the body. Dr Cooper did nothing wrong. Once he knew the woman was dead he had no medical duty to probe further, and the moment he became suspicious he was entitled to take the view that further investigation was better left to the police.

All's well that ends well, they say, and in the case of Carrie Sibson the proper action was taken at every stage, even if the truth came out in rather a fortuitous way. Detective Chief Inspector Butler and Detective Constable Locke took charge at 12 St Stephen's Way, and they were uninhibited by instructions to leave well alone. Turning the body over they discovered what the others had missed.

Whatever might have been suspected before, the evidence of the tied wrists brought virtual certainty. This was a case of murder and would have to be handled with a high standard of care. As the local man, Chief Inspector Butler would bear the brunt of the investigation but he was expected to inform Force Headquarters so that a team of experts could be formed to work with him in Colne. Chief Superintendent Beardsworth and Superintendent Wigham, in charge of Colne Division, came to see the body where it lay, but left the action to those who would follow.

Detective Chief Superintendent Joe Mounsey came to take overall command, bringing with him Dr Garrett, Home Office Pathologist, and Mr Handoll, Biologist, both attached to the North West Forensic Science Laboratory at Preston. After examining the body, the scientists took swabs and scrapings from the body and samples of hair and blood. Mr Handoll took possession of the bedclothes, the white pillow, the red cushion, articles of clothing and the packet of butter found on the body.

As soon as HM Coroner had been informed, the body was taken to the public mortuary at Nelson. There, Dr Garrett cut the ligature from the wrists, preserving the knot, and placed it with other samples before carrying out a postmortem examination. Apart from the distorted flesh of wrists and hands he found fairly extensive bruising on groin, breasts, shoulders and legs. There was purplish discoloration of the face, indicating deficiency in oxygenation of the blood, accompanied by fluidy swelling. The eyes were badly congested, the lower lip was bruised and there was bruising also on the tip of the tongue, which protruded between the lips. Both genitals and anus showed signs of bruising and interference and the skin of the genital area was greasy with what appeared to be butter.

Dr Garrett diagnosed the cause of death as asphyxia, due to suffocation.

In the meantime scene-of-crime officers had carried out a careful search of Carrie Sibson's bungalow. A few fingerprints had been found and various control samples of fibres, hairs and dust packaged for comparison. They confirmed that a theft had accompanied the murder: the old lady's piggy-bank had been forced open and was standing empty, and although its contents were not known it could be safely assumed that some money had been there, or the intruder would not have bothered to break it open. Whether anything else was missing from the bungalow could not be known, since none of her neighbours could say what property she had.

With no definite lead to follow, the police began their enquiries in a standard pattern, knocking on doors over as wide an area as possible and asking questions of people who just might have useful information to give. One of their primary interests was the man reported to have been in St Stephen's Way on the previous evening, calling at bungalows and asking the whereabouts of different people. There could easily be an innocent explanation for this: the man's genuine enquiries timed to the murder by mere coincidence; but he would have to be eliminated from the list of suspects and teams of detectives were sent out to cover this angle.

On the afternoon of Tuesday 16th June, Detective Sergeant Ackers and Detective Constable Taylor called at 57 Oak Street to interview a family named Hall. Mr and Mrs Hall were at home, but their son Barrie was out. The officers made arrangements to call again to see him.

Barrie Anselm Hall, an unemployed weaver aged 26, was born at Colne on 29th July 1943. When he was questioned at 7.40 that evening, in his father's presence, he told the two detectives a story which, if true, placed him many miles away from the scene of the crime: 'I went to Newcastle yesterday with my mate Harry Brown, in his van. I went to see them at the Ministry of Social Security about my cards, because I'd got a job at Spencers' Mill and I was down to start that day. The van broke down at Darlington and we had to leave it there. We hitch-hiked and got ourselves back to Keighley, then we had to wait for an early bus. We didn't get back to Colne till six o'clock this morning.'

He was asked a number of supplementary questions and said in reply that he did not know the old woman who had been killed and had never been anywhere near 12 St Stephen's Way. That was not unlikely even though he lived so close to the old people's estate, since Carrie Sibson's bungalow was at the farthest point from the access road and people would not pass near it unless they had business there. Asked about where he had been earlier that afternoon when the police had first called, he told them he had taken a book up to the "rough" (a fallow field some distance from his home) and spent the time reading.

As a matter of routine, the officers embodied all this information in the form of a witness statement which they asked Hall to sign. It was their intention that the document should join hundreds of other witness statements in a file, begun that day at Murder Control, which was thickening as they worked, and that all the points raised would be checked out to determine their truth or otherwise. But somewhat abruptly, that part of their work was rendered unnecessary. As the statement was being signed, Hall's mother came into the room and had a short conversation with her husband, after which both parents went out. The moment the door closed behind them, Barrie Hall said, 'What I've told you there isn't true, but I had to tell you that because my father was here. I'd already told that story to him to explain why I'd been out all night.'

Lies! Coupled with an admission of having been out all night! There could hardly have been a circumstance more likely to arouse suspicion. Suddenly the officers were very interested in Barrie Anselm Hall. DC Taylor invited him to go with them to a place where he could tell the truth in comfort. He agreed and they took him to Murder Control, which had been set up in the Youth Centre in Byron Road. He was settled in a waiting-room and began to make another statement, still only on a "witness" form.

'I'd been with a woman all night,' he began. 'I'd been on the beer all afternoon when I should have started work at Spencers' last night as a cotton weaver. I met this woman called Jean at the "Pigeon" Club and she took me to her home and I stayed the night with her. Her husband was on nights, so I left her about half-past five this morning and walked home through Barrowford. I don't know where this woman Jean lives, but I can point the house out to you.' [The "Pigeon" Club is a local name for the Jubilee Club in Peter Street, Colne.]

Checking the details in this statement was anything but routine, since Hall had already given the police a strong whiff of a lead. They grabbed the nearest police car, piled Hall into it and promised to follow his directions. The house he took them to was 9 Haworth Street, Nelson. 'That's where she lives,' he said, 'but don't go now, because her husband will be at home.'

Up to a point, the officers were satisfied. Hall seemed to be backing up his claims without evasion, and if he really had been womanising, well, extra-marital dalliance was of no great interest to them. They took Hall to Spencers' Mill in Rose Grove, Burnley, where he was due to start work, and dropped him off.

But they were soon back to interview him again. Unafraid of angry husbands they had gone directly to make enquiries at 9 Haworth Street, Nelson, and then to other houses in the vicinity. At the mill,

Hall was brought from his loom to speak to them.

'There's nobody called Jean at that house or anywhere near it,' Sergeant Ackers told him.

'Well, that's what she told me her name was,' Hall said, putting on a show of indignation, 'and that's the house she took me to.'

'We are not satisfied,' Ackers went on. 'We want you to come with us back to Colne to sort this out.'

'All right, I'll come,' he agreed. 'I'm still sure that's where she lives, though. Is there another street up there that looks like it? I was well gassed [drunk] at the time.'

In an office at Murder Control they searched him, and of £1.9s.5d found in his pockets there were eighteen separate shilling pieces. To have so many shillings at one time would be enough to make many an old detective suspect gas-meter breaking, but Hall had a ready explanation to offer. They were from change he had received in pubs. He saved up all his shillings to use in the juke-box and in food-dispensing machines at work.

Sergeant Ackers and DC Taylor began to question Hall once more, taking him over the story he had told and sifting it for fresh flaws, and they were engrossed in the task when Detective Chief Superintendent Mounsey came into the interview room. Mounsey, too, was very interested in Barrie Anselm Hall. He had the feeling that comes to many policemen when they believe they have the right man but still lack the evidence. After listening to the cross-talk for a while, he spoke to Hall himself.

'We'll need to check what you're saying,' he said, 'and that means making a lot more enquiries. It will take some time. Do you mind waiting here while we do it?'

'No, I don't mind at all,' Hall told him.

The story he had told was not completely false but he had changed it quite radically to suit his own purposes. Mounsey's men were able to identify "Jean" as Violet Harrison, aged 40, of 36 Forest Street, Nelson; and Hall had not lied about her name, as she explained when the police interviewed her.

For the past eighteen months, she said, her friends had got into the habit of calling her "Jean" for some reason not known. She knew Hall fairly well. Until

322

five years previously she had lived not far from his home in Oak Street, Colne. She remembered being in the Jubilee Club [the "Pigeon" club] with her friend, Denise Kemp, on the previous day, when Hall had come in and joined the company. The three had a few drinks together in an ordinary, friendly atmosphere, until Jean decided she would move on to the Derby Inn at Colne. Hall wanted to go with her, but explained that he had no money to buy drinks. 'I don't mind standing you a drink,' she said, so they went to the Derby Inn together. At one stage he had kissed her 'in a friendly way,' and while at the Derby he squeezed her about the waist but soon let go. That was all that happened between them, because a short while later she met a man whom she knew quite well, a Mr Wheeler, and shortly after Wheeler joined them Hall 'simply disappeared.' She did not see him again after that, and she certainly had never taken him to her home.

Violet Harrison's story was confirmed by Richard Frederick Wheeler, aged 59, lodging at 23 New Market Street, Colne. He had been with the woman—though he always called her by her proper name,

Violet—in the Derby Inn at the time under enquiry. There had been another man talking to her but he had left almost at once. After they had had a few drinks he drove Violet in his van to Nelson. He dropped her outside the Engineers' Arms in Nelson but did not go into the pub himself.

Denise Mary Kemp, aged 20, a domestic worker of 44 Sackville Street, Nelson, said she was in the Jubilee Club with Jean and a man called Hall, but when they left to go to Colne she stayed in the club. Later she moved on to the Engineers' Arms at Nelson *and she was in the Engineers' Arms much later, when Jean came in on her own.*

By these witnesses, Barrie Hall's account of his actions and movements on the night of the murder proved to be fiction. Mounsey and Detective Sergeant Ackers saw him again, still at Murder Control, and faced him with it. Hall conceded at once that his claim to have gone to Jean's home and spent the night with her was a lie. The Chief Superintendent cautioned him, and Hall said, 'I didn't tell you the truth because if I had done you wouldn't have believed me.'

It sounded like a breakthrough but it was nothing of the sort. He agreed that his story was a pack of lies, but promptly told them a new pack of lies to put in its place. 'There's an old broken-down caravan by the quarry up in Bluebell Woods,' he told them. 'I found it some time ago when I was walking round up there and saw it off the road. I went up there last night and slept in the caravan, but no one saw me there.'

The police did not believe a word of this. Their suspicions were crystallising at a rapid rate and Barrie Hall was "in the frame" for the murder entirely on his own. But lies have to be investigated as deeply as truths, and before they could make progress they would have to discount his story.

'Obviously we'll have to check this,' Mounsey told him, 'and it's too dark to go messing round quarries now. So do you mind staying the night? We'll fix you up with a bed.'

It was the classic ploy of a policeman not yet convinced that an arrest would be justified but reluctant to turn the suspect loose. Fortunately for Mounsey, Hall raised no objection.

'I don't want to go home anyway,' he said.

They took him to Nelson Police Station to bed him down for the night, arriving there at 2.55 am on Wednesday 17th June.

By 11.15 am on the same day, DS Ackers and DC Taylor were there again to see him.

'You've told us three different stories and at least two of them are false,' Ackers said. 'Now what about the caravan story?'

Though he had slept on it and some hours had passed, Hall was still sticking to his guns. 'I got very drunk so I couldn't go home,' he said. 'I went up the quarry like I said, to the old caravan. Nobody lives in it. I climbed in through a gap and went to sleep.'

When they asked him again about the murder, his reply was: 'I don't even know the woman and I certainly didn't kill her.'

The police were by this time following a new line. 'We're proposing to take you to see the police surgeon,' DC Taylor announced. 'He'll want to medically examine you. Do you object to that?'

Hall offered no objection, so they took

326

him to Dr Palin's surgery at Briarfield. He grumbled a little when he was asked to undress, saying, 'What is this for?' DC Taylor explained that the doctor wanted to give him a thorough, all-over examination, and added, 'If you know nothing about the murder you have nothing to fear, and this examination can help you.'

With that he undressed and the examination took place. The doctor took nail scrapings, a penis swab, pubic hair, chest hair, scalp hair and samples of blood and saliva. All these were handed to Detective Constable Lord, exhibits officer at Murder Control.

They took Hall back to Nelson Police Station, where DC Taylor began to take down Hall's new story in statement form at his dictation. There had been no change in what he wanted to say. He was making no admissions. When Taylor was joined by Sergeant Ackers the statement was halted and the two detectives took Hall up to the quarry area, near Bluebell Wood, to point out the old caravan.

They must have been a little surprised to find there actually was a caravan. It was derelict, almost collapsed, but Hall still insisted he had slept there during the night of the crime. There were no tell-tale signs either to support or condemn his story. The officers tried a subterfuge: standing near the caravan they asked Hall to point out to them the approximate place on the road from which he had first been able to see the caravan. He pointed with some confidence and they drove him to that place. As they had hoped, it was impossible to see the caravan from where they were now standing and they faced Hall with the dilemma. He was unmoved, not giving way at all. 'I'm getting mixed up a bit,' he said. 'It must have been from the other road.'

Nothing could rattle the man, it seemed, but by this time he had told so many lies, only to have them thrown back in his face, that he must have been weakening. Taken back to Murder Control and lodged in an interview room, he was given a meal and left to eat. When he had finished the meal, Detective Chief Superintendent Mounsey went in and began to question him again. The usual denials were all he would give at first, but eventually, after a period of silence, he said, 'I didn't mean to kill her.'

At that stage Mounsey called for

Detective Inspector Clegg to join him, both as witness to the interview that followed and as note-taker. It was time to warn Hall that he need not say anything unless he wished to do so, and this was done, but it made no difference. He was talking now: describing how he had gone to the old folks' homes in St Stephen's Way and forced an entry into one of the bungalows. It was put to him that he might make a voluntary statement under caution.

'Somebody can write it for me,' he said.

Mounsey then brought in the local men, Detective Chief Inspector Butler and Detective Sergeant Murphy, and after he had introduced them to Hall, Mounsey and Clegg left the room. With DS Murphy as witness, DCI Butler wrote down Hall's statement.

On Monday, that is the 15th of this month, I had been out all day drinking in pubs and in the "Pigeon" Club in Colne. I had been with two girls, Jean and Maureen Scott, until about 6 o'clock, when we left Maureen at the "Pigeon" Club. I was very drunk. My next recollection is finishing up at these homes. I knocked at a door and asked for Heseltine. Nobody came to the door so I knocked on another, and this lady opened the door. I pushed my way in. She screamed so I put my hand over her mouth. The next thing I know I was putting her onto the bed. She kept saying 'stop it' and all that. I was saying 'I don't want to hurt you.' She quietened down. She stopped struggling. The next thing I'm undressing me. I tried to have intercourse with her but I couldn't, so I tied her wrists with something. I was undressed and lay on the bed with her.

Hall described finding a packet of butter in the kitchen and rubbing some of it between her legs. As he told this part of the story he was crying. Afterwards he did manage to have intercourse with her.

I was throwing pillows and blankets on top of her. I think my hand was over her mouth for a long time. She was still alive then and I was just feeling her, then she went quiet. After that I fell asleep and when I woke up she was dead. I could see she wasn't breathing. I touched her belly to see if there was any movement

330

but there wasn't. I turned her over and back again, then picked the bedding up from the floor and covered her with it. I put a cushion and a pillow on her. I was scared then. I knew what I had done so I left the house by the front door. I went up to the quarry at Red Lane. I spent some time hoping she wasn't dead, then I walked home.

The false story of having been to Newcastle was invented first for his father, to cover up for the fact that he had stayed out all night. He had been obliged to tell the same story to the detectives because his father was standing by, listening. Hall's statement concludes:

At no time did I intend to kill the old lady. I realise what I have done and regret it. I have never regretted anything so much in my life.

A prisoner now, he was transferred to Colne Police Station and there he admitted having stolen money from the bungalow, some from drawers and the rest from the piggy-bank which he forced open. The eighteen shilling-pieces found in his pockets were the contents of the piggy-bank.

At 6 pm on Wednesday 17th June, at Colne Police Station, Detective Chief Inspector Butler cautioned and charged Barrie Anselm Hall with murdering Carrie Sibson, between 7.20 pm on Monday 15th June and 11 am on Tuesday 16th June 1970. Hall replied, 'I'm terribly sorry.' On the charge form he wrote: I'M TERREBLE SORRY I HAVE COMMITTED THIS CRIME AND ALSO WISH TO SAY I'M SORRY TO ANY FAMILY MRS SIMPSON [Sibson] HAS.

He appeared before Reedley Magistrates' Court on the same date and was remanded to Risley Remand Centre to await trial.

Granted legal aid, he was represented by Derek Lambert of Messrs Donald Race and Newton, Solicitors, of Nelson, and it seemed that the defence intended to contest the case against Hall, since one of their first moves was to ask the well-known pathologist, Dr George Bernard Manning, to perform a second postmortem examination on the body of Carrie Sibson.

But there was to be no court battle in this strange case. When he appeared at Lancaster Assizes on Wednesday 4th

November 1970, Hall pleaded guilty to murder. He was sentenced to imprisonment for life, with the judge's direction that he must serve at least fifteen years.

And now for a brief epilogue.

Because the court would not have been told very much about the background and character of Barrie Anselm Hall, details have been deliberately excluded from this account until now.

After leaving school at the age of fifteen, Hall had worked as a labourer or weaver for various companies at Colne, Nelson and further afield at Loughborough. But these jobs were mainly for short periods and in the interim he had many convictions for crime, ranging from assault and unlawful wounding through traffic offences (including stealing motor vehicles) to breaking offences and theft. He had last been convicted at Lancaster Assizes on 1st November 1967 for felonious wounding and had been sentenced to four years' imprisonment. When he committed the murder Hall had been a free man for only four days, having been released from prison on Thursday 11th June 1970.

And as a final touch of irony, all the

time Hall was denying the crime, fate was rushing to engulf him from another direction.

His fingerprints turned up on the door of Carrie Sibson's bedroom.

Peter N Walker

THE UNKNOWN LADY OF SUTTON BANK

Sutton Bank is one of North Yorkshire's most famous inclines. It lies upon the A170 road as one leaves Thirsk and travels towards Scarborough. Some five miles out of Thirsk, this famous hill ascends Whitestone Cliff as a tortuous climb which extends for about one mile in three distinct gradients, 20% (1–in–5), 25% (1–in–4) and again 20% (1–in–5). The steep road presents no worries to local motorists but it does cause immense problems to those who drive up while towing trailers such as boats, or attempt the bank with heavily-laden lorries and coaches. Happily, since 1984 caravans have been forbidden to use this stretch of the A170, which means that there are fewer blockages and local drivers can have a clear passage up and down their bank.

At the summit, known as Sutton Bank

Top, there is one of England's finest views and probably the best in the whole of Yorkshire. The vista is truly breathtaking and extends towards the distant Pennines. It is possible to look across the Yorkshire Dales to the west, then over to Teesside in the north and towards York and West Yorkshire in the south. A telescope on a pedestal which bears a map helps to identify the distant places. For centuries, this panoramic view has attracted visitors and sightseers, while the hilltop carried ancient routes, including the noted drovers' road which stretched from Scotland into England.

It was at the foot of Sutton Bank in 1138 that Gundred the Bountiful of Thirsk gave to some wandering monks a piece of land near Hood Hill, easily recognised today, and said to have been a place of human sacrifice in pagan times. These were the monks who later built Byland Abbey, their first attempt being at Old Byland and their second, fruitful one near Coxwold.

Near Sutton Bank Top Robert Bruce led the Scots to battle in 1322 against the English at Scots Corner, which should not be confused with Scotch Corner on the A1. The fight became known as the Battle of Byland and the English were well and truly beaten; their king, Edward II, fled to the protection of Byland Abbey in the valley below but left just before the Scots raided it, sacked it and stole the king's jewels. They then turned their attention to nearby Rievaulx Abbey.

Other famous people who came this way included John Wesley in March 1755, and William Wordsworth in July 1802. He came with his sister Dorothy and paused to admire the view on his journey to Brompton near Scarborough where he was to be married. After his wedding in October the same year, and now accompanied by his new wife Mary (*née* Hutchinson), he paused once again at Sutton Bank Top, this time at dusk, before going on to Thirsk. He wrote a sonnet about the view in which he mentioned 'an Indian citadel, Temple of Greece and Minster with its tower, substantially expressed.' Dorothy, in her Journal, also mentions 'a minster unusually distinct, minarets in another quarter and a round Grecian temple.' The Minster is clearly that of York, but identification of those other points will cause the viewer a good deal of puzzlement.

Tucked into the woodland below Sutton

Bank Top is the silvery water of Lake Gormire. There is a steep but delightful walk and a nature trail leading down to the lakeside. This tarn-like lake is about one third of a mile in circumference and is remarkable because no streams run into or out of it. The mystery of its formation has given rise to some legends—one says the lake is bottomless and another claims that it conceals an entire village, complete with church and spire. The Devil is also linked to the lake. One story says that he leapt from the cliff behind the lake while astride a white horse, and crashed to earth to form the crater which then filled with water. Another legend says that a white mare carrying a girl leapt to its death over the cliff behind Gormire, and that the body of the girl was never found.

The pale cliff in question is known as White Mare Crag and one theory is that the name comes from the white or silvery surface of the lake, ie White Mere Crag. This "white mare" link has no connection with a huge white horse which is carved into the hillside about a mile to the south. That is the famous White Horse of Kilburn, carved there in 1857 by the people and schoolchildren of that village.

It is now a landmark and can be seen from seventy miles away.

In the valley below Sutton Bank is Nevison House, once the home of the notorious seventeenth-century highwayman, William Nevison. He was nicknamed "Swift Nick" by no less a person than Charles II, and lore says it was he and not Dick Turpin who rode the famous Black Bess from London to York.

On top of Sutton Bank there is more of interest. In the centre of the huge car park, the North York Moors National Park Information Centre contains a wealth of detail about the district, especially about Sutton Bank and other parts of the National Park. There is a stunning cliff-top walk around the edge of the Yorkshire Gliding Club's airfield towards the White Horse of Kilburn, while the long-distance footpath, the Cleveland Way, also passes through here. Half a mile or so from the top of the bank is the Hambleton Hotel, behind which broad plains stretch towards the distant moors. These continue to serve as gallops for racehorses, and this was the location of the legendary Black Hambleton races between 1715 and 1770. The turf here is said to be the best in England for training racehorses, and strings of them at exercise continue to be a regular sight.

The ancient drovers' road passed this way too. Joining what is now the A170 close to the Hambleton Hotel, it ran from Scotland to enter the North York Moors near Swainby. From there it passed along the heights of Black Hambleton as it approached Sutton Bank Top. This drovers' road forked at Sutton Bank, with one route descending into upper Ryedale, near Oldstead, and going on to the village of Coxwold and then York, and the other turning along what is today the route of the A170. It bore right at Tom Smith's Cross, where a highwayman of that name was gibbeted, and led along what is still known as Ampleforth High Street. This is not the main street of that village but the route of a Roman highway, which descends into Ryedale to proceed via Oswaldkirk Bank Top and Hovingham into Malton, a town rich in Roman history.

Although cattle driving had been practised on the drovers' road since mediaeval times, it reached its peak in the eighteenth and nineteenth centuries. To feed London's rapidly-increasing population, hundreds of thousands of cattle were required and so they were driven on foot from Scotland and the north of England to be sold at local markets. Some of the processions were two miles long. On the road's fifteen-mile stretch across this part of the North York Moors, there were four halts, all inns. Parts of that ancient track continue to serve as a road, but only one halt remains as an inn—and that is the Hambleton Hotel at Sutton Bank Top.

Fairly recently, Sutton Bank Top featured in a national celebration. A massive bonfire was lit nearby on 6th June 1977 to commemorate the Silver Jubilee of Her Majesty Queen Elizabeth II. This was the 82nd in a chain of 103 fires stretching from Jersey in the Channel Isles to Saxavord in the Shetlands. The first fire was lit at Windsor Castle and I was present when the Sutton Bank fire was lit twenty minutes later.

Sutton Bank is certainly a place of history and legend, and I was involved in two mysteries at this place. The first is a ghost story dating to the reign of James I, and the second concerns the body of a woman found in 1981. She has never been identified.

With reference to the ghost story, I write a regular *Countryman's Diary* for the *Darlington & Stockton Times* and use my pseudonym of Nicholas Rhea. In January 1980, I heard from a motorist who had been driving late at night along the A170 near Sutton Bank Top. He had seen the figure of a woman in seventeenth-century dress dart across the road and into the forest beside the road, after apparently begging a lift or seeking help. So concerned was he for her safety, that he halted to search for her. She had been dressed in dark clothing, but he never found her and later heard that he might have seen a ghost. I mentioned his sighting in my column.

As a result, I was informed that this could have been the ghost of Abigail Glaister. Abigail lived at Kilburn, not far from Sutton Bank Top, and during the reign of James I, she was suspected of being a witch. She was pursued by men and hounds who wanted to capture her for execution, but she leapt over Whitestone Cliff near Lake Gormire and was killed. Since that time, her ghost has been seen many times near Sutton Bank Top, often seeking help from passers-by.

Upon mentioning this, I received a letter

from a lady who lives near Northallerton. When towing their caravan over Sutton Bank Top late one night, she and her husband had seen the figure of a woman apparently begging for a lift. She was dressed all in black, but when they pulled up to give her a lift, she vanished. Friends following in another car also saw the lady in black, and together they all made a search of the area, but found nothing. Recorded sightings of this ghost and its probable identity have regularly been published and it is just another in the long list of legends and mysteries which can be linked to this famous Yorkshire beauty spot.

But surely the most fascinating and puzzling is the identity of the mysterious woman whose body was found close to Sutton Bank Top in August 1981. The most exhaustive, skilled and prolonged enquiries have failed to identify her.

The story began on Friday 28th August 1981 at 8 am. A man telephoned Ripon Police Station and said that there was a decomposed body beside the minor road to Scawton and Rievaulx Abbey, not far from its junction with the A170 Thirsk-Scarborough road. In a well-spoken voice, with perhaps a trace of a local accent, he gave precise instructions on how to find the body, saying it lay among weeds on the left of the road as one drives from the A170 to Scawton, and added that it was very close to the entrance to Scawton Moor House Farm.

When the duty police officer asked for his name and address, the man declined and produced a curious response by saying, 'I can't identify myself for reasons of national security.'

At first, these words suggested a crank call. It seemed odd that anyone would ring Ripon Police Station with this information, because Thirsk was nearer. Then it was remembered that Thirsk Police Station was not manned for the entire twenty-four hours. Any telephone calls made to Thirsk when it was unmanned were automatically diverted to Ripon, and so it was felt that the caller had intended to ring Thirsk with his news.

The local village constable, who knew the area intimately, was directed to investigate this strange and anonymous report. When he arrived, he found no obvious sign of a body, but he began a more meticulous search. Eventually, after a great deal of patience and skill, he found what appeared to be one or two pieces of slender, well-weathered wood deep beneath a huge bed of rosebay willow-herb. These were barely recognisable as human bones, but the sparse remains of a skull convinced him that these were the remains of a human body. He called in the CID and the scene-of-crime experts for what was clearly going to be a very difficult investigation. Even at this stage, it was highly improbable that anyone could have stumbled across the remains and recognised them as human. The most observant of people could have walked across them and never known them as human remains. So did the caller know of their presence before he claimed to have found them? Indeed, had he placed the body there? It seemed that the caller knew far more than he was prepared to admit.

Led by Detective Chief Superintendent Strickland Carter of North Yorkshire Police CID, a team of detectives visited the scene. The remains of the skeleton were most difficult to locate and examine. At the entrance to Scawton Moor House Farm, there is a small concrete hardstanding once used for accommodating milk churns as they awaited collection by milk lorries.

From that point and running for several hundred yards along the wide verge of this narrow lane is a vast bed of rosebay willow-herb. In August they are well over six feet high and they grow so densely that one cannot see between their stems. At the base, the thick growth obliterates everything on the ground. Immediately behind the rosebay willow-herb is a close-growing plantation of coniferous trees, while between the two is a low, almost ruined dry-stone wall.

The area near the concrete hardstanding was often used by families as a parking-place for picnics, and so the verge immediately surrounding it was devoid of willow-herb. Children would play here and parents would sit outside their cars enjoying the moorland breezes, the scent of the conifers and the sunshine. And less than five feet away from them lay the unidentified body. It was lying almost parallel with the dry-stone wall, only some two feet away from it.

It was evident from the beginning that the body had been there for a considerable time, but none the less, the customary caution and attention to detail was never abandoned. Detective

Chief Superintendent Carter and his team began a very methodical investigation of the scene, eventually clearing a huge area of willow-herb so that the ground, and the bones, could be more closely examined. Every tiny object was labelled and retained, and Dr Michael Green, the Forensic Pathologist from the University of Leeds Department of Forensic Medicine, was called in to examine the body in the position in which it lay.

My part in this enquiry was that of press officer, my task being to create the necessary publicity which might help in identifying the body and solving the crime, if indeed a crime had been committed. That a crime had been committed was by no means certain—the death might have been from natural causes. I arrived at the same time as Dr Green and watched him carry out his fascinating forensic investigation. By this time—around 4.30 pm—the entire width of willow-herb had been removed and the scene had been examined and photographed, with all the found objects listed and preserved for scientific investigation.

The meagre remains of the body were now exposed, though they could still barely be recognised as human. But they did provide a lot of information for Dr Green. The surviving pelvic bone told him that these were the remains of a woman while the residue and insect larvae which had bred within the skull told him that she had lain here for about two years.

Having completed his on-site examination of the body, Dr Green took the remains to his laboratory for a more detailed examination, and officers of the Task Force then began a fingertip search of the scene and surrounding area. I felt it might be prudent to withhold publicity about this discovery until later that evening. If we did not announce the discovery on the evening television and radio bulletins, we felt that the anonymous caller would wonder whether his call had been taken seriously and that he might be tempted to return to the scene to see if his telephone call had produced any positive police action.

For these exceptional reasons, I did not announce the finding of the body until all the regional evening news bulletins had been broadcast. Perhaps a lack of news about police activity near the body would prompt the caller to take further action?

Maybe he would make another telephone call? Officers were concealed in the nearby woods to record any visits to the scene and although their all-night woodland vigil did, from within those forests, produce some startling results from the world of illicit love affairs, it did not produce a suspect. At nine o'clock, therefore, I informed the Press Association of this discovery and the publicity was thus set in motion.

In the meantime, the microscopic examination of the verge by the Task Force had produced results. The lid of a jar of meat paste was found directly beneath where the body had lain, and later, some two inches into the ground, they found a solitary toenail, painted red. On the low dry-stone wall immediately behind the body, the Task Force found a cardboard box containing six empty wine bottles. One of them had contained red wine bottled on 3rd October 1980. Whoever placed that box on the wall must have stepped over the body. We appealed for that person to come forward, but our appeals produced no one; by that time, the body had lain there for one year and could by then have been decomposed and the bones concealed, even at close range.

Examination of the meat paste lid showed that the contents of the jar had been sold by the manufacturers on 6th October 1979, and it was probably discarded shortly afterwards by someone having a picnic in the vicinity. The red varnish on the toenail was identified as being a Max Factor cosmetic of the Maxi range. The date of the lid told us that the body had been placed there *after* 6th October 1979, while the insect larvae told us she had lain there for about two years. So it seemed she had been placed among the rosebay willow-herb sometime during the autumn of 1979.

This date was later confirmed by a jockey who daily exercised racehorses; he rode past the body's resting-place every day, and during the October of 1979 he had become aware of an awful smell which emanated from among the willow-herb. He thought it might be the rotting carcase of a fox, dog or larger animal, and after two or three days, felt he should investigate its source. Unfortunately, before he got around to doing so, he fell from his horse and broke a leg; he was in hospital for a few weeks and by the time he resumed his riding, the smell had gone. He had forgotten about it anyway and did not carry out his intended investigation. None the less, at the time police enquiries began, he could pinpoint the date because he kept a diary of events.

As the police began their search of all records of missing women, both locally and nationally, Dr Green's analysis of the few bones produced a surprising amount of information. He could say that she was an adult, around 38–40 years of age and about 5′ 1″ tall. She was very slender and had had natural dark brown hair, cut to a length of about four or six inches. A few strands still adhered to the skull, but most of the other bones of the body had been carried away, probably by wild animals. She had borne children, probably three but certainly two, and she had an abnormality of her spine which would have caused backache at some stage of her life. She took size 4 shoes and, as already noted, used Max Factor nail varnish on her toes. She had false teeth in her upper jaw and six natural teeth in her lower jaw, these being stained, probably by nicotine.

Later examination of her teeth by the Dental School of Newcastle University confirmed the age of the woman, and suggested she had neglected the hygiene of her mouth and teeth. We did learn, however, that her formative years, until about the age of seven, had been spent in an area with a high degree of natural fluoride in the drinking-water.

Two local areas which qualified in that respect were the towns of Hartlepool and Grimsby, and this prompted detailed enquiries in those towns, particularly to trace any missing women.

It was also noted that the body had been completely naked, with no item or remnants of any clothing being found upon or near it; nor had we found any jewellery, watch, rings or other adornment. This suggested the body had been placed there with a deliberate purpose of concealing it and it had been done in such a manner that identification would be difficult, if not impossible. The cause of her death was never revealed to the press or the public, although we did announce that the death was, for obvious reasons, *suspicious*. It was stated that she had met her death by unnatural causes, and so a murder-type investigation was launched.

The nation's registers of missing women were scanned and assistance was given by a whole range of sources, both official and unofficial, through which a woman's absence might be noticed. Children's homes were contacted in the hope that some children might have missed recent visits by their mother, and the public was asked to report the absence of any single woman who may have been a friend, neighbour or work colleague. Employers were asked to check their registers and teams of detectives contacted all the local places where such a woman might have been employed or might have been missed.

One aspect affecting this locality was the number of holidaymakers who came here: caravans, campers, bed-and-breakfast establishments, hotels and boarding-houses were all considered, and all proprietors were asked to check their registers in the hope it might jog a distant memory. Motorists were asked to recall if they had given a lift to a lone woman, while the Salvation Army, hostels for the homeless and the various welfare organisations were asked to scan their records for missing women who might fit the vague description of the lady at Sutton Bank Top. Dentists were provided with details of the woman's teeth in the hope that someone might recognise his or her own workmanship.

And then we turned up something dramatic and exciting. At about the time we believed the body had been placed beside that road, we learned that a woman prisoner from Askham Grange Open Prison near York had escaped. She had been sentenced to a term of imprisonment for manslaughter. More than two years had passed since she had escaped but there weren't any reports of her having been seen. When her physical description was examined, it was found that it matched that of the Sutton Bank body in six respects. Age, height, colour of hair and build were similar; she had had children and, more amazingly, she had had trouble with her back. It seemed we had found a name for our corpse. But with such scant relics to work on, how could this be proved or disproved?

The only way was to find the escaped prisoner; she had been absent now for some two years and it was highly unlikely that she would voluntarily come forward for elimination. To do so could result in her being taken straight back to prison. One added problem was that she had come originally from Eire, and enquiries there had failed to trace her.

With the consent of the Home Office, therefore, we decided to publicise this new line of enquiry, and I got the task of alerting the newspapers, TV and radio stations, particularly those in Eire and Northern Ireland. We issued a plea to the prisoner that, if she were still alive, she should obtain a piece of white paper and imprint it with her fingerprints. Having been subjected to the police arrest procedure, she would know how to do this. We asked her to send those prints to Detective Chief Superintendent Carter at the North Yorkshire Police Headquarters. He would be able to compare them with her criminal record, and thus confirm that she was alive. We stressed however, that this course of action and any assistance she might give could in no way absolve her from any future legal action. In other words, she would be returned to prison if she was located.

It must be said that none of us expected a response; if she were still alive, what finer cover could she hope for than for everyone to assume she was dead? Was it likely she would blow her own cover to assist the police in this enquiry? Would she risk capture and the possibility of being returned to prison?

She did. Shortly after our appeal, Mr Carter received two neat pieces of white paper, each bearing fingerprints and accompanied by a friendly little note. When these were compared with the escapee's criminal record, it proved she was still alive and now we knew she was living somewhere in Eire. She had blown the perfect cover, and we had still not identified the body. The escapee has continued to evade capture.

It was inevitable that a widely-publicised enquiry of this nature would attract cranks. We received lots of time-wasting calls and letters from those odd people who insist on providing dubious help and advice, or even confessing to the *crime*. One crank wrote to claim he knew the killer's name, the woman's name and the identity of our anonymous caller. He said that Superintendent John Carlton, Mr Carter's deputy, had to broadcast on Radio Hallam, Sheffield, using a code supplied by the writer, when all would be revealed. Mr Carlton did this, but no one contacted us with the correct information; the writer was traced and eliminated from the enquiry. It was a time-wasting exercise but one which had to be undertaken just in case it proved genuine.

A clairvoyant then claimed to link this corpse with that of a man found in West Yorkshire the same day, the link being the figure A170. This was the road near to which our body was found but our enquiries showed that there was no possible link between that man and our dead lady. Oddly enough, however, the father of that West Yorkshire victim did regularly drive along the A170, right past the scene of our discovery.

These were just some examples of dozens of false trails that were presented to the investigating teams, and their hopes were lifted soon afterwards by the discovery of a woman's clothes in a wood only a mile from the scene. These comprised a black evening gown, a bra and some pants; they were hanging from a tree, but we could not link them with the dead woman. No one came forward to claim them. Then a macabre touch of humour occurred during our searches of the scene—as the Task Force conducted their patient search of the woods nearby, a hearse arrived, complete with plastic flowers and a coffin. It was accompanied by a film crew, and was part of a sequence for the TV comedy series *In Loving Memory*, starring Thora Hird. We felt that neither party knew of the other's presence.

By November of that year, it seemed that all possible avenues of enquiry had been exhausted; the records of several hundred missing women had been examined without success and it seemed there was nothing further that could be done. Then Chief Superintendent Carter announced a unique development.

Experts from the Department of Medical Illustration at Manchester University had studied the remains of the skull and had measured it. They felt it would be possible to construct a life-size model of the woman's head, by adding wax to a replica of her skull so that realistic features would be reproduced. Although there could be no guarantee of accuracy, it was felt that this might produce a passable image of what she had looked like in life, and so the model was made.

The make-up was done by the staff of Granada Television, and a news conference was arranged so that photographs of the model head would be widely circulated in the newspapers and on television. It was a macabre sight; the life-size head was complemented by short, dark brown hair and brown eyes set in a natural flesh-coloured face of considerable character. So far as we knew, this was the first time such a model had been used by the British Police in an attempt to identify a body. Other similar attempts have since been made, including one in 1988 in an effort to identify a victim of the terrible fire at King's Cross tube station, London.

The publicity prompted callers to provide several more names and some new lines of enquiry, but in spite of everyone's efforts, it did not achieve a positive identification. And that is the present situation. After years of investigation, the name of the mystery lady of Sutton Bank Top remains unknown. The identity of the mystery caller and his role are also unknown, but the police continue to search their files in the hope that, one day, the name of a missing woman will match the remains found on the morning of 28th August 1981 near Sutton Bank Top, one of Yorkshire's finest beauty spots.

Barbara Whitehead

SIMPLE WHEN YOU KNOW

Detective Chief Inspector Robert Southwell hadn't been along Norgate for some time, and he wouldn't be going along it now if it wasn't the shortest route from where he was to where he was deeply disinclined to be. The street had been a building site as long as he had lived in York. Once it must have been a pleasant old-fashioned place, because a number of buildings had been scheduled as worthy of preservation, but mostly they weren't there any more, and neither was most of the charm.

It was a sunny day in early June and he was going to the office-block where a rather nasty murder had happened the week before. On his earlier visits he'd gone the other way, from Lendal Bridge, close to where an earlier murder had taken place by the riverside, under the weeping tresses of the big old willows. The willows which had been chopped down since then.

The building site had gradually moved itself from one end of the street to the other. He walked first between a modern hotel and blocks of flats, fortress-like in the new style. Next the remaining pocket of old York, a church with a tall spire, gardens, a few period houses. Then he had to skirt the place they were excavating for new foundations, before he could reach the concrete ramp to a car park at first-floor level.

On the arid space where cars and bicycles were parked he paused, thinking that if he had to work in this office-block he would never be able to stand it, nerving himself to enter the back doors of the building, to infiltrate himself silently, to quietly witness the life of the occupants.

Why did he dislike the place so much? Police stations never disturbed him, perhaps because they had more sense of purpose.

He went in. The first door on the left was to the ladies' loos—they were in the same place on every floor. Next came the doors of the lift. At right angles, the door into the offices. Right angles again, the stairs. It was quiet but high above he could hear the faint clatter of someone's feet.

The lift was on another floor; he walked lightly up flights of stairs and stood once more at the door of the small square office where a man had died, apparently by the hand of God, for no human agency had yet proved to be responsible. But the hand of God, in Southwell's opinion, would not wield a letter-opener in the shape of a dagger, nor stick it with precision into someone's back. The hand of God would find some more subtle way to manage things. The fact was, though, that they hadn't yet found out who had done it, in the middle of a busy afternoon without being seen or leaving fingerprints on the weapon.

' 'Morning, Inspector,' said a bright young girl as she swung towards him with an armful of computer print-outs. 'Is it all finished? Have you come to tell us who the criminal is? Not that most of us aren't grateful to him,' and she smiled at Bob Southwell in such a way that any sting in her words was replaced by humour.

'None of you seem to regret him much,' he replied.

'It was rather horrid having a murder.' She looked serious for a moment. 'But if it had to happen to someone, he was the most popular candidate for the post.'

'We gathered that.'

'Why have you come, then?' she persisted.

'Oh... To see you again, of course,' he responded gallantly.

She giggled, then asked again, 'No, truthfully, now.'

Southwell wasn't sure himself, but as he answered her it became clearer to him.

'Sometimes if a case is sticking I find it helpful to go back quietly to the scene of the crime, and stand and think for a while in the ambience associated with it. That's what I've come to do, if I don't get distracted by the office juniors.'

As she listened, the girl looked serious and intelligent. When he finished, she put on her infectious smile again and said she had better let him carry on with it, then, but he wasn't to go arresting any of her friends.

Southwell listened to her footsteps clicking down the stairs and into the post room on a lower floor. He thought he knew the layout now as well if not better than those who worked there. One floor was Accounts, another mostly Sales; there were various other departments on two more floors, together with conference room, canteen, kitchen and so on.

The whole structure was concrete and glass and bare thermoplastic-tiled floors and metal filing cabinets and he decided that was what he disliked so much about it. Concrete was a very versatile building medium but no one could call it cosy. In spite of the carefully-planned pastel décor the place was sick, if ever a building was, a place for broken careers and pettiness.

The dead man, he had learned, had been both petty and tyrannous. A man who got kicks from blasting hopes. A man who would upset the plans of a department in order to demonstrate his superiority. A man who would take pleasure in keeping an employee doing work a trained chimpanzee could have done. A pettifogging boss who could always be relied on to let his staff down when they needed his support. There are many of that pattern. He was not unusual.

Southwell made his way up to the top floor where, as he listened to the sounds around him, footsteps and voices, he gazed for a while on a panorama of the river, the bridge, and high above at the top of the rise in the ground, York Minster, the grand

and gracious cathedral. The view was the saving grace of this building and when the new block next door was completed it would lose the view.

He slowly worked his way down again. The busy staff barely noticed his quiet progress. He spent some time in the dead man's office, which had not yet been allocated to anyone else. Last of all, he rang the bell for the lift and went down again to the entrance area which led into the raised car park.

On this floor he entered a small quiet room immediately below that of the murdered man. Here were two desks facing each other. One was empty, at the other a dark-haired young woman was sitting; he guessed she was in her thirties; she had an air of calm thoughtfulness.

'Where's Marie?' he asked, indicating the empty desk.

The dark-haired young woman looked up.

'She has the afternoon off,' she answered, and noticed him looking down at her hands. Claire was sorting through newspapers, cutting out the advertisements the office had caused to be inserted, and on her hands were transparent gloves.

'You're looking at my gloves.' She smiled. 'I've an allergy to newsprint, we aren't sure if it's the ink or the paper. When I'm doing this job I have to wear them.'

'I haven't seen them before, that's all, Claire,' Southwell said.

'I only need them for this job.'

Southwell perched on the edge of the empty desk and watched her idly as she worked, going through in his mind what he remembered of this attractive young woman, working so calmly in her casual clothes, jeans, T-shirt, trainers, unlike those of the staff who had to deal with the public and look smart. An open-air type, he decided. She had more reason to hate the dead man than perhaps anyone else in the office. Her fingerprints had been found in the room upstairs, together with those of half the staff. She was in the division controlled by the murdered man.

Claire's alibi had been cast-iron. When her colleague, Marie, left the room to take some file to their boss, she left Claire busy working. Marie went straight upstairs, without pausing to do any other errands. When she reached their boss's

367

office she found the man with his dagger-shaped paper-knife sticking out between his shoulder blades. When the alarm was raised, Claire had been found in this room, still busy working. There was no way she could have killed him.

Only there was.

'You had better tidy your things away, Claire,' he said. 'You're coming back to the police station with me.'

She looked up, still serene. 'Is this a joke?'

'No. I am arresting you for the murder of your head of division.'

'But I've been checked out. There's no way I could have murdered him.'

'Come along. We haven't got all day.'

Still protesting, she did as he asked.

When they were sitting either side of a table in an interview room in police headquarters she said in a duller voice, 'I don't see why you think I could have done it.'

'I have been spending time quietly in your office-block today. When I first came in, the lift was on another floor and so I walked upstairs. When I came down again I used the lift.'

'So?' said Claire, surprisingly curt for such a well-mannered, even-natured, quiet person.

'On the day of the murder Marie left the room to go upstairs, leaving you busy working. Marie is a decorative girl, very feminine. She always wears high heels. I don't suppose she's keen on climbing stairs. I've noticed she usually has a women's magazine on the go and takes stray peeps at it to refresh her in between her office work. Her mind is always busy on hair-dos and new clothes, wouldn't you say?'

'Yes.'

'So Marie went to the lift and rang the bell, then stood there waiting and taking a peep at her magazine.'

'Probably.'

'No probably about it. Your lifts are remarkably sluggish. She would have time to read several paragraphs before the lift came, and then it moves slowly. But you, Claire, you wear trainers. You move silently and you are a fit and energetic girl. There was plenty of time while she was waiting for that lift for you to slip up the flights of stairs behind her, without her noticing because she was reading her magazine and your feet make no noise, in at your boss's door, snatch up his paperknife and hey presto, before he realised what you were doing—and out again and down the stairs, the lift with its solid doors probably passing you going up as you were coming down. I suppose you were wearing those thin clear gloves of yours at the time.'

Claire shrugged her shoulders and bit her lip, but did not comment.

'It wouldn't be surprising,' Southwell went on, 'if you could run right to the top of the building up the stairs and still arrive there before the lift, if you rang for it before setting off.'

'There would be time to run up and halfway down again,' said Claire.

Douglas Wynn

WHO FIRED THE FATAL SHOTS?

This is a true story. It concerns the brutal murder of two unarmed police officers. But due to the largely-unavoidable manner in which the investigation was carried out, important questions have been raised. Did the man who was convicted receive a fair trial? And more importantly, was the right man convicted? Read the story and make up your own mind.

'Do you think he'll be long?' asked Police Constable Arthur Jagger.

Detective Inspector Duncan Fraser pursed his lips. 'We'll catch him tonight, never fear.' He turned up the collar of his coat and looked at the sky. There had been a forecast of rain. 'Probably get soaked as well. But we'll do it this time. Better take up our positions now.'

The two policemen set themselves some eighty yards apart on either side of a

371

footpath which led across the fields and up the hill, so that anyone coming up it would be intercepted. They were part of a team of ten officers surrounding Whinney Close Farm near the top of Cockley Hill, on the outskirts of Kirkheaton, a small mill town near Huddersfield. It was about 11.45 pm on the night of Saturday 14th June 1951.

The owner of the poultry farm was Alfred Moore. He'd only occupied the place, with his wife and four children, for about four months, but he'd already established himself in the eyes of the police as an active local burglar. They suspected him of being involved in a dozen break-ins at local mill offices and houses. But they had never been able to catch him with the loot—up to now. Tonight they knew he was out of the house and this time were going to intercept him as he came back across the fields.

There was heavy rain that night, but by the early hours it had stopped. Suddenly at about two o'clock the stillness of the dark night was shattered by the sounds of gunfire. Police Constable W Sellick, who was about a hundred yards from Inspector Fraser, heard five shots coming from that direction. He began running towards from where the shots had come and as he ran heard the faint sound of a police whistle. Sellick passed the place where the inspector should have been, but there was no sign of him. He ran on. As the constable approached a footpath he saw a faint glimmer of light, which proved to be a torch lying on the ground. Then he saw Inspector Fraser lying motionless on his back. PC Jagger was prone nearby, on his left side with his legs drawn up. He was conscious and in great pain.

PC Sellick summoned assistance by blowing his whistle and waving his torch. The injured men were taken down the hill on stretchers to an old derelict brickworks and transferred to an ambulance in the yard.

At Huddersfield Royal Infirmary the inspector was found to be dead. He had been shot three times from almost contact range. Once through the right wrist, once above the left elbow and once through the chest, penetrating the heart and killing him.

PC Jagger had been shot only once, but the result was a very serious abdominal wound. However, he was later able to make a statement.

He said that just before two o'clock he saw Moore walking towards his hilltop home. Jagger approached and obviously startled the man for he dived into the hedge. The policeman went up to him and shone his torch.

'I thought you were a cow,' mumbled Moore.

Jagger grabbed the man's left arm as DI Fraser came up. He too shone his torch on him. 'Are you Alfred Moore?' asked Fraser.

'Yes,' replied the farmer.

'We are police officers and you are coming with us.'

'No, sir. Oh, no, sir.'

And with that Moore pulled out a gun from his right-hand coat pocket. He began firing.

First he shot Jagger, who collapsed on the ground, but was able to see three more shots fired at Fraser, two of them with the gun almost touching the stricken man.

The fifth shot was explained later when it was found that the inspector had a red bruise on his stomach. Plainly the gun had misfired and the bullet, although hitting Fraser, had not enough power to penetrate the skin. It was later found near the spot where the attack had taken place and turned out to be a 9mm round, matching the others taken from the bodies—and forensic evidence showed later that all had been fired from the same gun.

Also discovered, later that day near the murder spot, were a double-ended skeleton key, two other keys, three keys on a string and a jack-knife.

Soon after the shooting, the officers remaining at the farm saw a light go on in the farmhouse. It was extinguished quickly. But the detective inspector in charge of the detail was in a quandary. He could rush the farm and try to take Moore. But the man might be armed and none of his own men were. He decided to send for armed reinforcements.

They duly arrived along with Detective Chief Superintendent Metcalf, who took charge. About four o'clock in the morning, Metcalf noticed smoke coming from the farmhouse chimney. It didn't come out in a steady stream, but in a series of short puffs, as though someone was throwing things on the fire. The police closed in around the farmhouse and one officer noticed a shadowy figure appear at one of the downstairs windows. He couldn't tell if it was a man or a woman, but it was crouching in the window. As he watched, it moved back out of sight into the room.

A short while later a curtain twitched in one of the upstairs windows. Suddenly they could see a woman, presumably Mrs Moore, standing there, with Moore behind her. Metcalf called out: 'Come out! We are police officers!'

Mrs Moore opened the window. 'What do you want?'

'We want to speak to Mr Moore.'

The woman was holding back the curtain. 'I'll come down.'

She soon appeared at the door, fully dressed, with her husband still standing behind her.

'Come here,' said Metcalf to Moore, stepping forward. He was taking a risk as he was unarmed, even though he was being covered by an armed officer.

Moore came forward slowly. He wore only a shirt and trousers. The Superintendent grabbed him. It was an action which would earn the brave officer an award for gallantry.

'Let him go!' cried Mrs Moore. 'Is it serious?'

'It's serious enough,' muttered her husband.

At the police station he said that he had gone to bed at about twelve o'clock and not gone out again that night. When asked about the smoke issuing from his chimney at four o'clock, he said that he had got up to burn some rubbish, but he wouldn't elaborate any further.

Asked what firearms he had, Moore said, 'Oh, my head is bad. Don't talk about it. It's awful.' And he refused to answer any more questions on the subject.

Up at Whinney Close Farm the police were conducting an exhaustive search of the house and the area around it. In the farmyard, under some loose bricks, they found a live 9mm round of ammunition. Then, in a tallboy in the front bedroom, they discovered a discharged cartridge case, also 9mm.

They also solved the mystery of the crouching figure at the window. Below this window they saw a cavity in the wall. In this cavity they discovered gold and silver cigarette cases, a platinum ring, a gold watch and 157 keys, which included safe keys and car ignition keys, Yale and double-sided skeleton keys. In addition, two more 9mm cartridge cases were found.

Under a bed were a pair of brown shoes which were still wet and had grass and grass-seeds sticking to them. These were subsequently shown to have come from the fields around the farm. A raincoat hanging in a wardrobe had a white hair on it, similar to those of the murdered DI Fraser.

The fireplace still contained hot ashes when the police raked through it and found evidence that hundreds of postage stamps and dollar bills had been burnt there. It was obvious that a desperate attempt had been made to get rid of incriminating evidence.

As Sunday wore on and the police continued their painstaking search of the farm, PC Jagger was fighting for his life at Huddersfield Royal Infirmary. An emergency operation was performed and he had a blood transfusion, but the doctors were not optimistic. The policeman might recover, but the odds were against it. Senior police officers realised that the constable's evidence would be vital. He had been the only one to have seen the assailant and live.

In the late afternoon Dr James Hall

Wrigley examined Jagger and gave his verdict. The policeman was fit enough to give a statement under oath and attend an identification parade. This was held at the sick man's bedside. Nine men in raincoats lined up in front of the bed. The constable picked out Moore as the man who had shot him and DI Fraser.

Asked if he was satisfied with the conduct of the parade, Moore said: 'Yes. But it wasn't me.'

A special court was then convened before Percy Crowther, a local magistrate. After Jagger gave his evidence of the shooting incident, Moore was asked if he would like to put any questions to the witness.

'Are you quite sure?' he asked the man in the bed.

'I am quite sure,' came the reply.

At 8.15 am the next day, Arthur Jagger lost his fight for life. He was forty-two, a married man with two daughters. Duncan Fraser, forty-five, was married with one daughter.

Moore was charged that day with double murder.

The search went on at the farm for several more weeks. All the grass was cut in the fields and soldiers with mine-detectors were called in. Feeding-troughs were emptied, walls knocked down and the crevices between bricks carefully examined. The house itself was practically taken apart brick by brick. But the gun which killed the two policemen was never found. And neither was any loot discovered which could be attributed to a robbery done that night.

The police also questioned Moore's brother Charles. He lived nearby and had been at Whinney Close Farm that fateful Saturday, helping his brother build a pigsty. He had stayed later than he intended and missed the last bus home. At about eleven o'clock that night he set out to walk home and Alfred went with him. They walked down through the fields, following the same footpath which was to be the scene of the tragedy a few hours later.

They parted at about 11.20 pm and Charles reached home at 11.35 pm. The police retraced Moore's footsteps and concluded he could not have reached Whinney Close Farm any earlier than 11.50 pm. They had set up their cordon by 11.45 pm or a little before. And it was their opinion that Moore could not possibly have got back home without first passing through the cordon.

Moore went on trial at Leeds Assizes on Monday 10th December 1951, before Mr Justice Pearson, with G Raymond Hinchcliffe KC prosecuting and the defence in the hands of Harry Hylton-Foster KC.

The prosecution case rested on the premise that the defendant could not have passed through the cordon undetected and therefore it must have been him who came up the hill and shot the two policemen. PC Jagger's statement was read out to the jury as was the report of the identification parade. Spent cartridges of the type used to kill the officers had been found at the farm, together with ample evidence that Moore had been carrying on a burglary business.

Counsel for the defence managed to establish that 9mm ammunition was one of the most common kinds and the cartridges found at the farm were of various dates of manufacture. And the white hair found on Moore's raincoat could not definitely be said to have come from Fraser.

But the jury of ten men and two women took only fifty minutes to return a verdict of guilty on both charges. Mr Justice

Pearson, whose first murder trial this was, had the black square placed on his head and pronounced the sentence of death.

Mr Hylton-Foster appealed against the verdict and the appeal was heard on Monday 21st January 1952, before Lord Chief Justice Goddard. It was disposed of in thirty minutes. Once again the evidence of PC Jagger was the difficulty the defence could not overcome. Although Moore's solicitor also petitioned the Home Office for a reprieve, it was refused. Alfred Moore was hanged at Armley Jail, Leeds, on Wednesday 6th February 1952.

But was he guilty?

The two main parts of the prosecution case were the identification by PC Jagger and the police assertion that Moore could not have passed through the cordon undetected.

This last point is surely open to question. The cordon was set by 11.45 pm or a little before and Moore could have reached home by 11.50 pm. A few minutes either way in each of the time estimates and Moore could have been home before the cordon was established. Here certainly there was a reasonable doubt.

But the crucial evidence was that of

PC Jagger. He clearly identified Moore as the man he saw in the field. But how clear can you really be when you see a person by torchlight on a dark night? Since it had rained earlier it was quite likely to have been cloudy with no moon when the sighting was made. Arthur Jagger had at most a fleeting glimpse of the man by the light of a torch, which can easily distort features, especially if it is held to the side. And the next day when the officer made his statement, as defence counsel pointed out at the trial, he had just undergone a serious operation and might have been suffering from the effects of the anaesthetic.

A serious omission, as far as Moore was concerned, was that at the court convened by the dying man's bedside, he was not represented by a lawyer of any kind. It was nobody's fault. It was a Sunday and the solicitor Moore asked for simply could not be found. The police could not wait as there was no telling how long Jagger would last. But the fact remains that the accused did not have the assistance of a solicitor, as he was entitled to, who might have been able to question the police officer about how much he could actually see by torchlight on that dark night.

All that Moore could think of was to say: 'Are you quite sure?'

And so the evidence of the police officer went virtually unchallenged, which may have cost Moore his life.

Yet if Moore did not shoot the police officers, who did? There is no doubt that he was a burglar. It was admitted in court that he had been responsible for a number of break-ins over the past few months and his house certainly contained stolen goods. Yet interestingly enough nothing was found by the police in exhaustive searches of the farm and the surrounding fields which could be proved to have been stolen that night. And since the gun was never found either it adds to the doubt that it was Moore who used the gun on the policemen.

But what if Moore was also a fence, a receiver of stolen goods? It might then have been another person who came up the hill that dark night and ran into the cordon. Another thief, possibly carrying loot which he had obtained from a burglary and wanted to sell to Moore. If he was carrying a gun and shot the policemen, he would presumably have gone back the way he came, taking the gun and the loot with him.

If there was such a man, then he brutally shot down two unarmed policemen and sent an innocent man to the gallows.

But if there wasn't such a man, then Alfred Moore richly deserved to be convicted and to pay the penalty prescribed by law.

Which was it?

Ngaio Marsh (1895–1982)

TWO TALKS

To celebrate the centenary of the birth of Ngaio Marsh, these talks are published for the first time, by kind permission of her Estate.

1. OUR PARTICULAR JOB

Broadcast on "Bookshop", Radio New Zealand, 1st January 1957

Strange beliefs are held by people who don't write books, about people who do. I suppose all professional writers come up against these beliefs and I suppose that we all get fairly well accustomed to them. There is, for instance, the conviction, firmly held by some of one's friends and a great many of one's acquaintances, that detective fiction writes itself. When these people ask a writer to visit them or to open a bazaar or to give a talk to their pet club, and the writer declines, giving work as the reason for the refusal, they obviously think they have been handed out a pitifully lame excuse. They are inclined to be hurt or huffy. 'Oh,' they say, 'you could come if you wanted to. *Working?*' they say. 'Oh, you mean *writing*. That isn't any trouble to *you.*'

This may be flattering but it also happens to be quite untrue. Writing is a hideous trouble.

Then there are the people who see libellous references in what one hoped was a purely fictitious creation. I have been accused of giving a cruelly accurate portrait of three entirely different persons in a single character. One of the supposed victims lived in England, one in the North Island and one in the South Island of New Zealand. In this case there was safety in numbers. They couldn't all sue me for libel.

Parallel with this is the attitude that supposes the writer to be a sort of scavenger (which, in a sense, of course one is) and to be perpetually geared-up for an assault. 'Don't put me in it,' some comparative stranger will cry when one proffers the usual shamefaced excuse that one is working. When I thought I was going to be a painter, I used to meet with the same sort of thing. I remember, many years ago, sweating away at a landscape by a roadside in South Canterbury. One of the then-current South Canterbury dowagers swept by in a cloud of dust at about fifty miles an hour in her chauffeur-driven limousine. As she did so, she screamed something at me from the rear seat. It was only after the dust had subsided that I realised what it was she had yelled. It was: 'Don't put me in it.'

In respect of detective fiction, perhaps the oddest notion (it is more prevalent than you might suppose) is the idea that the author is as much in the dark about the outcome of the story as the reader. More than once I have been asked if, while writing these stories, I myself know whodunit. I leave it to you, gentle listeners, to imagine the nightmarish dilemma of the crime novelist ploughing through a series of equivocal situations to which he or she doesn't know the answer.

The truth about professional writers is this. We worry and fumble and rehash. At two o'clock in the morning we get marvellous ideas and at eight o'clock the following evening we recognise these ideas for the nonsense they are. We have awful sessions when nothing goes right and brief but blissful sessions when everything seems to go well. We worry ourselves sick about income tax. We have responsibilities. We do not work in a light-hearted, carefree fashion, all for fun. We do not wait for inspiration. We work because we've jolly well got to.

But when all is said and done, we toil at this particular job because it's turned out to *be* our particular job and in a weird sort of way I suppose we may be said to like it.

2. SHAKESPEARE'S LOST WHODUNIT

The colloquial nature of this light-hearted piece derives from the fact that it was delivered as a talk to the Times Book Club during Ngaio Marsh's stay in London from 1949 to 1951. Her reputation as a detective fiction writer was high; a million paperback copies of ten of her novels had just been issued by Collins as the "Marsh Million", and she was much in demand as a broadcaster on the BBC. The text has been slightly adjusted for publication by Margaret Lewis.

One of the questions that I am most often asked is, where do you get your plots? This is an attempt to answer it. I'm going to concoct the bare bones and leave you to discover where they came from. The immediate source of my plots is generally some personal experience.

Suppose, on a motoring holiday in a remote part of the country, we have pointed out to us a famous chemical works, and not far away a sort of gothic castle and a smaller but still handsome house. We learn that the castle belongs to the family that owns the works and that the Works Manager, his son and his daughter live in the house. We've never seen these people but we begin to invent them. They emerge. This Works Manager is an elderly widower—shrewd, plausible. He has a talent for ingratiating himself with important people. His morals are of a conventional rather than a purely ethical character. His children are young enough to be his grandchildren: a high-spirited boy and an enchanting girl. We must find a name for them. The surname of Chamberlain occurs to me so, provisionally, let us call them the Chamberlains.

The chemical works belongs to an immensely wealthy family that wields a very great deal of power in the affairs of the country generally. They are king-pins of the industry, and perhaps as good a name as any to fix them in our memory will be the name King, especially as they live in a house like a castle. They consist of the Senior Partner, General King, his younger brother who is the Junior Partner, and the General's wife and son. The General is almost too good to be true. He had a most distinguished record as a soldier, he is incredibly good-looking and he is immensely able in an old-fashioned way that puts integrity at the top of the list. Under his direction the good name and high international fame of the great firm is absolute. He is married to a woman who has been a beauty of the ripe voluptuous kind and whose charms are now perhaps a little overripe. They have one son: an enchanting boy of charm and brilliance who is being brought up as a princeling but manages to remain comparatively unspoilt. He is being given a liberal education but his bent is scientific and he shows great promise in this area.

The General's brother and Junior Partner is utterly unlike him. He is a man who smells of good port, expensive cigars and the rarest kind of hair oil. He is a bon viveur and has an eye for a pretty woman when he sees one, and he sees one in his sister-in-law. He has great business ability but is much less conventional and fastidiously scrupulous than his brother.

Here then are the two families. The district is a remote one. It is natural that the three children should be very much thrown together; the Chamberlain boy and girl and young King tumble about together as naturally as kittens and with as few cares. When the boys get older they go to different schools while the girl stays at home with a governess. During the holidays they take up their friendship exactly where they had dropped it. Then one fine summer holiday young King comes home to find that the child he had left is no longer a child but suddenly a very attractive girl. The inevitable has happened. The brother half-senses this and resents it. The other two have become self-conscious. A shadow has fallen over the fellowship.

The inevitable has also happened elsewhere. General King's wife has never perhaps understood or appreciated him. She is a full-blooded woman of limited intelligence and she does like a man. She and her husband's brother understand each other very well and the understanding has ripened. The Works Manager, the astute Mr Chamberlain, knows what is going on but he thinks it expedient to look the other way. He has a great admiration for the ability of the Junior Partner.

Well, here we are. The whole thing is rather like the opening of a Somerset Maugham short story but we hope we can give it a turn towards a crime. Somebody has got to be a corpse. Let us find the likeliest candidate. Obviously the General. Old General King has got to die. How?

At this stage, it's a good idea to inspect the *mise-en-scène*, which is a huge chemical works. May not a huge chemical works run an experimental department? May that experimental department not concern itself with dangerous drugs and their antidotes? With poisons, in fact? What more lethal poison than the venom secreted by certain snakes? Let us decide that the experimental laboratories are experimenting with snakes.

I hear a cry of anguish from the reader as a modus-operandi snakebite ranks about as low as arrow-poison in detective fiction and, used in the ordinary way, is definitely out. But it can be rather fun to employ hackneyed material and then, if possible, with a bland smile, give it a twist. We shall attempt this feat.

The General is in the habit of spending an hour after lunch in his private garden at the Works. He takes with him his black cocker spaniel and the *Times* crossword puzzle. Very often he dozes off for ten minutes at a time. The reader must be familiar with the General's appearance. His taste in dress is old-fashioned and aristocratically eccentric. He likes to wear a suit of Old Boy's plus-twos and Newmarket boots and a tweed hat. In these he can often be observed on sunny days taking his post-prandial nap.

On what is always called "the day in question" he fails to turn up for a very important afternoon Board Meeting and a young man who works in the special laboratory is sent to find him. He does find him. Dead.

A doctor is brought from the Works hospital, examines the body, finds a double puncture inside the ear. Somebody says, 'My God, it looks like a snakebite.' The snake cage is inspected, a poisonous reptile is found missing—subsequently it is discovered in the garden and recaptured. This snake is not in fact a snake but a red herring.

The tragedy has come at a time when the firm is engaged with important European negotiations. These negotiations centre round a toxin called H/Q that the laboratory has isolated and on which young King has been doing specialised work. The representative of the European firm is staying with the General and they have fallen out over certain negotiations in connection with this toxin.

There is an inquest at which snakebite is found as cause of death and there is a tremendous funeral followed by the reading of the Will. The only Will that can be found was made before the son was born and everything has been left to the wife.

Time goes by. The son, young King, finds himself dependent upon his mother and uncle. He has been shocked beyond measure by his father's sudden death and driven into himself. He turns for comfort to the girl who has so much attracted him. But she begins to avoid him and this, on top of everything else, bewilders and maddens him. Her behaviour seems to him and to us strangely suspicious. On top of all this his mother announces her engagement to his uncle and their marriage takes place. There are Board Meetings which the boy is forced to attend and at which his uncle takes complete control. Young King tries to cut out for himself and go back to the University, but his mother dissuades him. He works moodily in the laboratories on the H/Q toxin.

Now I'm sure all of you can see what has happened. We thought we'd invented an original plot—instead we find we've fallen on perhaps the best-known story in the whole range of European writing. (Everyone by now must realise that we are talking about *Hamlet*.)

One of the night-watchmen, a superstitious Irishman, looking down on the old General's garden which has been locked ever since his death, sees, one moonlit night, something white stirring in the shadows. There is a rustle, the moon comes out from behind a cloud and there, at the very spot where the General's body was found, protruding from under a bush, is a Newmarket boot jerking as if the wearer was in his death-throes. The night-watchman bolts, finds his mates and one of the resident scientists, a fellow-student of young King. The young scientist is, of course, convinced there is a naturalistic explanation but without a key to the garden can't do much about it. He thinks it's best to talk to young King and next morning does so.

Young King says he's going to see for himself. The next night he does. Same thing. Moon, rustling, whiteness and the protruding and moving foot in the Newmarket boot. At considerable risk he climbs over the balustrade, hangs by his hands and drops into the garden. He finds the General's black spaniel with the General's Newmarket boot which it no doubt has taken from its old master's dressing-room and carried into the shrubbery. As the son stoops to pick it up he sees a shred of newspaper sticking to one of the bushes. It's the *Times* crossword. Written across it in pencil in his father's hand with the writing trailing off is the word "Murdered". It is a message from the dead.

This is the case so far, and it should occupy about 60–70 pages. So far it has followed the original pretty closely, but from this point it will tend to diverge somewhat, since this is a detective novel. Suppose our detective is to be an amateur, Hamlet himself. He may delay an approach to the police for a number of perfectly legitimate reasons: the horror of the exhumation, his fear that his mother may be implicated, or simply because the incident has so shocked him that he wants to give himself time to recover. He is indeed so overwrought that he is on the edge of a nervous breakdown. He tells his scientific friend Horatio that he is going to find out more for himself before he calls in the police.

Now, from the beginning, he has suspected his uncle, and so does the reader. We've got to do something about this. We can still use quite a lot of the original by letting the son stage a reconstruction of the murder as he imagines it to have taken place ("The Mousetrap"). His uncle can still leave the performance in a hurry. But it will be now, when the reader most strongly suspects the uncle, that we've got to introduce something that will seem to show that the uncle couldn't possibly have done it. There are lots of ways in which this gambit can be executed, but the simplest is suddenly to throw the weight of suspicion right over onto another character. This is best done by innuendo and in such a way that the reader will think himself a cunning dog to have spotted it.

Possibly the best man to draw suspicion is the Works Manager who is, of course, a reassembly of Polonius. He can turn out to have been heavily involved with Fortinbras, the representative of the European firm, and likely to make a very good thing out of it if the deal with H/Q, the isolated toxin, goes through, which was unlikely while the General was alive.

Young King encounters Ophelia, the girl with whom he is so much in love, and it looks as if they are about to clear up their misunderstanding when he catches sight of her father and realises that he is being spied upon. The father, Polonius, now begins to behave in a manner that, if properly handled, may seem very suspicious to the reader. He confides to the uncle and Hamlet's mother that he thinks the boy is deranged. He suggests that this is due to the unhappy love affair but the reader must be made to suspect that this is all unfounded and the old man is terrified on his own account. He is shown to be in the closest cahoots with Uncle Claudius and with the tycoon Fortinbras. We see him plotting and planning and persuading Hamlet's mother and his uncle that it would be a good thing if he were sent away for a rest-cure. Finally, he suggests to the boy's mother that she has a good talk with her son, and in doing so she must try to get out of him the reason for his extraordinary behaviour.

The meeting is to take place in the mother's boudoir, a room with a balcony high up in their enormous house. The mother, Gertrude, can be exactly like her prototype, a floppy sentimentalist completely dependent on the men. She is jolly glad to know that Polonius is hard by, hiding on the balcony. Her son comes and is now persuaded that she knows much more about his father's death than is good for her. He is determined to have it out with her and his manner terrifies her. She reacts hysterically and Polonius, alarmed, makes some movement that is heard by the son. He asks his mother for an explanation of the noise and she bleats out the extremely unconvincing suggestion that it might be a rat. Hamlet pushes open the doors onto the balcony and in doing so knocks Polonius on the head and he falls from the balcony and is killed.

You will perceive here several departures from the original, but we proceed nevertheless on somewhat similar lines. The distracted young man turns on his mother and treats her to an embarrassingly frank examination of the intimate side of her domestic life as he sees it. If we keep our wits about us we can at this juncture make her respond in an extremely suspicious manner, particularly as the next thing she does is to go straight to her husband and tell him Hamlet has just killed Polonius. Hamlet, in the meantime, has gone down four storeys into the shrubbery to see what can be done about the body. It now becomes clear to us that our detective novel is going to be laced with one of the ingredients of the thriller. I refer, of course, to The Chase.

The chase for Hamlet is led by two particularly revolting bureaucratic under-secretaries, a pair of sissies called Rosencrantz and Guildenstern. He is finally rounded up and brought before his uncle to whom he is so insultingly rude that any suspicions we may have had of the uncle are dispelled on a wave of irritated sympathy. Everybody is now all for the rest-cure. Our hero appears to consent and actually has his luggage packed and allows himself to be driven away hotfoot while somebody is sent off to book his passage at the nearest Tourist Agency. Polonius' body is discovered and as there is nothing to show to the contrary the police believe an account of a sudden attack of vertigo. A quiet funeral takes place. So, having brought forward and retired the uncle as a suspect in favour of Polonius, we find that we have suddenly got rid of Polonius. It is not unusual for a character to suddenly bolt like this. Let us have a look at what remains in the field of suspects.

We find quite a tidy number: the girlfriend, the mother and the two yes-boys as well as Fortinbras, the representative of the European firm, and a frightful little type called Osric who found the body. We will have been careful to touch in any number of little suspicious details. Fortinbras, of course, will benefit materially by the General's death because he will now get the formula for H/Q. Rosencrantz and Guildenstern can have jobs in the reptile department. Even the young scientist, Horatio, can be known to possess the key to the Reptile House. At this juncture we can pull in a bit of highly technical stuff which will take a lot of mugging up but is always effective. Hamlet, working independently, can discover that the poison that killed the General did not belong to the same group as that secreted by the escaped reptile. It is undoubtedly the H/Q toxin.

It would be beneficial at this point to let in some new blood to the field of suspects and the play provides it. Back comes the girlfriend's brother Laertes from a riotous party in Paris, filled with suspicion about his father's death and raring to go. He behaves in such an extravagant manner, trying to raise a general strike at the Works and ready to take on all comers including Hamlet and his uncle that we can, if we handle him properly, make the whole thing look like an act designed to cover his own complicity in the murder of the General. Perhaps the General gave him the sack for riotous living or he might even turn out to have had a violent adolescent passion for Gertrude herself. The uncle has a terrible job calming Laertes and does it with such courage and tact that really we find him becoming more and more sympathetic to the general reader.

Laertes has no sooner simmered down than his sister, Hamlet's girlfriend Ophelia, goes completely round the bend and sets him off again. She makes a number of extremely ambiguous statements and is found drowned by Hamlet's mother who now leaps to the forefront of the suspects. She gives the most extraordinarily circumstantial account of what she describes as a suicide. It is an eye-witness's account and as full of detail as a detective inspector's report. Ophelia, she says, had climbed out on a willow branch over a stream carrying a number of wild flowers, accurately catalogued by Gertrude herself. The branch, says Gertrude, broke and Ophelia, after floating rather like an inverted frogman downstream, singing as she went, finally went under for the third time and was drowned. What, the reader asks himself, was Gertrude doing all this time? Was no attempt made to fish the wretched girl out? There is admirable material here for suggesting a sub-motive for Gertrude.

There has to be another funeral; this is definitely a detective novel for people who enjoy a plurality of corpses. We vary this one with shock tactics. Hamlet, having double-crossed his escort at the airport, comes back in time for the funeral. This enrages Laertes and there is a really tough set-to between the two young men. We are, although you might not believe it, very nearly coming up the straight. Hamlet apologises to Laertes who appears to accept the apology. The scene takes place in the gymnasium. Each of the young men belongs to his University Fencing Club and Hamlet, in fact, has his Blue.

The uncle, in his hearty man-of-the-world way, suggests that to seal their reconciliation the boys have a friendly bout with the foils. Hamlet doesn't give a damn either way but Laertes seems to be quite keen. The uncle says they will make a party of it, drinks are brought in and all the suspects who remain alive are asked to the party. You all know what happens. They fight and Hamlet is clearly the better one of the two. Quite a lot of heavy betting goes on—the uncle in particular laying steep odds on Hamlet. A minor suspect, the aforementioned little type called Osric, is in charge of the foils but the uncle inspects them. Drinks are circulated freely, the uncle is in his most convivial vein and he insists on fixing a drink for Hamlet. Hamlet says he'll wait until after the bout but his mother, who enjoys her dram, takes charge of his as well as her own.

Hamlet has just scored his second hit. They are about to play the third bout when he notices that Laertes' foil has no safety button on it. With this discovery, if carefully handled, Laertes will look pretty suspicious to the average reader. Hamlet forces on the third bout. With a clever flick of the wrist he unarms Laertes, clamps his foot down on Laertes' foil and forces Laertes to take his own. Laertes, terrified, does so and gets a cut from the unbated weapon.

At this juncture there is a great rumpus from Gertrude, who, having finished her own drink, is about to help herself to Hamlet's. Her husband calls out to her not to touch it. She pays no attention to this but she suddenly notices as she drinks that the cocktail smells revolting. At the same time the most dreadful things are happening to the wound on Laertes. A condition described as a loathsome tetter has broken out. Laertes, in agony, manages to point out that the uncle examined the foils and must be responsible. The Queen, who has been seized with what appears to be colic, is being looked after by Hamlet who exclaims as he stoops over her, 'There is a characteristic odour—she has taken the H/Q toxin. I cannot be mistaken.' And then pointing dramatically at Laertes he continues, 'And there we have the unmistakable reaction of H/Q administered intravenously. There is only one hand that could have done this. The hand that mixed the cocktail bated the foil. O my prophetic soul, my Uncle!'

NOTES ON CONTRIBUTORS

ROBERT BARNARD spent most of his adult life teaching in universities in Australia and Norway, returning to Britain to become a full-time crime writer in 1983. He has written thirty books under his own name, of which the latest is *Masters of the House*. He also writes historical crime novels under the name Bernard Bastable, the latest of which is *Dead, Mr Mozart*. He and his wife live in Leeds.

CHAZ BRENCHLEY has earned his living as a writer since he was eighteen. He is the author of half a dozen novels, most recently *Paradise*, a long book about faith and power in a crime-ridden and decaying city. He is a prizewinning ex-poet and has also published three fantasies for children and more than four hundred short stories in various genres.

ANN CLEEVES is the author of two distinct crime series. George Palmer-Jones is an elderly amateur sleuth who solves mysteries with a background in conservation or birdwatching. Inspector Stephen Ramsey is based in his creator's home county of Northumberland. Ann Cleeves' most recent novel is *The Healers.*

BARBARA CROSSLEY has her roots in Saddleworth, on the Pennine hills, but she now lives in Blackpool, where she was a local newspaper journalist before taking up fiction full-time in 1992. Her crime novels, *Candyfloss Coast* and *Rollercoaster,* are based in a bright, brash Northern resort not unlike her home town.

EILEEN DEWHURST was born and brought up in Liverpool, read English at Oxford and has earned her living in a variety of ways, including journalism. She has written sixteen crime novels: twelve murder mysteries, three thrillers, and one experimentally combining the two genres.

MARTIN EDWARDS is the author of five novels about the Liverpool solicitor and amateur detective Harry Devlin. The first, *All the Lonely People,* was shortlisted for the John Creasey Memorial Award for best first crime novel of 1991. It has been followed by *Suspicious Minds, I Remember You, Yesterday's Papers* and *Eve of Destruction.* The series has recently been optioned for television.

ROGER FORSDYKE is a serving police officer who over the last twenty years has helped detect murders, and investigated (amongst other things) rapes, robberies and errant police officers. He is co-author of the police promotion aspirants' definitive study text and is currently working on his fourth novel.

REGINALD HILL has written more than forty novels including the well-known Dalziel and Pascoe series set in Yorkshire. His most recent book is *Born Guilty,* the second to feature the serendipitous Luton PI, Joe Sixsmith. Hill lives quietly in Cumbria with his wife, Pat, and his conscience.

MARGARET LEWIS published *Ngaio Marsh: A Life* with Chatto and Windus (UK) and Bridget Williams Books (New

Zealand) in 1991. She has recently written *Edith Pargeter: Ellis Peters* (Seren, 1994), a book about the life and work of this popular author. Margaret has had several short stories published and has read a sequence on BBC Radio Newcastle.

PETER LEWIS has lived in the North-East for more than thirty years and teaches courses in crime at one of the institutions for which Durham is famous. Among his books are "bio-critiques" of Eric Ambler and John le Carré, the latter receiving an Edgar Allan Poe Award from the Mystery Writers of America.

VAL McDERMID grew up in a Scottish mining community and then read English at Oxford. She was a journalist for eighteen years and is now a full-time writer living outside Manchester. She has published seven novels, the latest of which is *Crack Down*.

KAY MITCHELL was born in Wakefield and educated there and at Leeds University. She now lives near Wakefield with her husband and has two children. She has published three police novels under her own name and also writes private-eye stories under the pseudonym of Sarah Lacey.

STEPHEN MURRAY is perhaps the most southerly of *Northern Blood* contributors, and the most foolhardy, giving up salaried employment ten years ago to write his first novel. Seven others have followed, including *Death and Transfiguration.* He lives in the Marches with a wife, two small sons and a 1931 Sunbeam, though not necessarily in that order.

ALAN SEWART is the author of more than forty books on crime subjects. A retired police superintendent, he uses his own experience to produce novels with an authentic police background. He writes under his own name and two pseudonyms: Padder Nash and Alan Stewart Well.

PETER N WALKER is a retired police inspector. Under several pseudonyms, he has published almost ninety books, fact and fiction, the best-known being the *Constable* series. Written as by Nicholas Rhea, these inspired the hit ITV drama, *Heartbeat.* He is the present Chairman of the Crime Writers' Association.

BARBARA WHITEHEAD, born in Yorkshire, still lives there, ignoring the blandishments of all other counties. She has lectured for twenty years in adult education on Creative Writing and Family History. Her twelfth and most recent book, *The Killings at Barley Hall,* is the fifth in her York Cycle of Mysteries.

DOUGLAS WYNN worked as a research chemist and a technical college lecturer before retiring early to concentrate on crime. He has researched and written about many true murder cases and published three collections of real-life crimes, *Settings for Slaughter, Blind Justice?* and *The Limits of Detection.* His fourth, *On Trial for Murder,* will be published in October 1995. He lives in Lincolnshire.

The publishers hope that this book has given you enjoyable reading. Large Print Books are especially designed to be as easy to see and hold as possible. If you wish a complete list of our books, please ask at your local library or write directly to: Magna Large Print Books, Long Preston, North Yorkshire, BD23 4ND, England.

This Large Print Book for the Partially sighted, who cannot read normal print, is published under the auspices of

THE ULVERSCROFT FOUNDATION

THE ULVERSCROFT FOUNDATION

. . . we hope that you have enjoyed this Large Print Book. Please think for a moment about those people who have worse eyesight problems than you . . . and are unable to even read or enjoy Large Print, without great difficulty.

You can help them by sending a donation, large or small to:

**The Ulverscroft Foundation,
1, The Green, Bradgate Road,
Anstey, Leicestershire, LE7 7FU,
England.**
or request a copy of our brochure for more details.

The Foundation will use all your help to assist those people who are handicapped by various sight problems and need special attention.

Thank you very much for your help.